EARLY MORNING MURDER

When Savannah rang the doorbell, no one answered. After buzzing a couple of times, she knocked loudly.

Still no response.

She glanced at her watch. It was seven-forty. Maybe Lisa was still in bed and a sound sleeper. Perhaps if she tried the back door.

But she had no better luck there. After pounding until her knuckles tingled, she was about to give up and accept the fact that no one was at home, when she noticed something that sent a chill through her. Deep, jagged gouges in the wooden doorframe, just beside the lock.

Even as she tried to deny what she feared, Savannah pulled a tissue from her jacket pocket and used it to turn the knob. The door swung open easily. Carefully, she walked through the kitchen and into the living room. As she crept deeper into the room, a strange, irritating sound caught her attention. A high-pitched beeping, like a pager or . . .

It was the telephone receiver, lying on the floor beside the end table.

Slipping the Beretta from its holster, Savannah pointed the barrel at the ceiling and crept down the short hallway. She hurried to the first bedroom. Lisa's bed was disheveled, the spread lying in a heap on the ancient, gold shag carpeting. The top sheet was gone. The lower, fitted sheet that remained had been pulled loose and the right side was ripped. At the foot of the bed lay a pillow with a crimson darkness staining the linen.

Savannah didn't need to turn on the light to see what it was. She could smell the distinctive, coppery odor of blood. . . .

Books by G. A. McKevett

JUST DESSERTS

BITTER SWEETS

KILLER CALORIES

COOKED GOOSE

SUGAR AND SPITE

Published by Kensington Publishing Corp.

• G. A. McKevett •

BITTER SWEETS

KENSINGTON BOOKS
KENSINGTON PUBLISHING CORP.
http://www.kensingtonbooks.com

*This book is lovingly dedicated
to my grandparents*

Stella and Arthur McGill

*Better known and loved as
Ma and Pa Gill*

For their generous contributions of time, support and expertise, the author would like to thank:

Rob Ward
Brad Haskell
Bruce Watson
Ken Chapman
And a certain medical examiner, who wishes to remain anonymous, but she knows who she is.

CHAPTER ONE

"Just take a deep breath and dive right in there, sugar." Savannah Reid pointed to the body that lay in a pool of sunlight and red gore on the polished oak floor. "Welcome to Homicide 101."

The young would-be detective, who stood beside Savannah, crossed her arms tightly over her chest, crumpling the front of her impeccably tailored suit. She swallowed hard and turned a sickly shade of green that was a tad more chartreuse than the elegant jade silk she was wearing.

Savannah chuckled inwardly but kept a straight face. *What a wimp*, she thought. This one was nice and fresh. It didn't even smell. Wait until Miss Tammy Prissy-Pot had to examine a truly ripe corpse that had been lying around, unrefrigerated, for a month of Sundays. She'd be tossing her cookies for sure.

Savannah enjoyed the company of her new assistant, in spite of the fact that the two women couldn't have been more different. Tammy's strict attention to detail and left-brained approach to life irritated Savannah from time to time. Mostly because the contrast highlighted Savannah's own disorganization that sometimes bordered on outright sloppiness.

But Tammy was bright, curious, humble about what she didn't know, and eager to learn. Training her was turning out to be quite a pleasure for Savannah . . . if she could only get her past her queasiness.

"Come on, shake a leg," Savannah drawled in a Georgia accent as thick and sweet as peach pie filling. She knelt beside the body, which was lying on its side, sprawled across the office floor near a large bay window. The low afternoon rays of the California sun streamed in, illuminating the crime scene and leaving little to the imagination. "Let's get to it. What's first?"

"Well . . ." The petite blonde's usually squeaky voice with its distinctive Long Island twang had slid at least half an octave up the scale. "This . . . um, this guy . . . he's the victim, and . . ."

"No shit, Sherlock." Savannah grinned good-naturedly. "Get down here and check him out. He's not gonna bite you. Not now."

Gingerly, Tammy stepped a bit closer and chose a clean spot on the floor to place one shapely knee.

"Next time you might want to wear something a bit more casual," Savannah suggested, pointing out her own attire of slacks, sweater, and loafers. "Stiffs don't care how you look."

"God, Savannah, you're so crude."

"Who, me? Naw, I'm just a bit earthy. You should watch

an autopsy with Dirk. He's got some great one-liners that would make you split your bloomers laughin'."

At the mention of Dirk Coulter, Tammy wrinkled her pert nose. "Yeah, I'll bet he does," she replied dryly.

"All right, down to business, kiddo." Savannah's face changed in an instant, the teasing smile gone, her blue eyes intense and calculating as she studied the body on the floor. "The victim of a violent crime is often the only witness, other than the perpetrator," she began in a serious monotone, reciting by rote. "They can give you the most accurate account . . . that is, if they can talk when it's all over. Obviously, this guy ain't sayin' much. So . . . ?"

"We look to the crime scene to tell us what happened," Tammy supplied.

"That's right. Tell me, what happened?"

She quickly scanned the victim. "Somebody—or bodies— handcuffed this guy, blindfolded him, and shot him in the back of the neck."

"From a distance or close range?"

Tammy leaned over to study the entrance wound. "Close range."

"Because?"

"Powder burns."

She waved her hand, indicating the office in general. "Was our killer organized or disorganized?"

Tammy chewed on her lower lip for a second. "I'd say organized."

"Why?"

"The crime scene appears controlled, not chaotic. No signs of violence—other than the gunshot. Restraints were used."

She nodded toward the victim's hands, which were manacled behind his back. "I doubt those handcuffs were just lying around the office, so the killer must have brought his own. The murder weapon is gone and not much other visible evidence left behind. Looks pretty organized to me."

Savannah nodded. "So, what sort of guy are we going to be looking for?"

Tammy hesitated, searching for the right mental file to access. "Profile of an organized killer: high intelligence, socially and sexually adequate, probably lives with a partner, high birth order, controlled, masculine, charming."

Savannah grinned. "Sounds great."

"Yeah, really." Tammy relaxed for a moment, then resumed her recitation. "And he'll anticipate being questioned . . . if we can find him, that is."

"If we do . . . what will be our interviewing techniques?"

"Have a direct strategy and stick to it. Be certain of all your details; *he* will be. He'll only admit what he absolutely has to."

"You've been doing your homework," Savannah said, flashing the younger woman the dimpled Reid smile that never failed. Her feminine features—wide blue eyes, Betty Boop mouth and heart-shaped face, framed with midnight brown curls—were deceivingly demure. Southern belle daintiness stopped there. In her line of work, Savannah seldom had the opportunity to indulge the genteel side of her personality.

Thank goodness Granny Reid in Georgia didn't know what a tomboy she had become.

"I think I'm going to make a detective of you yet," she told Tammy.

The blonde's pallid cheeks flushed from Savannah's compliment. "Yeah, well . . . I've been hitting the books."

"How about a victim profile?"

Tammy's self-satisfied grin evaporated. "Victim profile? Oh, I guess I didn't get that far."

"The victim can tell us a lot. Before some bastard turned him into meat, he was a living breathing human being." With a brief, but almost-reverent expression on her face, Savannah reached down and gently brushed a lock of hair back from the man's forehead. "What kind of a person he was can tell us something about the individual who destroyed him. Tell me about our victim."

"He is . . . was . . . a large man. Well over six feet tall, probably close to two hundred pounds. Caucasian. I'd say mid thirties, dark brown hair, green eyes. Extremely handsome."

"You noticed that, too, huh?"

"Hey, you told me to be observant." With the tip of one finger she brushed the sleeve of his houndstooth wool jacket. "Expensive clothes, not wearing a wedding ring, quality haircut."

"Broad shoulders, slender waist, *great* buns," Savannah added salaciously as she leaned over and goosed the body's rear end.

"Sa-*van*-ah! For heaven's sake, have some respect!"

"Aw, lighten up, sugar," she replied, laughing. "Trust me, at this point he ain't gonna take offense."

The phone on the nearby desk jangled, startling both women.

"Good Lord," Savannah said. "A call. A real call! Could it be . . . ?"

"Maybe. It might be. Should I answer it?"

"Of course. That's what I'm paying you for."

Tammy sprang to her feet and hurried to the rolltop desk. After clearing her throat, she picked up the phone and spoke with what Savannah classified as a rather bad Lauren Bacall impression, "Moonlight Magnolia Detective Agency," she breathed. "May I help you?"

Excited, Savannah clutched the body's jacket sleeve and shook it. "Ryan . . . a call. We finally got a call."

"It's probably a wrong number," the corpse responded, raising his head and stretching his long limbs. "Mind if I get up now? This cursed floor of yours is hardwood, you know."

"Yeah, yeah, sure," Savannah said, grabbing him by the lapels and raising him to a sitting position. Absentmindedly she rubbed some of the stage blood off his face and began to undo his handcuffs while listening to Tammy's end of the conversation. It sounded promising. *Hallelujah! Their first client!*

"Yes, Mr. O'Donnell," she was saying, "I'm sure we could help you find your sister. But I think you should speak to Ms. Savannah Reid herself. Yes, she's the owner of the agency . . . a retired, thrice-decorated, police detective. That's right. One moment please."

Tammy cupped her hand over the mouthpiece and "cut a rug" as Savannah's Granny Reid would say, wriggling her diminutive butt and jumping up and down on her three-and-a-half-inch heels. "We've got a case, we've got a case."

"Glory be," Savannah muttered as she grabbed the phone out of her assistant's shaking hand. "Maybe we won't starve after all."

Brian O'Donnell. Medium height, slender build. Distinctive dark red hair, brown eyes and curl-tipped mustache. Forty-seven years old. Residence—Orlando, Florida, fifteen years. Occupation—real estate broker. Married. Looking for sister.

Savannah glanced down the yellow legal pad on her lap at the notes she had taken over the last twenty minutes. Sticking the end of her pen in her mouth, she chewed it thoughtfully, then—remembering that she was trying to quit—she returned her attention to the man sitting in the matching wing chair across from her.

His eyes met hers over the rim of the mug as he sipped the steaming coffee. "Do you think you can help me, Ms. Reid?" he said, after licking a drop from his mustache. "Do we have enough to go on?"

"Actually, you aren't a bad detective yourself, Mr. O'Donnell. You've given me more here than I would have hoped for."

"Good. I'm glad to hear that. Finding my sister means a lot to me."

Savannah watched as his hands closed around the mug. Although his posture was casual with one sneaker propped on the opposite knee of his semiworn jeans, he held the cup handle more tightly than necessary. She jotted the fact down on her mental legal pad.

That was the main reason why Savannah had decided to offer her clients coffee or tea when she first interviewed them here in her private office—a small area that had, until recently, been her sun porch. The steaming beverage of their choice and Cadbury chocolate-dipped tea biscuits were more than a token of Southern hospitality. While eating and drinking, a person often allowed his or her carefully constructed facade to slip, revealing a candid glimpse of what was going on behind the scene. Experience had taught her that a lot could be learned about a person just by watching the way he seasoned his coffee or chewed a cookie. Brian O'Donnell had inhaled his three biscuits without stopping to savor a single crumb. Definitely *not* a hedonist, like herself.

Savannah had worked hard at convincing herself that the silver tray, bearing coffee, whipped cream, cinnamon sticks, various liqueurs, and chocolate curls had nothing to do with the constant cravings of her own sweet tooth. Of course, she knew better, but she didn't really care.

Setting her own china cup aside, she picked up the stack of papers which O'Donnell had laid on the coffee table between them. "This may seem like a rather personal question, but I'd like to know why finding your sister is so important to you," she said, flipping through the assorted documents.

Brian's face was haggard with harsh, angular lines, a bit pale, with smudges under both eyes. Within the first two minutes after they had met, Savannah had surmised that, either he didn't spend enough hours in bed, or he spent more hours tossing and turning than snoring. But, at the mention of his sister, his expression softened and he turned to gaze thoughtfully into the blaze of the gas log fireplace, which she had turned on for his benefit. Another cozy touch designed to set a client at ease. It seemed to be working.

"My mother died when Susette was five and I was seven," he said. "A sudden illness . . . some sort of flu, I think. Dad wasn't really sure. He didn't feel adequate to raise two children on his own, thought a girl should have a mother to teach her . . . girl things, you know."

Savannah nodded. "Go on."

"So, he put Susie up for adoption. I remember the day they

came to take her away. She and I both cried a lot, begged Dad not to go through with it. I know he loved her. But I guess he had to do what he thought was best."

He was silent for a long moment, staring into the flickering blaze. Then, he cleared his throat and took a brisk slurp of coffee.

"Susie was a pretty good kid . . . for a girl." He gave Savannah a sideways glance. "No offense."

Savannah shrugged. "Some of us aren't too bad."

"She couldn't fish worth a darn, but we had a tree house and . . ."

As his voice faded away, Savannah decided not to push it any farther. His reasons for wanting to locate his sister, spoken and unspoken, were pretty clear.

"Is the tree house still there?" she asked softly.

"Yeah. And I still live on my father's property, where we were when she was given away. I have three boys of my own now. There's a picture of them there with the other stuff I brought you. They've made some improvements to the old shack—they call it a fort—but I think Susie would still recognize it. I want her to see it. If she's got kids, I want them to meet my boys."

"I understand." Savannah thought of her own brothers and sisters in Georgia—all eight of them—and felt a pang of homesickness. "But why now?" she asked. "Is this your first attempt to locate Susette . . ." She referred to the papers. ". . . or Lisa, as she's called now?"

"Oh, no. I've tried off and on for years without any luck. Then, a couple of months ago, my dad passed away. He wasn't wealthy, by any means, but he did leave some money for Susie

. . . I mean, Lisa. Before he died, he asked me to try one more time."

O'Donnell's face eased into a tired, sad smile. "But he wouldn't have had to ask," he added. "I would have looked for her again anyway. I don't think I'll ever give up . . . not until I find her. She's the only family my boys and I have anymore. Other than my wife, of course."

"Of course." Savannah studied the pile of papers in her lap. Work. Finally, a job to sink her teeth into. It had been too long. "One more thing, Mr. O'Donnell. Why did you choose our agency?"

He smiled and for a moment he didn't look quite so tired. "Like I said, I traced Lisa to San Carmelita. I know she was living here three months ago, but now I've lost her trail. While I was in the library, trying to find some records, I came across an old newspaper article and . . ."

He paused and looked slightly embarrassed.

Savannah decided to let him off the hook and supply the rest. "You read about my little ruckus with the police chief and the city council."

"Ah . . . yeah."

"And about me getting kicked off the force."

"Yes, but you solved your case anyway. That's what counted. I figured if you could whip City Hall, you could solve a little problem like mine."

Savannah leaned over and offered him her hand. "Thank you. I hope I can live up to your high expectations."

"I'm sure you will." He took her hand and they shook solemnly.

"Mr. O'Donnell, you've hired yourself a detective agency,"

she said. "And we're going to do everything we can to find your sister for you." *Hot damn*, she thought as she watched the stress melt from his face. It sure felt good to be back to work, to be doing something useful in the world.

She reached for his mug. "Now, how about another cup of coffee? This time let's do it right. We'll dose it with a slug of Bailey's and slap some whipped cream on it."

Although Savannah had migrated to the Southern California seaside years before, she prided herself on the fact that you could never quite squeeze the last drop of juice out of a true Georgia peach. Southern California or southern Dixie, it didn't matter when it came to entertaining friends and family.

Like her Granny Reid and generations of ladies before her, Savannah lived in mortal fear that someone, somewhere, might suffer a pang of hunger while in her presence. It simply wasn't allowed.

Except, maybe, for Dirk.

Facing him across her dining room table at this, the first official personnel meeting of the Moonlight Magnolia Detective Agency, Savannah was beginning to get a bit peeved as she watched him reach for his sixteenth chocolate chip and macadamia nut cookie. She had baked a plateful. There were two left.

After having served as his partner on the San Carmelita Police Force, and having been his closest personal friend for years, Savannah had to admit, she loved the guy. But she harbored no illusions about him. Dirk was a real pig, in more ways than one.

"Would you like me to put this meeting on hold for half

an hour or so and go fix you a meal, Dirk?" she asked. "I could whip up a leg of lamb with mint jelly, prime rib and a creamy horseradish sauce, or maybe Chateaubriand?"

He lit up like the Rockefeller Plaza Christmas tree during a power surge. "Would you? That'd be great!"

Shaking her head and sighing, Savannah shoved the plate down the table and out of his reach.

"Have a cookie, Ryan," she said to the previously expired corpse. She turned to his companion. "You, too, Gibson, while there's still some left."

Savannah knew better than to offer anything with a calorie in it to Tammy, who sat there, demurely sipping her cup of decaffeinated coffee, flavored with sugarless sweetener, nonfat creamer, and carob powder. Okay, Savannah admitted that the younger woman did wear a petite size three and would probably live forever without one cell of plaque to block her arteries.

But she had no boobs.

Savannah took a small measure of consolation in this fact: Tammy Hart would live long and die without ever knowing the hedonistic pleasure of savoring a sip of pure cholesterol-laden sin, or experiencing the womanly thrill of overflowing her bra cups. Both of which Savannah enjoyed every morning of her life.

Finally, Savannah had convinced herself that she felt sorry for Tammy and her sleek, slender figure. So terribly sorry.

But it hadn't been easy.

"Tell me, dear," said John Gibson, the elegant, silver-haired British gentleman sitting at the end of the table beside Ryan, "Exactly how can Ryan and I assist you with this new case of yours? We are, as always, at your disposal." In a knightly gesture, he waved a hand toward his younger friend.

Dirk made an unpleasant snort which, Savannah surmised, had nothing to do with his sinus infection and more to do with his acute case of homophobia. She shot him a warning glance.

"Nothing at the moment, Gibson, thank you," she replied as she rose to add hot water and another tea bag to the older man's individual pot of Earl Grey. "This will be a pretty cut-and-dried search. I don't think we'll be needing your special surveillance skills or equipment."

"If you do, you'll let us know?" Ryan said, smiling up at Savannah with a face that still took her breath away. Tall, dark, and outrageously handsome, Ryan Stone had provided the inspiration for many of Savannah's midnight fantasies. If he had not been so happily involved with Gibson for so many years, she would have employed every one of her considerably feminine wiles to try to reorient his sexual preference.

Fat chance.

Seeing the way that Tammy was gazing at him like a lust-besotted cocker spaniel, Savannah guessed that the same thoughts had crossed her mind. Oh, well . . .

"Tammy and I can handle this one . . . at least for the time being," she said as she returned to her seat and plopped a dollop of chocolate-flavored whipped cream into her coffee. From the corner of her eye, she saw Tammy cringe. "Starting tomorrow morning, you can begin checking on Brian O'Donnell," she told her. "Just the usual stuff to see that all his ID is legit, that he's who he says he is. He seems sincere and all that, but we want to make sure before we go searching for someone on his behalf."

Tammy's prissiness disappeared and her expression turned businesslike as she flipped open a notebook and began to scribble furiously. "Got it, boss," she said with an eager, if a bit naive, enthusiasm that went straight to Savannah's heart. *Tammy is a good kid*, she reminded herself. *A little young, a little skinny, a tad self-righteous, perhaps. But a good kid.*

"And what about me?" Dirk said, still wearing a pout that looked ridiculous on a forty-plus man's face. A face that was endearing for its character, but had that street-worn look, as though he had been dragged around the block a time or two on his overly robust belly. "Why did you haul me over here if you don't need me?"

"Because, darlin' . . ." Savannah blew him a sexy kiss across the table. ". . . we love you and we wanted you here to celebrate our first case with us."

He blushed all the way up to his receding hairline. It occurred to Savannah that Dirk needed to get a life if something like a little Southern flirtation gave him a hot flush.

"Besides," she added in a quiet monotone, "I want you to run some DMV plates and do a couple of record checks."

"I knew there was a catch," he growled, fighting back a grudging grin. Dirk was never more happy than when he could complain of being used. "What's in it for me? I mean, I'm not exactly on your payroll here."

"A ham sandwich."

He considered, then shook his head. "I don't think so. It's the leg of lamb and mint jelly or nothin'."

"With cheese . . ." she bargained. He didn't budge. "And a smear of dijon."

"Deal."

In a car parked in the shadows half a block away, a silent figure sat and watched as, one by one, Savannah's guests filed out the door. For the past hour, the spy had been observing their shadows on the dining room curtains; a meeting had been in progress. It didn't require a vivid imagination to guess who and what had been the subject of the conversation.

Having recorded the "comings" and "goings" of the household for the past four hours, the person in the shadows was well satisfied.

So far, so good. Everything appeared to be going as planned.

Scribbling on a note pad, aided by the dim glow of a penlight, the voyeur paid special attention to the dynamics between each departing attendee and their hostess as they wished her good-bye. The tall guy and the older man left together, each giving her an affectionate kiss on the cheek. The young blonde hugged her, then puttered away in a hot pink, perfectly renovated, Volkswagen bug.

A more colorful character, the fellow who looked like a bedraggled cop, had merely socked her on the shoulder before climbing into a battered 1962 Buick Skylark. Unlike the Volkswagen, the Skylark could be described by a tactful phrase commonly used in classified ads—"restorable." But barely.

This surprised the note-taker, who had pegged the guy in the Buick as Savannah's lover and had expected him to stay the night.

So, Savannah Reid didn't live with a man; she was alone.

Good, that might make things easier later.

As the last of the cars drove away, Savannah disappeared inside the quaint, Spanish-style cottage, and turned out the porch light. Moments later, a series of shadows on blinds and the dousing of more lights signaled that she was retiring. Finally, only one window glowed—upstairs on the left. Her bedroom.

That's all for tonight, folks, the individual thought, turning the key in the ignition and firing up the engine. *The wheels are turning now. It won't be long.*

So far, things were going much better than hoped. Who said the game of murder was complicated?

CHAPTER TWO

On a morning like this, it wasn't difficult for Savannah to remember why she had relocated fifteen years ago from Georgia to Southern California. As she guided her red Camaro northward around the twisting turns of Buena Vista Road, she could see the Pacific Ocean glittering, diamond-dusted turquoise, to her far left.

Along the shore lay San Carmelita, the small, quaint village where she had finally settled after a brief and somewhat unpleasant stint as a rookie on the Hollywood Police Force. It was a tough beat to lose your virginity.

On the other hand, San Carmelita was small and personal. Savannah knew the owners of the shops and restaurants she frequented, and occasionally met a friend on the streets.

All in all, Savannah liked San Carmelita. Except for the

occasional pang of homesickness, the periodic longing for the smell of a Georgia pine, and the PMS craving for a couple of airy-light Southern biscuits smeared with sorghum and fresh butter, San Carmelita felt like home.

The golden, morning sun shone on the foothills that rose to her right, gentle slopes which, from a distance, looked as though they were covered with soft, tan suede.

Heavier than usual spring rains had kept the hills green for months, but the recent Santa Ana winds had dried the new brush to fire-crisp tinder.

Not for the first time, Savannah marveled at the logic which drove people to build the most expensive homes in town there on the crest of the hills. Sure, the view was terrific, but when the seasonal brushfires started in the fall, they would be on the front line of the assault. Not to mention the prospects of instantaneous relocation downward in event of a major earthquake.

As she drove higher into the exclusive neighborhood, Savannah assured herself that her opinions were solid and had nothing to do with the fact that *she* couldn't afford to live in one of these fine, custom homes with the breathtaking view. Certainly not on a recently-fired-police-detective's nonsalary, or on a recently-established-private-detective's income.

Referring to her notebook, which lay open on the passenger's seat next to her, she checked the address—1513 N. Lotus. The last known residence of one Lisa Mallock, formerly known as "Susie" O'Donnell.

Brother Brian had given Savannah this information, his final lead in his search for his sister. He had told her that, when he had knocked on this door, he had been informed that Lisa was no longer living there. The door had been slammed in his face by a somewhat austere, elderly gentleman with an enormous dog.

A cheery prospect to look forward to.

But not one that bothered Savannah. Hell, in her line of work a slammed door was nothing. If they didn't shoot, stab, punch you, or insult your genealogy, it was usually considered a satisfactory interview.

"Hmm-mmm . . . not bad," she mumbled as she pulled in front of the pseudo-Swiss chalet, trilevel home. The design might have been a tad outdated, but the home was well kept, freshly painted, the yard immaculate, with flowers blooming in orderly profusion.

She decided not to park the Camaro on the spotless driveway; it had an embarrassing habit of dripping oil.

The moment she rang the doorbell, she heard a dog begin to bark. Considering the bass tone and deep resonance, she decided that Brian hadn't exaggerated. It was a very large dog, who obviously took his job seriously.

When the door opened, a bundle of bristling, black fur burst through and charged toward her. Bared teeth glistened in a face that looked like a cross between an Akita and a grizzly bear.

Instinctively, Savannah slipped her hand inside her jacket to her shoulder holster and the handle of her Beretta. But she resisted the compulsion to draw. Shooting the family beast on the porch was hardly a way to get on anyone's good side.

"Beowulf, sit!" growled the equally determined, male voice of a human as the door swung wider.

"Yes, please, do have a seat, Beowulf," she whispered, feel-

ing the dog's hot breath on her calf through the thin linen of
her slacks.

Obedient, he stopped barking but continued to growl, his
teeth inches from her leg, his lips fluttering like a window shade
in a stiff breeze.

"Beowulf, that's enough. Knock it off," said the handsome,
elderly man whose broad—if slightly stooped—shoulders nearly
filled the doorway. For his age, which was probably around seventy, he was an exceptional physical specimen. He was tall,
well over six feet, steel gray hair cut in a short buzz, and pale
blue eyes that were unnerving in their intensity.

Only the arthritic swelling and distortion of his finger
joints gave any hint of disability or special challenge.

But, apparently, his problems didn't prevent him from pur-
suing his interests. Judging from the soil on his jeans and tee
shirt, and the smudge of peat moss on his right cheek, she had
interrupted his gardening.

He reached down, grabbed the dog by the abundant scruff
of the neck, and gave him a gentle shake. "Don't worry, ma'am,"
he told her with a slight Southern accent, reminiscent of her
own. "The old fellow is just trying to earn extra doggie treats by
acting like a tough guy. His bark is worse than his bite."

Doubtfully, she looked down at the gleaming incisors. "Really?"

The man chuckled. "No, not really. But he doesn't eat
anyone without my permission."

"I'm so pleased to hear that." She extended her hand to
him. He took it and gave her a firm shake. "My name is Savannah Reid. I'm trying to get in touch with Lisa Mallock. Is she
at home?"

Instantly, he dropped her hand. "No."

The open, friendly expression slid off his face as he crossed his arms over his broad chest and scowled down at her.

"I see." She hesitated, then plunged ahead. "When do you expect her to return?"

"Who's asking?"

Shrugging her shoulders, she gave him her most winning smile, the one that deepened her already-charming dimples, and she turned up the Southern Comfort in her voice. "Why, just me."

He wasn't impressed. In fact, he was beginning to look as irritable as his dog. "What do you want with her?"

Savannah dropped the Georgia peach routine and fixed him with her most official eyeball lock. He wasn't the only one on the porch with intense blue eyes. And hers were a few shades darker. "I'd rather not say, sir, but it's regarding some very important family business."

"Yeah, I'll just bet it is." He took a step back, dragging the dog with him. "Lady, you can go to hell!"

A split second later, she was staring at the slammed door, four inches from her nose, and her ears were ringing from the concussion.

So much for *that* interview and whatever it might have revealed.

She supposed she was lucky.

At least he hadn't given Beowulf permission to eat her.

As Savannah walked through the front door of the San Carmelita Main Street Police Station, she wondered if she would ever enter this building again without feeling queasy and more than a little sick at heart.

Probably not.

She had enjoyed being a cop. *Well . . . maybe "enjoyed" wasn't the word*, she thought, reconsidering. There had been plenty of nightmare experiences, too. Dark, painful, infinitely sad and downright terrifying times. But she *had* thrived on the stress and reveled in the satisfaction that she had been good at her job.

Too good.

She had solved the wrong homicide case, exposed the wrong individuals, and gotten her butt canned. When the "truth" involved the chief of police and a prominent council-woman . . . one's investigatory skills could prove detrimental to one's career advancement.

Since she had been unceremoniously dismissed from the force, she had limited her trips to the station to after hours. This way, she could be assured of avoiding Chief Hillquist and Captain Bloss, her two least-favorite people in the world.

She nodded to Denise Harmon, who held down the fort—or more specifically, the front desk—during the night shift. Like most of the department personnel Savannah met from time to time, Denise greeted her warmly. It was a commonly held opinion among the rank and file that Savannah had been badly mistreated and unfairly dismissed.

"Hey, Savannah. How are you doing?" she said with a bright, open smile that was her most attractive feature. Maybe it was Denise's only attractive feature—she was a bit streetworn and rough around the edges—but Savannah had stopped noticing that a long time ago. Some people were just so nice and good-hearted that such things didn't matter.

"How am I doing?" Savannah responded, donning her thickest Southern accent. "Thanks for asking. As a matter of fact, I'm just sweeter than peee-can pie, darlin'."

"And nuttier, too," said an underly enthusiastic male voice.

Savannah turned to see Dirk standing in the squad room doorway, a goofy grin on his face. He spotted the brown bag in her hand and the smirk widened.

"You brought it!" he exclaimed.

"Of course." She held out the bag to him. "I know better than to appear around here without a sacrificial offering of burnt flesh for the beast."

"Burnt flesh?" He crinkled his nose.

"Honey baked ham and smoked turkey. I realize it's a departure from your usual three-pounds-for-a-dollar bologna, but—"

"I'll take it."

"Somehow I thought you would."

He ushered her into the squad room with more aplomb and respect than usual. Much more.

Long ago Savannah had discovered that food was the most tried-and-true way to any human being's heart. There was hardly any soul so hardened that it couldn't be softened with a Black Forest cake or a piece of apple pie.

Besides, the more generous individuals sometimes shared the gift with the giver.

That wasn't going to happen, she realized as she watched Dirk walk over to his desk, unwrap the sandwich, and bury his face in it. When it came to food, Dirk never shared.

"So, what do I have to do for this?" he asked around the mouthful of ham and turkey.

"Run a name for me."

"Only one?"

"To start with."

Having consumed half of the sandwich in three bites, he laid the rest aside and rolled his chair in front of the computer. She grabbed a nearby chair and sat beside him.

"Who?" he asked, trying to sound gruff. Early in their relationship, Savannah had figured out the rather simple psychic puzzle that was "Dirk Coulter." Dirk would do anything in the world for anyone, but he wanted them to feel at least a wee bit guilty for squandering his precious time and interfering with his life.

As though he *had* a life.

"Lisa Mallock," she replied, then spelled the last name. "Date of birth: June 13, 1951."

He accessed the Department of Motor Vehicles records first. Peering anxiously at the screen, Savannah was disappointed to see the same address as she had just visited, 1513 N. Lotus. But at least she had a physical description and picture— her first look at the lady in question.

Lisa Mallock was an attractive redhead, with hair that was the same rich auburn as her brother's. Like Brian O'Donnell, she had dark brown eyes. That was where the family resemblance ended. Her features were far more delicate, though she had the appearance of a woman who was growing old faster than her forty-five years suggested.

Height: Five feet, six inches

Weight: 130 pounds

"Any previous convictions or outstanding warrants?" she asked.

He punched some keys, brought up a new screen. "Nope."

"None?"

"Notta single one. A very good girl."

"Yeah." Savannah scowled and tapped her "Flaming Desire" crimson fingertips on the desk top.

"Something wrong with that? You *want* her to have a record?"

"Not really. But she does move around a lot. According to my client, her brother, he's traced her to five addresses in the last year, this one being the last. Either she's extremely unstable, or she's running from something. I was thinking maybe it was the law."

"Bill collectors?"

She nodded. "That would be my second guess. I'll have Tammy run a credit check on her."

"Anything else?" Dirk's eyes glowed, and not just from the sickly green light of the computer screen. He really did enjoy being a cop; it was something Savannah had always loved about him. It was what she missed most about no longer being his partner. They had shared the same obsessions—food, and solving whatever crime they were working on at the moment.

"Yeah . . . one more thing." She pulled a slip of paper from her purse. On it, she had scribbled the license plate number from the late model Lincoln Continental that had been parked in front of Beowulf's master's house.

"Run this plate for me?"

"You got another ham sandwich in your purse?"

With a sigh, she reached into her bag again and, this time,

pulled out one of her favorite things in the world, a dark Swiss chocolate bar with hazelnut and maraschino cherry cream filling. She bought them by the dozen at Trader Joe's; one never knew when one might be seized with a chocolate fit, and they were the only known cure.

This was her last bar, which made it precious, indeed.

She thrust it toward him, and he happily snatched it from her hand. "Now, give," she muttered.

More punching on the keyboard, two-finger typing. The computer clicked, beeped, and displayed a new screen.

"Forrest Neilson," Dirk announced.

"Yep, that's Beowulf's master, all right," she said, gazing at the picture, the buzz of gray hair, the intense eyes. "And his license was renewed about the same time as Lisa Mallock's, at the same address. Seems they were living together at one time, if not now."

"The woman you're looking for lives with Forrest Neilson?" Dirk said, staring at the picture on the screen.

"Maybe. Don't know for sure. When I asked, he didn't really say, one way or the other. He just made it clear that she wasn't available. Why? Do you know him?"

"Sure I do. He's *Colonel* Forrest Neilson, a Congressional Medal of Honor recipient, retired, very active in local vet programs. I met him at the American Legion last year. A great guy."

"A colonel? Really? Hmmmm. . . ."

"And you know what else?"

"What's that?"

"He's got a grown daughter . . . his only kid . . . adopted, I heard. Saw her from a distance one night . . . across a parking lot."

"Redhead? About five-six, 130 pounds?"

He nodded and shoved the last bite of chocolate into his face. "Yep, just about that size," he said around the mouthful. "And a real carrot top."

The next morning, as Savannah walked into the Moonlight Magnolia Detective Agency office—formerly known as her den—she saw Tammy snatch a pair of tortoiseshell framed glasses off her tiny face and stash them behind the computer monitor.

"Aha! Caught ya!" she said, chuckling at the young woman's vanity. She had been vain once, too. Long ago . . . when she had been much younger and cuter.

Tammy giggled self-consciously. "Well, you know what they say about men not making passes at women who wear glasses."

"Yeah, I've heard that. But they also say that guys don't leer at gals with big rears." She placed her hands on her ample hips and struck a seductive pose. "But I'm here to tell you, darlin', it just ain't so."

Savannah leaned across her assistant, retrieved the glasses, and held them out to her. "The opposite sex isn't all that picky . . . so, we have to be. Put those back on, sugar. You need to be able to tell the good ones from the bad ones at a distance . . . while you've still got time to run."

With a sheepish smile, Tammy slipped the huge glasses onto her small face. Everything about Tammy Hart reminded Savannah of a valentine. Delicate, sentimental, ultrafeminine . . . but passionate, Tammy had a soft pinkness about her personality that was endearing, but Savannah believed she had the capability to flash fiery red under the right/wrong circumstances.

"By the way," Tammy said, running her fingers through her pale blond hair that fell, straight and glossy, to her shoulders. "I'm finished checking out Brian O'Donnell for you. He's who he says he is. Sounds like a really good guy."

"I'm sure you were very thorough," Savannah said. "Bring your notes into the living room and we'll go over them. But first things first. I have a cup of mocha blend and a cream cheese Danish with my name on it waiting for me in the kitchen. Would you like a . . . ?" She glanced up and down the young woman's slender figure. "No, of course not. How silly of me. May I offer you a stalk of celery in a glass of Perrier?"

Savannah sat in her favorite spot in the world, her overstuffed, wing chair with Diamante in her lap and Cleopatra curled on the footstool at her feet. Both cats were purring contentedly.

As though she needed anything to make her more comfortable, she was surrounded with soft, floral print, satin-fringed pillows. Unable to discard the atrocious flowered housedresses that Granny Reid sent to her regularly from Georgia, Savannah had fashioned them into cushions. Sitting among them, she could almost feel as though she were receiving a hug from the octogenarian darling.

Perched on the edge of the sofa, Tammy sat with her notebook in hand, an alert expression on her pretty face. Eager. Very eager.

"I checked with the phone company in Orlando to verify the number and address that Brian O'Donnell gave you," she was saying as she happily rattled away. "And then I called and talked to his family. His wife seemed sweet and happy to speak to me.

We compared physical descriptions and they matched down to his handlebar mustache. She made it perfectly clear that she supports Brian completely in his search for his sister."

"Then she knows he's here?"

"Oh, yes. She said he left four days ago for California. I think she said something about him driving and—"

"Driving? I thought he told me he flew."

Tammy pursed her lips thoughtfully. "Oh . . . okay . . . maybe I misunderstood. Anyway, she wished us luck in finding Lisa. Said it would mean a lot to them all. Isn't that nice?"

"Very."

"But there's something else. . . ."

"What's that?"

"He has a reason, other than sentimentality, for wanting to find his sister right now."

Savannah stopped stroking Diamante and gave Tammy her full attention. "You mean the inheritance money?"

"Oh, you knew about that already?" Tammy looked a bit disappointed.

"Brian mentioned it, said it wasn't much."

"Not much? Well . . . I guess it depends on how you look at it, but fifty thousand seems like a lot to me."

Savannah thought of the stack of unpaid bills on her kitchen counter. "Yeah, sounds like a lot to me, too. I wonder why Brother Brian felt the need to underplay that aspect of his story."

Tammy shrugged. "Maybe he thought you would look harder if you thought it was only a mission of love."

"Perhaps."

A prickling of premonition and apprehension ran along the

back of Savannah's neck, a feeling she was well acquainted with, but hated. Mostly, because it had proven to be painfully accurate at portending disasters.

She tried to push the sensation to the back of her mind, to ignore it. This was her first job as a private detective. It felt wonderful to be working again.

And she didn't want anything to interfere with that sense of pride and fulfillment.

Shut up! she told it. *And go away! You don't know everything. This could turn out just fine.*

"Is everything okay, Savannah?" Watching Savannah closely, Tammy looked nearly as worried as she felt.

"Sure." She gave a little shrug and chuckled, but the sound wasn't very cheery. "Everything's fine."

But no matter what she told Tammy or herself . . . that feeling of unease just wouldn't go away.

About twenty-five miles out of town, in an isolated resort cabin on the shore of Lake Arroyo, another person was trying to believe that, in spite of misgivings, everything was fine.

Reid is good at what she does. She'll find her. It won't take long.

Nervously pacing the old cabin which smelled of mildew and fish, the individual marked time. Waiting, hoping, aching for the moment to come, when so many carefully laid plans and cherished fantasies would be fulfilled.

But everything hinged on Savannah Reid's ability to locate Lisa Mallock. And Lisa had no intention of being found.

Carefully, the person examined the paraphernalia spread on the threadbare chenille bedspread: thin copper wire, wads of cotton batting and silver duct tape, the all-purpose hunting knife, and . . . of course . . . the pistol.

The scene was set.

All that was needed . . . was the not-so-innocent victim. It wouldn't be much longer now. The waiting was almost over.

CHAPTER THREE

When Savannah had begun to canvass Lisa Mallock's neighborhood that afternoon, she could have sworn that her face had been three-dimensional. But with every door that had been slammed on it, she could feel her profile becoming more and more flat.

There had to be an easier way to make a living.

Once, she had thought that people opened up to her because of her charm, her good looks, her warm wit. Now she realized that they had only talked to her because they'd had to. She had been a cop. Without that badge hanging on its gold chain around her neck, the members of her adoring public weren't nearly so accommodating.

She stood on the sidewalk, roasting in the heat of a dry, Santa Ana afternoon. The weather man had predicted smog warnings, bad air quality that might be harmful to sensitive persons. *No kidding*, she thought, tasting the pollution on her tongue. *Sensitive people or anyone with a set of lungs.*

Glancing around her, she made a quick mental tally of the houses visited. Eight in all. The ones on either side of the colonel's home and several across the street.

Lisa Mallock's neighbors were extremely suspicious . . . far more than normal, even in typically paranoid suburbia . . . and very protective of her.

"Why do you want to know?" and "What do you want with her?" were the questions Savannah had received instead of answers. So far, no one would even confirm or deny that Lisa still lived with her adoptive father, the colonel.

Ever the hopeful heart, Savannah strolled up the walk of a house four doors north. The flowers in the yard, the children's rope swing that dangled from a sturdy oak limb, the tole-painted birdhouses, all seemed to suggest warmth, hospitality, and welcome.

Maybe.

The woman who answered the door wore a bright smile and a white apron. Savannah didn't think that anyone wore those anymore. She felt as though she had stepped back in time into a 1950s Frigidaire commercial.

"Hello, may I help you?" the lady asked.

Savannah could smell the wonderful fragrance of chocolate chip cookies baking.

"I certainly hope so," she said, trying not to sound too discouraged. "I'm trying to get in touch with Lisa Mallock. Can you tell me if she lives around here?"

The beautiful smile froze on the woman's face. "Not anymore," was the reply. "She moved a couple of weeks ago."

Well, at least that answered one thing.

"I really do need to speak to her. Do you know where she is now?"

"I . . . ah . . . I really don't think I should tell you. Lisa asked us not to say because . . ."

"Yes? Because?"

"Nothing. I don't think I should discuss her with you. She's a really nice person, one of the best people I've ever met, and she's had such problems lately with . . ."

"With?"

The woman shook her perfectly styled head of hair. "No. That's all I'm going to say. Good-bye."

At least she didn't slam the door in her face. She simply closed it. Firmly, decisively, if apologetically, she closed it.

Same difference, Savannah thought as she dragged her body—which suddenly seemed bone tired—down the sidewalk.

"Hey, lady," said a soft, barely there voice behind her.

She turned and was surprised to see a small fairy princess, about ten years old, standing on the porch of the house she had just visited. Instantly, she knew it was a fairy, because of the pink tights and leotard, the lacy skirt, and, of course, the glitter-spangled wand in the child's hand.

"Yes?" she asked, smiling down at the dainty apparition as it tiptoed toward her on pink satin ballet slippers.

"You were asking my mom about Christy's mom, huh?" the girl said, a slight pout on her pixie face.

"Christy's mom?" Savannah's mind raced.

"Yeah, Christy Mallock, the girl who used to live down the street."

"Lisa's daughter?"

"That's right. She's the same age as me, and we used to go to ballet class together, but now she moved across town, and we have to go to rehearsal in different cars. I miss her."

"I'll bet you do." Savannah's heart beat wildly. She was embarrassed by her eagerness to extract whatever information possible out of this innocent, unsuspecting child. "But you still see her in dance class?"

"Oh, sure. Christy gets to be the queen of our pageant."

Savannah cast a furtive, guilty look at the house, but Mommy Perfect seemed to be nowhere in sight. She was sorely tempted simply to ask the girl outright where Lisa and Christy were living now. But, having just been refused the information by the mother, it seemed down and dirty to use the child that way. Even a P.I. had to draw a line somewhere.

But there were other ways. . . .

"Your pageant? That sounds very exciting," Savannah said. "When are you having it?"

"Day after tomorrow, in the gymnasium at our school."

"And where do you go to school?"

"Channel Islands Elementary."

"What time is the recital?"

"It's at two o'clock in the afternoon."

"May I come?"

The girl beamed with pride at Savannah's interest. "Sure. Anybody can come, if you pay three dollars."

"Thank you . . . and what is your name?"

"Marilee."

"Thank you, Marilee. I'll be looking forward to it."

"Are you really going to come?" the girl cried after her as Savannah climbed into the Camaro.

"Sure, and thank you for the invitation," she replied. "I'll be there. I wouldn't miss it for the world."

Savannah lay in her bed, trying to enjoy her new rose-sprinkled sheets and her latest Victoria's Secret acquisition, an oversize, silk poet's shirt. The ruffles spilled over her wrists and tickled the backs of her hands. The deep vee in the neckline revealed softly rounded femininity.

Here, in her own bedroom, she had always indulged her female side . . . a part of herself that was often neglected in her day-to-day work. In the course of being a detective, she saw some pretty horrible aspects of society, revelations that would have made her hard and cold before her time. But every night, she could walk into this cozy room with its antique brass bed, the turn-of-the-century French armoire, the floral wallpaper and crisp, ruffled linens, and she could feel pampered and soothed.

But tonight, it wasn't working.

She sat up in bed, propped against half a dozen pillows, Tammy's latest reports spread across the duvet. And the facts she saw there in black and white disturbed her.

Name: Lisa Mallock
Age: 45
Previous occupation: Registered Nurse
Military history: Nurse in army hospitals, 23 years

Divorced: Ex-husband's name, Earl Mallock
Children: One daughter, Christy, age 10, full custody
Credit rating: Excellent

Savannah continued to scan the report. Nothing seemed out of the ordinary. Lisa Mallock appeared to have led a responsible, productive life, until a year ago, when she had begun to move from one place to another about every three months. She had left her long-standing, well-paying job at the Veterans' Hospital and had worked for a string of temp agencies, providing in-home nursing for less than half the money.

Why?

Usually, people didn't pull up stakes and move households every three months just because they got an itch. Being on the run was a lot of work, especially with a child.

What was Lisa Mallock running from?

More importantly, *whom?*

Earl Mallock seemed the likely person. Mothers were seldom given full custody of a child, unless the court deemed the father unsuitable for some reason.

Savannah thought of the man who had sat, sipping coffee and eating cookies in her den. Brian O'Donnell . . . biological brother in search of his sister.

Tammy had said that he checked out, that he was who he claimed to be.

All the same, Savannah decided to proceed carefully, paying close attention to that voice inside that was warning her about this situation. She had no intention of being a pawn in some bitter ex-husband's game, or anyone else's for that matter.

From what she could see on paper, Lisa Mallock was a decent person, a hardworking mother.

Someday the devils who were chasing Lisa would probably catch up to her; that was the way life usually worked. Savannah might not be able to prevent that from happening, but she sure as hell didn't want to be the cause of it.

Saturday afternoon, at one-thirty sharp, Savannah stood in line outside the gymnasium with her three dollars in hand, eager to see "The Snow Fairy Queen" pageant in all its glory.

With the golden California summer sun beating down on her dark hair and perspiration pooling in the cups of her bra, it wasn't easy to get into the "winter" mood, but she was trying.

Fifteen minutes later, she was allowed in and found herself an excellent, if uncomfortable, seat on the bleachers . . . four rows back in the center.

As the giggling cast of dozens scurried about on the makeshift "stage," wearing pink satin, ruffles of stiff netting, glistening with bits of iridescent glitter, Savannah felt a twang of regret. Here she was, forty years old, no kids of her own, not even a marital prospect on the horizon.

Loving children, she hadn't exactly planned her life this way. Like most women she knew, she had nurtured fantasies of home, hearth, husband, and a handful of hellions. But "Life" had a way of happening while you were busy coping with the present and dreaming about the future. And when today's problems were settled and tomorrow arrived, it seemed to always have a new set of concerns all its own. Either way, she was discovering that the "future"—once it had arrived—wasn't all it was cracked up to be.

Shaking herself out of her somewhat depressing reverie, Savannah searched the crowd for the hundredth time, looking for the red-haired woman whose picture she had seen on Dirk's computer screen.

But the moment the presentation began, it was Christy Mallock who first caught her attention.

The child, who twirled across the stage on her tiptoes, was the image of her mother. Dark, copper hair fell in shimmering waves to her waist. Her pretty face reflected the same strength of will, the same enthusiasm for life, as her mom's.

And there was no mistaking the costume with its extra ruffles, excess glitter, and the jeweled crown perched on her head. Christy was, indeed, the personification of a Snow Fairy Queen.

A second later, Savannah spotted Lisa Mallock, sitting a few rows behind her and to the left, wearing an infinitely proud smile on her tension-tight face. At that moment, Savannah envied her . . . despite whatever personal problems she might have. Savannah would have given anything to have felt that kind of pride, even for a moment, to take that little girl home with her and spend the evening baking chocolate chip cookies and maybe watching *Beauty and the Beast* on home video.

She had intended to approach Lisa Mallock here, after the show in the parking lot, to attempt to give her the information about her brother and his search for her.

But she couldn't bring herself to interfere with this event, which obviously meant so much to both mother and daughter. If Lisa Mallock had been living under even half the stress that Savannah supposed, she would need this fanciful interlude to enjoy some of the precious aspects of life.

No problem. Savannah had tailed more than one person from place to place. She would follow them home, and then, only then, would she intrude on their lives. If worse came to worst, she'd just get another door slammed in her face, right?

Wrong. It was worse. Much worse.

That evening, when Savannah knocked on the door of the modest duplex, it opened promptly, and she found herself staring down the barrel of a gun.

The face at the other end of the pistol had the same basic features, but bore little resemblance to the proud mommy at the dance recital.

"I wondered how long it would take someone to show up here," Lisa Mallock said, sighting down the barrel. "Get away from my door and leave me alone."

Savannah had a long-standing policy: If they're pointing a gun at you, do whatever they say . . . within reason.

She had been at gunpoint before, but each time, she had previously anticipated the problem and had been somewhat emotionally prepared. When you went barging into a major cocaine dealer's house with a dozen ATF officers, you expected trouble.

She hadn't seen this one coming.

The thought deeply disturbed her. Mistakes like that could leave her dead.

She was getting old and sloppy . . . at least, complacent. Not a comforting realization.

If she were smart, Savannah knew that she would turn on her heel and march away from the door, tell Brian O'Donnell where his sister lived, wish him luck—he would need it—and collect her money.

But she didn't work that way.

Why? Because she was a compassionate, caring person.

Or maybe just stupid. Time would tell.

"Lisa," she said in what she hoped was her most cajoling, soothing tone. "I'm not here to cause you trouble of any kind, really. I just—"

"I know why you're here. *He* hired you, just like he hired all the other ones."

"He? He who?"

"Earl, my ex-husband. He wants to kill me and kidnap my daughter. He's certainly threatened to often enough." Anger blazed in her eyes, but beneath the fury, Savannah saw the fear, the pain. Lisa shook her head and for a moment, Savannah thought she might start to cry. "I don't understand," the woman said. "How can you people help someone like that?"

Savannah's heart went out to the woman, in spite of the weapon pointed at her. In Lisa Mallock's shoes, stalked by a vengeful ex, with a child to protect, she might do the same thing.

No "might." She would.

"I'm not working for Earl," Savannah told her. "I've never met him, I swear. The man who hired me is Brian O'Donnell, your natural brother. He wants very badly to get in touch with you."

For a brief moment the woman's eyes softened, a look of hope crossed her face, but it quickly dissolved into bitterness. "It's Earl, all right. He lied to you."

"I don't think so. He's—"

"A fat guy with dark brown hair, blue eyes and a beard, right?"

"No, kinda skinny with dark red hair, like yours and Christy's, and brown eyes. No beard. Just a curly mustache. Looks like a barbershop quartet tenor."

For the first time, the hand that held the gun began to tremble. Savannah was immensely relieved to see Lisa lower the pistol to her side.

"Really?" Lisa's eyes searched hers, begging her to be telling the truth.

Holding up two fingers, Savannah said solemnly, "Scout's honor."

"Were you ever a Girl Scout?"

Savannah shrugged and gave her a sheepish grin. "No, but I was a Blue Bird for six months in '62."

"Close enough." She opened the door wider. "Come on in."

Usually, Savannah refused any form of refreshment when conducting an investigation in someone's home. But the fresh peanut butter and M&M cookies on the kitchen table were too great a temptation to be denied.

"I put the candies on myself," Christy bragged, still prancing around in her regal, fairy queen attire. "Four on each one and all different colors."

"I can see that. You did an excellent job." Savannah smiled at her and once again felt the twang of loss. *Dang those biological urges*, she thought. "You're almost as good a baker as you are a dancer."

Christy blushed with pride, but Lisa seemed less affected

by her comments. Silently, she stepped over to the stove and poured two mugs of coffee. Joining them at the table, she slid onto a chair across from Savannah, pushing some piles of bills aside.

Overdue . . . considering the red envelopes.

But then, Savannah wasn't going to judge the woman. Recently, her own phone had been scheduled for disconnection, and she had been granted a reprieve only by the grace of Brian O'Donnell's retainer.

With only a modicum of civility, Lisa shoved the mug of coffee across the table at Savannah.

"Chris, go to your room now and play or something. This lady and I have some business to discuss."

Christy's face crumpled into a pout, her bottom lip protruding to the extreme that Savannah thought pigeons might have been tempted to perch on it. "I don't wanna play right now," the child said, casting a curious look at Savannah.

"Then go into my room and watch television."

"I'm not supposed to watch TV until I have all my homework done."

"So, do your homework first . . . in your room."

"But . . . but it's that hard stuff . . . long division . . . and you said you'd help me. I can't do it by myself."

"Christina Louise."

"Okay, I'm going. I'm going."

Savannah wiped her hand across her lips, trying to hide her smile as the once-graceful pageant queen stomped away to her bedroom, ruffles bouncing indignantly.

"Do you have kids?" Lisa asked as she took a sip from her mug. Savannah noticed that, in spite of her forced nonchalance, her hands were still shaking. Savannah didn't think it was from a caffeine overdose.

"No, I'm sorry to say I don't. But I practically raised my eight younger brothers and sisters back in Georgia. Do I get credit for that?"

Lisa nodded, and a bit of her hostility seemed to slip away. "*Eight* of them? Yes, tons of credit. That must have been a lot of work and responsibility for a young person."

"It was. But I wouldn't have missed it for the world. I really love kids."

Across the table, Lisa's eyes met hers with an intensity born of fear and determination. "Then you can understand why I have to protect my daughter from a man who would destroy her life and mine."

"Yes, I can."

Lisa paused and took a long drink of her coffee, as though fortifying herself for the rest of the conversation. "Tell me, Ms. Reid, do you think some people are really evil? Not just misguided, but truly evil?"

Having been a cop for fifteen years, Savannah didn't have to think long to answer Lisa's question. "Yes, I do. Thankfully, I think they are rare. I believe that most folks mean well, that the majority live by some sort of moral code, however warped their philosophy might be. But I have come across a few individuals who I would say are evil to the core."

"Well, my ex-husband is one of those people. He doesn't care who he hurts as long as he can control everything and everyone around him. I left him. I divorced him. I removed myself and our daughter from his control. He'll never forgive me for that. And he will never accept the situation."

Savannah liked to believe she knew people. After years of dealing with the best and worst of humanity, she could usually read a person and know what was going on behind the facade they presented to the world. This woman was telling the truth.

Savannah's heart went out to Lisa and her little fairy princess daughter.

"Have you been running from him for long?" she asked.

"It seems like forever. He always finds us, and then we have to move. A new house, another job for me, a change of schools for Christy. Thanks to that bastard, we're a couple of nomads." She sighed, and Savannah could see the depth of her fatigue. Lisa Mallock wasn't just tired; she was deeply, dangerously exhausted.

"It isn't fair," Savannah said, feeling the impotence she had always experienced when confronted with this situation. Even as a peace officer, she had been unable to do much in these circumstances. The law protected men like Earl Mallock far better than it did the women and children they terrorized. A restraining order was a flimsy bit of paper that did nothing to protect a victim from a bullet or the blade of a knife.

In Savannah's career, it had been one of her most profound frustrations.

"No, it isn't fair," Lisa agreed, her voice as hollow as her eyes. "But it's the way things are. And for right now, all I can do is be careful. That's why I'm so reluctant to trust what you're telling me about my brother."

"I understand. But this could be a wonderful opportunity for you and your daughter. With all that's going on in your life, it might be nice to be reconnected with your brother, to have a sense of family. He lives in Orlando, Florida, with his wife and children and—"

"Brian has kids of his own?" Lisa's eyes misted.

"Three boys. He said he wants them to meet your children, to play with them."

The moisture on Lisa's lids puddled and spilled down her cheeks. "We used to have a tree house," she said wistfully. "I remember playing in it . . . before my mom died . . . before my dad gave me away. . . ."

"Your dad . . . oh, yes, by the way . . ." Savannah swallowed, wondering how the already-stressed woman would take this news. "Part of the reason why Brian is looking for you now is because your father recently passed away. It seems he left you with an inheritance."

"My father included me in his will?" Lisa looked pleased and touched.

"Well, I'm not certain of all the facts, but I do know that Brian wants to make sure that you get your share."

Savannah glanced around the sparsely furnished duplex. Nomads couldn't afford luxuries. "I understand it's around fifty thousand dollars. That much money might help you and your daughter, too," she added.

Lisa nodded, studying her coffee as though the swirls of cream—like a fortune-teller's tea leaves—might tell her something. "Mostly," she said, "I just want to see Brian again. I don't have many memories of him, but the ones I have are some of the happiest of my life."

Setting down her coffee mug, Lisa covered her face with her hands and began to cry softly. "I don't know what to do," she said.

Savannah reached across the table and placed her hand on the woman's arm, trying to impart some degree of comfort and reassurance.

"We've checked this guy out, Lisa," she said, "from top to bottom. This time it isn't Earl. It's Brian. This time it's something good coming into your life, not something bad. It's true. You can trust me."

Lisa uncovered her face and stared at Savannah with a haunted, hunted look that Savannah would never forget. "Trust isn't something that comes easy for me anymore," she said.

"I can understand that." Savannah patted her arm. "But can you bring yourself to do it . . . for yourself, for Christy . . . one more time?"

Slowly, Lisa Mallock nodded her head and a light of hope entered those tired eyes. "Okay," she said with quiet conviction. "I'll trust somebody. One more time."

By the time Savannah left Lisa Mallock's home, the hour was much later than she had thought. Once Savannah had convinced the worried mother of her child's safety and Savannah's own altruistic intentions, the visit had turned more social. The two women had shared a few more cups of coffee and enough personal information to convince Savannah that she would like to pursue a friendship with this gutsy, compassionate lady. Apparently, being a nurse had required some of the same personality traits as law enforcement. They had found they had a lot in common.

Feeling good about the turn of events, Savannah left the house and strolled down the deserted sidewalk toward her parked car. The air currents had shifted, the Santa Ana winds abated, and an onshore flow of evening breeze had covered the city with a thick layer of fog.

The streetlamps glowed golden, haloed by the mist, their haze-diffused light casting a dim, surreal glow over the quiet neighborhood. Children, parents, and pets had deserted the streets and were behind closed doors, attending to homework, late evening meals, and the perpetual television viewing. Only the trash cans—beige for recycling, green for normal—stood, silently waiting for the morning collection.

As Savannah approached her car, a particularly cool breath of evening air whirled around her, invading the thin linen jacket she wore. The tiny hairs on the back of her neck rose and she shuddered.

It was a feeling she had experienced several times before, a distinct, unpleasant sensation that had little to do with the weather.

Pausing, she stood still in the middle of the sidewalk and studied her surroundings.

Silence.

Stillness.

But for all the quiet, the air didn't seem empty. She didn't feel alone.

Straining to hear, she listened for anything: the sound of muffled footsteps, movement in the nearby shrubs . . . even the sound of another human being breathing.

But there was nothing. Nothing, except for her overpowering premonition that someone, somewhere was watching, waiting, listening . . . even as she was.

"Who's there?" she asked, knowing there would be no response.

But there was.

From the darkness behind the closest house came the deep, bass growl of a dog. A big dog. Probably about the size and temperament of Beowulf. Then the animal began barking in earnest.

As it was hidden by the shadows, Savannah couldn't see the creature, but she didn't have to. She wasn't interested in being introduced. One ferocious beast per day was her quota.

Without wasting another moment, she hurried to the Camaro, jumped inside, snapped down the door locks, and started the engine. A few seconds later, she was headed down the street and out of the neighborhood.

There wasn't anyone there, she told herself as she pulled onto the better lit, more heavily traveled Harrington Boulevard. *It was just the dog. That's what you sensed. The dog. It was looking at you and . . .*

Sure, that was all it had been, she decided. But a voice inside told her not to believe it. That little something inside knew better.

You know it wasn't just the dog, she warned herself.

It was just the dog . . . and Lisa's stories about her creepy husband, came the comforting reply.

Since when do you lock car doors against stories and watchdogs?

Okay, she admitted, it had her there.

Steering her car toward home, she decided it was too late to try to contact Brian O'Donnell. He had waited all these years to get in touch with his sister. Surely, he could hold out until morning.

Besides, Savannah had already decided that she had to sleep on it before turning the information over to him.

Lisa and Christy Mallock were trusting her. And Savannah knew she was going to spend a fitful night, wrestling with the demon—or maybe it was her own intuition—who was telling her that she was about to do something she would regret.

CHAPTER FOUR

Savannah woke with a start and sat up in bed, gripping her sheets with shaking hands. Her new silk nightgown clung to her perspiration-soaked body. It was a cold, clammy, sick sweat. She was deeply frightened, her pulse pounding in her ears, her mouth dry. Probably the residue from a nightmare . . . but she couldn't remember many details.

The last time she had awoken this abruptly and this unpleasantly had been during the Northridge earthquake, an event that she and her fellow Southern Californians weren't likely to forget anytime soon. But the fern hanging in the corner was still, not swinging wildly, as before. The pictures remained on the wall. The same walls were intact and basically vertical . . . always a good sign.

So, why did she feel as though she needed to throw up?

She wasn't sure, but her dream had been inhabited by tiny, star-spangled dancers in pink ruffled skirts and a dark, menacing presence, that had somehow gained access to the innocents by way of her own actions.

Earl Mallock. She couldn't get him out of her mind. Dark hair, heavy set, blue eyes. And pure evil. That had been Lisa's description of her ex-husband.

Brian O'Donnell. Dark auburn hair, slender, soft-spoken and brown-eyed.

They couldn't be the same person.

But what if the man in her office had been working for Earl Mallock? Perhaps he was a misguided friend performing some sort of grim favor?

No, he had seemed sincere enough. Savannah prided herself on being an astute judge of character, and she could have sworn that she had seen only honesty in his face, that she had heard only love and concern in his voice.

But then, she had been fooled before. Good judgment or not, no one was infallible. Not if a con was good at his job.

Either way, she couldn't simply lie there in bed, thinking, worrying. The hope of going back to sleep was a futile fantasy.

With a sigh she threw back the sheets and duvet and stared at the alarm clock on her bed stand as though it were a mortal enemy—1:25 A.M. Great . . . she had been asleep a whole hour and a half.

Dragging her tired body from the warm, soft bed, she walked to her closet and pulled on some jeans, a sweatshirt, and a pair of sneakers, sans the socks. Then she headed downstairs to get her purse and car keys.

She wasn't sure where she was going, or what she was hoping to accomplish at this time of night. But she knew she had to do something. She had to make sure everything was okay with Brian O'Donnell. Because, in eight hours, she was supposed to tell him where to find Lisa Mallock and her daughter.

And before she gave him that precious information, she had to be absolutely, positively sure.

Just outside the San Carmelita city limits—fifty yards outside, to be exact—sat the Blue Moon Motel. The sign in front of the establishment boasted easy access to Lake Arroyo, the best fishing, boating, and skiing in the county. But, cynical as she was, Savannah had long suspected that its location had been chosen because it was beyond the jurisdiction of the San Carmelita Police Department.

With only occasional interference from the county sheriff's deputies, the Blue Moon owners provided a convenient, out-of-the-way, no-tell motel for those individuals engaging in clandestine meetings. Twenty-five bucks would buy you three hours of uninterrupted debauchery beneath mirrored ceilings, on vibrating beds with blue crushed velvet spreads—circa: 1972.

And if you weren't fortunate enough to have company in your room, any one of four X-rated cable television stations would show you what you were missing.

Fourteen units long, the building glowed an anemic blue-white in the light of the flickering neon sign which announced that there were, indeed, vacancies.

Each dark blue door bore a crescent moon, reminiscent of a couple of outhouses Savannah had known as a child in Georgia.

Savannah pulled her Camaro into the parking lot, gravel

crunching under her tires. The area was dark and located behind the motel. No doubt to provide even more privacy for nervous customers.

As she entered the squeaking front door, she spotted the innkeeper sitting behind the counter, his feet propped on a table beside a chrome coffeepot. From beneath the rim of a battered fishing cap, he was staring at a small, black-and-white television set, which had been shoved onto an overhead shelf, above the ancient cash register.

"Yeah?" he asked without taking his eyes off the TV. She couldn't see enough of the picture to know what had him so entranced, but from the groans and moans that issued from the set, she assumed he was watching one of his own cable channels.

"I need—" she began.

"How long?"

She stepped closer and caught a glimpse of exaggerated male anatomy on the screen. "I beg your pardon?" she asked.

"How long do you need the room for?" he replied, still not looking her way. "We rent by the hour. I got one with a king-size water bed and—"

"No, thank you. I just wanted to visit one of your guests."

"Fine with me." He finally turned toward her and shifted the cigarette from one corner of his mouth to the other. "But, you visit, you pay."

"I'm just going to talk to him."

"Yeah . . ." the guy grinned unpleasantly, revealing teeth that looked as though they hadn't been acquainted with a toothbrush in a decade or so. They appeared to be wearing tiny yellow-green sweaters. ". . . you just wanna talk. Now, don't they all."

Unconsciously, Savannah reached for the badge, which she had worn for so many years on a heavy chain around her neck. The badge which had been stripped from her, along with her authority as a peace officer. It certainly made moments like this more complicated.

"My name is Savannah Reid," she began, opening her purse to produce her private investigator's license, "and I—"

"Savannah Reid? Well, why didn't you say so?"

Mmmmmm . . . he had heard of her; she wasn't sure if that was good news or bad.

"I didn't know it would matter," she replied.

"Of course it does." His grin widened, revealing gaps between the rows of "sweaters." "I got a message for you, right here."

He bent over and began to riffle through the pile of papers on his desk top. After tossing aside an assortment of ancient phone messages with curling edges, musty girlie magazines, and wadded gum and cigarette wrappers, he produced a fairly fresh-looking slip of pink paper.

"A message, for me?" she asked. Her stomach began to churn, as though she knew she wasn't going to like what she was about to receive. "Who is it from?"

Do you really have to ask? she told herself.

"It's from a fellow who was staying here for a week or so."

"A red-haired guy."

"That's him."

"You say he *was* staying? Does that mean he's gone?"

"Yep. Checked out a couple of hours ago. Don't know why he'd leave so late. Might as well have stayed. I'd done charged him for the night. He seemed to be in a hurry to get on his way."

Adrenaline flooding through her veins, Savannah unfolded the pink slip of paper and read three simple words:

Thanks for everything.

"That's it?" she asked, staring at the writing, which looked as though it had been scrawled in haste. "He didn't even sign it?"

"Guess not," the clerk said with a shrug as he leaned over the counter to glance at the note. As though he hadn't already read it.

"What did he say when he gave it to you?"

"Just said something like, 'There's gonna be a lady come in here by the name of Savannah Reid. She'll be asking for me. Give her this.' Then he sorta grinned and handed that to me."

"He *grinned?* What do you mean, he grinned? Was it a nice, friendly smile?"

"Nope. It sure wasn't. It was one of those weird grins like people give you when they're enjoying something they shouldn't."

Savannah mentally digested that for a moment, then pushed a bit further. "Do you mean like a mischievous gr—"

"I don't know, lady." The clerk settled back into his chair, obviously tired of the subject and eager to return to his television viewing. "Just a weird look. That's all I can tell you. That and . . . well . . . it kinda gave me the creeps."

"Gave *you* the creeps," Savannah muttered as she turned to leave, clutching the terse note in her palm, which had suddenly grown moist and cold.

Her client had disappeared abruptly, without collecting

the information he had hired her to uncover, without paying her the remainder of what he owed, leaving behind only a three-word message and a smile which even a weirdo had described as "weird."

Not good, she decided.

Definitely not good.

"Don't cry, Christy. Everything's all right. Mommy's here now and you don't have to worry about anything."

Cradling her sobbing daughter in her arms, Lisa Mallock tried to sound more calm and confident than she felt.

That ghostly, nocturnal creature, the Night Mare, had galloped across the landscape of more than one victim's dreams tonight, it seemed. Lisa herself had been plagued with disturbing images of violent confrontations, off and on all night. Perhaps most disturbing of all was the fact that in her dreams she was losing those battles. And there was so much at stake; she simply couldn't afford to lose.

Just before dawn she had awakened to find Christy standing beside her bed, weeping. She had pulled the shivering child into her bed and snuggled her close. Lisa didn't want to think about how much she needed that comforting contact herself. How weak and vulnerable she felt at this point in her life.

"Daddy's gonna find us again." Christy buried her face against her mother's neck. Lisa could feel the child's tears, wet and warm, tickling down her skin. "He's going to hurt us. I know, because I saw him in my dream."

"A dream is just a story that your imagination tells when you're asleep, honey." Lisa stroked the glossy copper curls, so like her own, and kissed the girl's forehead. She tasted salty with sweat. "Dreams are like fairy tales. Some are pretty, and some are scary. But none of them are real."

"Then Daddy isn't going to find us, ever again?"

By the light of the bedside lamp, Lisa saw the innocence, the trust in her daughter's eyes. She couldn't bring herself to lie to the child. "I don't know if he will or not. But even if he does, you don't have to worry. I'll keep you safe."

The words seemed to have little effect on the girl. Reaching up with her small hand, Christy stroked her mother's cheek. "I know you will. But Daddy's really big and strong. Mommy, who's going to keep *you* safe?"

Who, indeed? Lisa wondered, trying to find an honest answer that would reassure her daughter. And herself.

The courts? The police? They hadn't been much help in the past.

"My husband is going to kill me someday," she had told them, again and again. "Really, he will. It's just a matter of time."

"Get a restraining order," they would suggest.

"I have one."

"So, when he shows up at your door, give us a call," they had replied. "We'll be there within ten minutes."

Great, she thought, *he could kill me five times in ten minutes.*

Maybe, God would protect her. Maybe He would remember all those mornings she had spent in Sunday school as a child, all the Bible pictures she had colored oh-so-carefully, all the quarters she had placed in the offering plate. Maybe He would send a host of angels to rescue her when the time came.

But somehow, Lisa Mallock didn't think so. *She* had chosen to marry Earl Mallock of her own free will. *She* had ignored that wiser, inspired voice inside that had warned her about him. Now, she had the sinking feeling that God had decided to let her deal with the consequences of her actions alone. She had no one to blame but herself.

And she had no one else to protect her. Just she, herself . . . and the pistol locked in her nightstand . . . if she could get to it in time . . . if her aim was straight . . . if she could summon the courage to shoot someone she had once loved more than life itself.

If.

Lisa felt the child in her arms go limp, relaxing at last as her breathing slowed and her eyes closed. Christy had drifted off to sleep without an answer to her question: Who would protect her mommy? And Lisa was thankful, because she didn't have an honest answer, for her precious daughter, cuddled warm and trustingly against her side . . . or for herself.

"I can't believe you would haul me out of bed at four in the morning and not even bring me an apple fritter and some java." Usually, Dirk's voracious appetite was a source of mild amusement for Savannah, but, under the circumstances, she wasn't in the mood.

"Don't hassle me, Coulter," she said as she slid onto the chair in front of a police station computer and began to type furiously. "Take my word for it, this isn't the time."

"That bad?" Dirk asked, the pout dissolving from his face.

"Yeah, that bad."

"Whatcha looking for?" He leaned over her shoulder to study the blue screen that quickly switched to green. She had accessed the Department of Motor Vehicle files.

"Earl Mallock."

"Your lost sister's old man?"

"Yeah, but she isn't lost anymore. I found her last night."

"Good work."

"Maybe. Maybe not."

Savannah's pulse pounded in her ears as she punched in the necessary codes to find what she was looking for . . . what she hoped to high heaven she wouldn't find.

Mallock's name appeared on the screen, along with his basic identification stats.

> *Name:* Mallock, Earl R.
> *Address:* 312 Elm Street, San Carmelita, CA
> *Height:* 5´ 10˝ *Weight:* 220 lbs.
> *Hair:* Dark brown *Eyes:* Blue

"That's the same description Lisa Mallock gave me last night," Savannah said, trying to feel better.

Dirk read over her shoulder. "So, what's the problem?"

"I'm afraid I might have helped Lisa's abusive ex-husband find her." She peered at the screen. "But the guy who hired me looked completely different."

"Maybe he's a friend of the husband's, trying to help him out."

"Could be, or . . ."

She waited for the photo to appear, her hands and insides shaking . . . and it wasn't only because she needed a cup of coffee.

A face materialized before her on the screen. Round, double-chinned. If he had been wearing a white beard and red suit,

Earl Mallock could have been a department store variety Santa Claus. Unless you looked into his eyes.

Savannah had seen that look before, too many times. Flat, emotionless, frightening more for what wasn't there than what was. No sense of happiness, excitement, sorrow, or pain . . . all the components that made up most lives. All that was reflected there was a void, a profound emptiness of the soul.

She shivered.

"Recognize him?" Dirk said.

"Well, not really, but . . ."

Yes, she did. As much as she didn't want to, she did recognize him.

"If you change the hair and eye color," she muttered, staring at the screen, "if you take off the extra pounds . . . oh, God. . . ."

"Is it him?" Dirk placed strong, warm hands on her shoulders. But, rather than imparting comfort, as he obviously intended, the intimate gesture nearly made her burst into tears of fear and anger.

"That son of a bitch. He dyed his hair and cut it short."

"And his eyes?"

"Colored contacts, I'll bet."

"But you said he was fat."

"He was. But apparently he lost the weight. Fast. That's probably why he looked so haggard and run-down. This picture was taken less than a year ago, and he's about 160 pounds now."

"Wow, you'll have to find out what kind of a diet he was on," Dirk replied.

"Shut up," she snapped. "Your timing stinks and you aren't funny."

Instead of verbal retaliation, he continued to rub her shoulders. "You didn't know, Van," he said softly.

"That doesn't matter," she said, jumping up from the chair and throwing the switch on the computer. "I *should* have known."

She headed for the door.

"Where are you going?" Dirk hurried after her.

"To see Lisa Mallock. To warn her. To tell her she was wrong about trusting me. In this world you can't trust anybody. Not even yourself." Tears flooded her eyes as she strode down the hallway and out the back door of the station. "Dammit," she muttered as she got into the Camaro and peeled out of the parking lot, leaving Dirk standing alone and looking concerned on the station steps. "I *should* have known. I'm sorry, Lisa . . . Christy. Dammit, I'm so sorry."

CHAPTER FIVE

When Savannah had left the police station, she had fully intended to drive straight to Lisa Mallock's home, ring the bell, and warn her about a possible contact from her ex-husband. But after arriving at the address, Savannah checked her watch and realized it was only five-thirty in the morning.

Lisa would be distressed enough about the information, without being summoned out of bed to receive the news.

Sitting in the Camaro, Savannah studied the surrounding parking lot, play area, and laundry room. No one was stirring. All was silent and still. With the first pink and lavender rays of dawn tinting the sky, it seemed hard to believe that anything sinister was likely to happen soon.

Seven-thirty, she decided. *With a child in the house, she'll probably be up and about by then.*

After drinking a cup of coffee or two, Lisa would be forti-
fied, at least a bit, to hear the bad tidings.

Checking everything once more, Savannah headed home.
She intended to spend the next two hours combing the information that she and Tammy had uncovered . . . or the *misin-
formation*, as it had turned out to be. She needed to see what
had gone wrong and how she might redeem the situation.

But another shock greeted her as she hurried up the walkway to her house. At first she thought it was Earl Mallock,
standing there on her front porch, partially hidden by the
bougainvillea. The red hair, the slender build, were all too familiar.

But when the man turned toward her and she could see his
face, she had an instant idea who her early morning visitor was.

"I'm sorry for the early hour," he began, "but—"

"It's all right. Let me guess," she said dryly, holding out her
hand to him. "You're Brian O'Donnell. The *real* one, that is."

He looked genuinely confused as he accepted her handshake. "I beg your pardon?"

"Your sister's name is Lisa Mallock, and I'll just bet you're
looking for her. Right?"

"How did you know?"

"Just a lucky guess." With a tired, defeated sigh she opened
her front door. "Come inside, Mr. O'Donnell. It's about time you
and I put our heads together."

Savannah offered the man one of the wing chairs in her office,
and she sat in the other opposite him. There was no time to mess
with coffee, cookies, or Southern hospitality. "Talk about a

creepy sense of déjà vu," she muttered as she stared at the red-haired man across from her.

"What?"

"Never mind. Let me ask you a question," she said. "First, why were you on my doorstep so early in the morning?"

"I couldn't sleep. I was worried." The dark circles under his eyes attested to the fact that he was weary, but Savannah wasn't ready to believe anything too readily anymore.

"It's a condition that's going around," she replied. "Why were *you* worried?"

"I talked to my wife, back in Orlando, Florida, last evening, about eight o'clock Pacific time. She told me that you, or someone from your office, called her."

"That's true."

"She said that someone who looks like me came here and asked you to find my sister."

"Someone did. We called her to verify that it was you, and we compared physical descriptions. She confirmed that you were in San Carmelita, searching for your sister, and that she wasn't surprised you had contacted a private investigator. I'm very sorry, Mr. O'Donnell, if that's who you really are. Everyone thought our visitor was who he claimed to be . . . specifically, you."

"I think I might know who he was," Brian O'Donnell said.

Yeah, you and me both, Savannah thought, but she kept it to herself. "Who?" she asked.

"I'm afraid it might be Lisa's ex-husband, a guy by the name of Earl."

"Is that right?" Savannah cleared her throat. "And why do you think that?"

"Because I'm afraid I may have made a mistake by talking to him about her. You see, I've been searching for my sister for a long time and about eight months ago I traced her here to San Carmelita. I contacted her husband—he's her ex now, but I didn't know it then—and asked him about her. He didn't let on that they were even separated, let alone divorced. He said that if I'd come to town, he might convince her to see me."

"You came then . . . eight months ago?"

"Yes. I flew right out, and he met me at LAX. We had a drink there in one of the lounges and he told me that she refused to see me. He asked me a lot of questions about our childhood, my life, our family. I was flattered that he was such an interested brother-in-law, considering that my sister wouldn't even see me."

"Yes. He can be quite convincing," Savannah agreed, shifting uncomfortably in her chair. "Please, go on."

"We continued to correspond, and when my father died recently, I asked him to talk to my sister again, to tell her how important it was that I see her. I was hoping that, maybe, the inheritance money would make a difference."

He blushed, a deep, natural redhead flush and shrugged his shoulders. "I wasn't proud. I wanted to see her any way I could, no matter what her motivation."

"I can understand that. But you haven't seen her yet?"

"No. I just arrived in town last night. And after I spoke to my wife, I decided I'd better come over here right away and ask you what was up. Besides, I don't even know where my sister is. Last night I drove by the address that Earl Mallock gave me and it's just one of those postal centers with PO boxes."

Savannah felt the first spark of hope she had experienced

since visiting the Blue Moon Motel last night. Maybe things weren't quite so bleak, after all. Along with the bad news that she would have to deliver to Lisa Mallock in another hour and a half, she could bring her a blessing . . . a real, flesh-and-blood brother.

"I know where she is," Savannah told him with a tired smile. "I'm going to spend the next ninety minutes making absolutely, positively sure that you are who you say you are. And if it's true, I'll introduce you to your sister. Believe me, you couldn't have arrived at a better time."

"Is this it?" Brian O'Donnell's ruddy face glowed with anticipation as Savannah pulled the Camaro into the driveway and cut the key. "Is this my sister's house?"

"That's it. The unit 'A' on the left. And that's her Tempest under the carport, so I'd say she's home."

Brian was already opening the car door and swinging a leg out.

"Ah . . . you might want to wait just a minute," she suggested, "and let me go first. I think I should tell her that you're with me."

He looked only slightly disappointed. "Oh, okay. I'm just anxious, that's all."

"Perfectly understandable. I won't take long. Promise."

But when Savannah rang the doorbell, no one answered. After buzzing a couple times, she knocked loudly.

Still no response.

She glanced at her watch. It was seven-forty. Maybe Lisa was still in bed and a sound sleeper. Perhaps if she tried the back door.

But she had no better luck there. After pounding until her knuckles tingled, she was about to give up and accept the fact that no one was at home, when she noticed something that sent a chill through her. Deep, jagged gouges in the wooden door-frame, just beside the lock.

"No," she whispered. "No, don't let it be. . . ."

Even as she tried to deny what she feared, Savannah pulled a tissue from her jacket pocket and used it to turn the knob. The door swung open easily.

Lisa Mallock would never have slept with the door un-locked. With the threat of her ex-husband hanging over her, Lisa wouldn't even have been awake in her house with the door unlocked.

"Lisa?" Savannah stuck her head inside the kitchen and looked around. The bills were still spread across the table. The remaining M&M cookies on the plate had been covered with plastic wrap. "Lisa, Christy?"

Instinctively, Savannah's hand went to the Beretta that she carried in a shoulder holster beneath her jacket. Not wanting to scare Lisa or her young daughter, she didn't draw the weapon, but she was ready if necessary.

"It's me, Savannah Reid. Anybody home?" she called. The house had a heavy, uneasy stillness about it that made the back of her neck tingle.

Carefully, she walked through the kitchen and into the liv-ing room. With the shades and curtains drawn, the room was fairly dark, and she could only discern basic shapes: the sofa, a bean bag chair, the television on a TV tray in the corner.

As she crept deeper into the room, a strange, irritating sound caught her attention. A high-pitched beeping, like a pager or . . .

It was the telephone receiver, lying on the floor beside the end table. As a matter of habit, she reached for it, to return it to its cradle, but caught herself. Although she was hoping against hope this wasn't a crime scene, she knew better than disturb anything.

"Lisa?" she called again, knowing it was pointless. No one slept that soundly. If Lisa Mallock were here and able to speak, she would have done so already.

Slipping the Beretta from its holster, Savannah pointed the barrel at the ceiling and crept down the short hallway. One glance into the bathroom told her that it was empty and nothing seemed amiss.

She hurried on to the first bedroom. Inside she saw the twin bed with its Little Mermaid spread, spilling onto the floor. The only other piece of furniture in the room was a small dresser. The drawers were gaping open and appeared to be empty.

Pink tights and a spangled crown lay crumpled on the floor. No fairy princess would have left such a prize like that. Not willingly. "Oh . . . Christy," Savannah whispered to the silent room.

Across the hall, Lisa's bed was equally disheveled, the spread lying in a heap on the ancient, gold shag carpeting.

The top sheet was gone—another fact which Savannah noted with alarm. Lisa Mallock had been a nurse. It was probably just a silly stereotype, hospital corners and all that, but Savannah couldn't imagine a nurse sleeping without a top and bottom sheet.

The lower, fitted sheet that remained had been pulled loose and the right side was ripped. At the foot of the bed lay a pillow with a crimson darkness staining the linen. Savannah didn't need to turn on the light to see what it was. She could smell the distinctive, coppery odor of blood.

"What's going on here?"

She whirled around, gun in hand, to find Brian O'Donnell staring at her with a stricken face. He looked past her to the bed, and she heard him draw a ragged, strangling gasp.

Returning the pistol to its holster, she placed one hand on his chest and gently coaxed him backward. Maybe he hadn't seen the ripped sheet or the bloody pillow. "I'm not sure," she said. "But it doesn't look good."

"Do you think her ex-husband did something to her?"

"I don't know. We'll have to call the police and—"

At that moment they heard a loud noise; someone had thrown open the front door. Heavy footsteps. Male voices.

"Stay here," she whispered to Brian as she pulled her gun again. Pushing him aside, she crept along the wall and took a peek around the corner into the living room.

By the light of the open doorway, she saw three silhouettes, a trio of men, standing in the center of the room. As her eyes adjusted to the brightness, she recognized the one nearest her.

"Dirk?" she asked.

He whirled around, obviously as shocked to see her as she had been to identify him. "Van?"

"It's me. And who are . . . ?"

Even as she uttered the words, she realized that the fellow by the door was Colonel Forrest Neilson, and the third was one of her least-favorite people.

"Why, Captain Bloss," she muttered with saccharine sweetness, "what a pure dee-light to set eyes upon you again."

"Yeah, right," he replied with that grating nasal voice and

perpetual liquid sniff that had always made her hate him . . . along with a few other hundred reasons that came immediately to mind. As her superior, Bloss had forced her out of the San Carmelita Police Department for grossly unfair reasons. That was her foremost reason for wanting to see him roasting on a spit at a country barbecue, and she knew at least a couple dozen individuals who would eagerly stand in line for the chance to turn him.

"Why are you in my daughter's house?" Colonel Neilson took a step toward her and she fought the urge to back away from him. In spite of his age and disabilities, he was still an intimidating figure.

"I had an appointment with Mrs. Mallock," she replied evenly, stretching the truth only a bit. Lisa hadn't exactly been expecting her, but she had promised to be in touch soon.

Close enough.

"At what time?" Bloss said.

"Five minutes ago."

"You saw Lisa five minutes ago?" Dirk asked.

"No," Savannah had to admit. "She doesn't appear to be at home."

"Of course she isn't home," the colonel interjected, his bass voice booming through the eerie silence of the house. "Why do you think we're here?"

"Why *are* you here?" Savannah addressed the question to Dirk, who was looking unusually miserable, even for him.

"Because Colonel Neilson believes his daughter is missing," he said quietly.

"She *is* missing." Neilson took another step toward Savannah, his arthritic hands curled into impotent fists. "That no-good son of a bitch has her . . . and my granddaughter, too, thanks to you, Miss Reid."

"Do you know that for a fact, sir?" she asked, deliberately keeping her voice even, despite her rising pulse rate.

"Don't you get smart with me, young lady. Everything was fine until you came along and—"

"Excuse me. . . ." A soft voice interrupted and Brian O'Donnell stepped from the hallway, where Savannah had left him, into the living room.

The colonel jumped, Bloss snorted, and Dirk's hand went to his gun.

"Did I hear you say that Susie O'Donnell is your daughter?" Brian asked Neilson.

The colonel said nothing for a long moment. Even in the dim light, Savannah could see him turn pale beneath his deep California tan. Then he snapped, "Who the hell are you?"

"Brian O'Donnell." The younger man held out his hand to Neilson. "I'm Susie's brother, Brian. I've been looking for you a long time . . . and for Susan."

"Her name is Lisa now." The colonel's voice was brusque, but Savannah could hear the emotion beneath the clipped words.

"I understand," Brian replied, lowering his hand when the colonel refused to shake it.

"Well . . ." The colonel cleared his throat and pulled himself to attention. ". . . it seems we're all looking for her right now." He pushed past Brian and Savannah and headed down the hall toward the bedrooms.

"Since when does a citizen get a police captain and a detective all to himself, just because his daughter isn't answering her telephone?" Savannah asked, keeping her voice low.

"Since he's Colonel Forrest Neilson," Bloss returned, his round face flushed a bit darker than usual. "He's a close and personal friend of the chief's."

"Gee, that explains everything," Savannah said sarcastically. "Let's see now . . . the last time I investigated one of the chief's 'close and personal friends' I was fired. Right?"

"You aren't too swift; are you, Reid?" Bloss sniffed again, then carelessly swabbed the used tissue across his sweaty forehead. "You got one of them learning disorders or something?"

Savannah shrugged and gave him a demure, if somewhat insincere, smile. "Not all of us are cerebrally gifted, like yourself," she said. Dropping her voice, she added, "Not to mention phallically challenged and testicularly limited."

He gave her a quizzical look, followed by a scowl. Even if he hadn't understood her words, her smirk was enough to let him know that he had been insulted.

"You'd better watch yourself. If anything has happened to Mrs. Mallock and I find out you had something to do with it . . ." he muttered as he brushed past her and followed the colonel down the hall.

Savannah's brief sense of satisfaction was followed by a wave of misgivings. Once again, her smart mouth had provided her with a high-ranking position on Bloss's "shit list." An honor she didn't relish.

"*Has* something happened to my sister?" Brian asked, looking miserable, bewildered, and upset.

"I certainly hope not." Savannah wished she had some

genuine words of comfort, but she couldn't lie to the man. Under the circumstances, she couldn't even lie to herself.

She found herself wishing she had never heard the name of Brian O'Donnell. By now, his sister surely wished she had never heard of Savannah Reid. Everyone would have been better off unacquainted.

"They aren't going to like what they're going to see in there," she said softly to Dirk as Neilson and Bloss disappeared into Lisa's bedroom.

His eyes widened a little, registering a question mark. "Not a body . . . ?" he whispered.

"No."

"Good."

"Bloody sheets."

"Oh." Dirk's face sobered. "*Not* so good."

Savannah glanced at Brian and noted that he looked as though he were about to be sick. She thought of Lisa Mallock and little Christy, the ballerina snow queen. "No," she said, her throat tightening, a bitter taste welling up from her stomach. "Not good at all."

"Charge me or release me. Now!"

Savannah rose from the rusty metal chair and shoved away from the table where she had been sitting, getting grilled, for the past hour and a half. She had enjoyed about as much of Captain Norman Hillquist's charming company as she could stand.

"Sit down!"

"No!"

He towered over her by at least ten inches, 180 pounds of barbell-inspired bulk, but Savannah was past caring. He was chief of police of the city of San Carmelita and capable of doing her great harm—heaven knows, he had done so in the past— but she didn't give a damn. Enough was enough.

He made a move as though to shove her back onto the chair. Instinctively, her karate training came to the fore and she snapped into a defensive stance.

Great move, Reid, she told herself. *Are you really stupid enough to chop a police chief?*

Of course, the answer was "No." But she kept her position until he took a step backward. It was all such a stupid game they played.

So what if she had investigated his city councilwoman girl-friend for murder last year, had exposed their affair and caused the woman to lose her council seat? So what if she had uncovered the greatest scandal ever to rock the sleepy hamlet of San Carmelita? So what if she had nearly caused him to be ousted from his precious job and ruined his life? Was that any reason for him to hate her forever?

Okay. Maybe so.

"Now, chief," she said, trying to sound reasonable, patient . . . anything but furious. "In the first place, we don't know that Lisa has been killed. So, we both know that you can't honestly threaten to charge me with being an accessory to murder. Secondly, even if—God forbid—something has happened to her, you have no proof that I had anything to do with it. Because I didn't."

Hillquist's jaw tightened, and the sun-leathered, golf course lines at the corners of his eyes crinkled. "Do you deny that you were working for Earl Mallock?"

She sighed. "We've been over that a dozen times. I was, but I didn't know it at the time."

"And you expect me to believe that?"

"What I expect . . ." she said, fixing him with a level, blue-eyed gaze that had, occasionally, caused weaker souls to quake in their sneakers, ". . . is that you are going to put our differences in the past, where they belong, and handle this like the professional we both know you are."

When he said nothing, she continued, "I haven't broken any law—"

"That we know of."

"That you know of, and you can't continue to hold me." She glanced at her watch. "So, if you'll excuse me, I have a nail appointment. Thanks to you, I've already missed my pedicure."

To her surprise, he allowed her to pass. He didn't say another word as she left the stuffy confines of the tiny interrogation room.

But she could feel his eyes boring into her back, could sense the rage building inside him, the still-hot ache for revenge. If someone had messed with her life the way she had interfered with his, she would have wanted to get even. She had always been a bit nervous, waiting . . . anticipating his next move. Somehow, she knew that Hillquist's idea of vengeance would be more dramatic than just seeing to it that she received more than her share of traffic tickets.

As Savannah got into her Camaro and headed back toward Lisa Mallock's house, her sense of apprehension grew by the mile. Fear for Lisa, for Christy, and an uneasiness about her own immediate future.

Deep in her gut Savannah knew something terrible had

happened—or was about to happen—to Christy's mom. And somehow, it was her fault.

Chief Norman Hillquist wasn't about to let a chance like this slip by.

Savannah just had to make sure that her own sense of guilt, misplaced or otherwise, didn't make it any easier for him to nail her to the nearest wall.

Through a red haze of pain, fear, and fury, the woman stared up at the face of her tormentor and wondered what had gone wrong. Once, she had loved and trusted this person.

A lifetime ago.

"I want to hear it," the voice was saying. "I want to hear you admit that you aren't the saint you've always claimed to be."

One twist of the wire. Then another. The agony in her wrists compounded. A hot, searing sensation shot up her arms and into her shoulders and neck.

Any minute now, her soft moans would give way to screaming. She wouldn't be able to help herself. Not even for Christy in the next room.

Another twist. More misery. This time in her ankles. Her calf muscles began to knot in twitching spasms, more painful than anything she could ever remember.

She heard the voice again, but this time it sounded farther away.

"Say it, you self-righteous bitch. We both know you did it. Admit it!"

When this had begun, hours before, she had hoped that numbness or shock would take hold, dulling the sharp edge of the pain. But it hadn't. Somewhere, in the dark recesses of her consciousness, she remained a nurse, and she knew it was because the wire was so thin. Her inquisitor had chosen well.

Another twist at her wrists. It was too much. A scream welled up from deep inside her, bringing the bitter taste of bile into her mouth. Choking her.

She thought of Christy, terrified, listening in the next room.

She thought of what this monster might do to her child, if all its rage hadn't been spent after finishing with her.

The nurse inside whispered, *You're going to lose consciousness soon. If you're going to do it, you have to do it now.*

I don't have a chance, she told the logical, still-rational nurse. *If I try, I'll die.*

If you don't try, you'll die anyway. What do you have to lose?

Her ex-husband had accused her of being all intellect, no emotion. Maybe he had been right.

At that moment, she wanted desperately to throw all reason aside. To naively believe that maybe her abuser would tire of the game and let them both go. To scream and beg for mercy. To admit anything and everything . . . whether it was true or not. To give in to the pain, the horror of her circumstances and just be a terrified child.

But she knew she couldn't afford the luxury of hysteria. She was a nurse and, more importantly, a mother.

Do it! Now! For yourself. For Christy!

She gathered everything within her, stood on her swollen, bleeding feet, and struck out at her attacker with wire-lacerated hands.

Susie O'Donnell had always been a fighter.

And old habits die hard.

CHAPTER SIX

"Oh, my dear Savannah, how perfectly dreadful for you." John Gibson sat beside Savannah on the diamond-tucked, burgundy leather sofa, patting her hand and giving her more sympathy than she could have hoped for in a month of Sundays.

She loved coming here to this elegant apartment, high in the foothills overlooking San Carmelita. Among the classic antiques, gilt-edged books in mahogany cases, and paintings of sylvan English countrysides, she could truly appreciate the art of fine European living. It was such a genteel pleasure to drop by, sip Earl Grey tea, and nibble on scones warm from the oven.

John Gibson and Ryan Stone might be gay, but they surely knew how to treat a lady.

Looking like a model from a GQ ad, Ryan sat in the wing

chair across from them, holding his own mug of tea, an equally concerned look on his face. "You don't believe that any of this is your fault, do you?" he asked.

"At the moment, I don't even know what 'any of this' is. Until I find out what's happened to Lisa Mallock and her little girl, I won't know how guilty to feel . . . or not feel . . . or whatever."

"If any harm has come to Mrs. Mallock," John said, continuing to stroke the back of her hand with his perfectly manicured fingertips, "I'm certain it will be in spite of your diligence, not as a result of your neglect. Savannah, you are truly one of the most responsible young women I've ever known."

"Thank you," she said, suppressing a case of the sentimental sniffles.

"But you *are* responsible," he repeated, "and it is my pleasure to say so."

"No, I mean, thank you for calling me young."

Ryan reached across the cocktail table to refresh her cup of tea. "How can we help?"

Savannah started to dab at her eyes with her napkin, then remembered it was monogrammed linen. Instead, she dug into her purse for a tissue. "Earl Mallock," she said. "I need to know everything you can find out about him. All I have is a birthdate, a DMV photo, and basic physical description that isn't even close anymore."

She began to feel better already. As former agents in the FBI, Ryan Stone and John Gibson seemed to be perpetually flowing founts of information regarding almost anyone she asked them to investigate. Although John had retired and Ryan had become a highly paid bodyguard for the rich and famous, she wouldn't want either one of them on her trail if she were trying to play hide-and-seek.

"Do you have an address for Mallock?" Ryan asked, taking notes with a gold-trimmed, rosewood fountain pen.

"The one I have is obsolete. Neither he nor Lisa have lived there since they divorced. The place was sold; I checked."

"He has to have been living somewhere," John said. "Has the police department assigned a detective to investigate?"

"Yes, and fortunately for us, it's Dirk."

The looks exchanged between the two men were less than enthusiastic. With Dirk's homophobic views and caustic comments, he hadn't exactly endeared himself to either of them.

"Detective Coulter is a . . . talented . . . investigator," John replied carefully. "And he's very fond of you. I'm sure he'll share whatever information he has with you."

Notably less impressed with Dirk's "talent," Ryan continued to jot information on his pad. "You work on Mallock," he told John, "and I'll look into Colonel Neilson."

"The colonel?" Savannah asked. "Why?"

"Let's just say I've met him a time or two, and I find him an interesting character . . . one I would like to know better."

"Good luck. Don't let Beowulf take a plug of flesh out of you."

"Beowulf?"

"I'm sure you'll have the pleasure of making his acquaintance soon, if you begin to investigate the colonel."

Savannah turned to look out the window at the sinking sun that was setting crimson fire to the hills, the islands, the sky, and even the ocean waves. Ordinarily, she would have thought it a beautiful, peaceful scene, but this evening it looked angry.

Maybe it was just her mood.

"I've gotta go," she said, rising and folding her napkin neatly on the tea tray. The time for chivalrous pampering and luxuriant sympathy was over. She had work to do.

Ryan walked her to the door, his large hand warm and comforting against her back. "What's next on your agenda, Savannah?" he asked. She could hear the concern in his voice and loved him for it.

"Don't ask," she replied, giving him a dimpled smile.

"I don't think I like the sound of that." He tweaked her chin. "What are you up to?"

She donned her most beguiling Southern accent. "Little ol' me? Why, just a friendly bit of . . . shall we say . . . minor trespassing."

He laughed and opened the door for her. "Knowing you, it's probably more like breaking and entering."

Standing on tiptoe, she kissed his cheek. "Now, I guess that just depends on how you look at it."

Savannah knew how Captain Bloss and Chief Hillquist would "look at it."

Terms like: Felony "B" & "E", Crossing a Police Barricade, Compromising the Scene of a Crime, occurred to her as she sneaked through the back door of Lisa Mallock's duplex. It would be a bit difficult to pretend that she hadn't seen that bright yellow tape surrounding the property, or the large notice taped to each door.

And, of course, it would be hard to explain away the flashlight in her hand and the latex gloves she was wearing.

A couple of good reasons to get in and out, she told herself as she creaked the door closed behind her and snapped on the flashlight.

The narrow cone of white light swept around the room, illuminating every dark nook and niche, until she was satisfied that she was the only illegal entrant.

So far, so good.

The place smelled of undumped garbage, and the air was thick and stale. At least, that was the reason Savannah gave herself to explain her shortness of breath.

This place gave her the shivers. She would find what she was looking for and get the hell out, back into the fresh, moist night . . . away from things like little Christy's lunch pail sitting on the counter and Lisa's love note to her daughter stuck to the refrigerator.

Yes, this was definitely an "in and out" sort of situation. Short and sweet . . . or at least not too bitter.

As usual, when searching a possible crime scene, Savannah wasn't sure what she was looking for. But experience had taught her that she would recognize it when she saw it.

At least, one could always hope.

She recognized it. A bright red-orange notice lying folded atop the stack of papers on the kitchen table.

The bit of mail had caught her eye before when she had sat here, eating M&M cookies and trying to gain Lisa Mallock's trust. It wasn't just your standard overdue bill. Those types of salutatory greetings Savannah was all too familiar with these days.

This one was protruding from an envelope which was marked as registered mail. Lisa had signed for it. Someone had paid about five bucks to have that signature.

Why?

Tucking the flashlight under her arm, Savannah reached for the red paper and unfolded it.

She read the bold type which warned of impending legal action.

THIRD NOTICE
OF
INTENTION TO LIQUIDATE

This will serve as final notice that Cracker Box Storage, located at 903 Harrington Boulevard, will auction the contents of locker number 17, unless the three months overdue rental fees are paid in full within ten days.

Examining the envelope, Savannah noted with interest that it had been addressed to Mr. and/or Mrs. Earl Mallock.

One glance around the sparsely furnished duplex told Savannah that Lisa Mallock probably wouldn't have needed a storage unit. If she had owned any material goods in the world, besides the ones inside these walls, she would have been using them, not surviving with only the barest essentials.

Earl Mallock's storage unit.

The thought stirred Savannah's curiosity. One could learn a lot about a beast by viewing the contents of its habitat. And until she could find out where Earl Mallock lived, his locker would have to do.

The rows of identical, drab, beige buildings reminded Savannah of some chicken coops she had seen down South. The storage lockers might smell better than Uncle George's poultry farm, but they were far less interesting.

Nothing was happening. No one, nothing. Savannah was getting antsy.

Sitting in the Camaro, she had been waiting twenty minutes for Dirk to arrive with a court order in hand, giving him permission to search Earl Mallock's unit. Since she had supplied the lead, Dirk had been kind enough to allow her to watch the process.

Plus she had promised him another honey-baked ham sandwich and a peanut butter milkshake, which was growing lukewarm on the dash.

She had just finished applying the second coat of "Flaming Desire" red polish to her nails when he appeared, chugging down the street in his battered old Buick Skylark. Judging from the car's rumbles, creaks, and groans, he needed to drive it off the nearest cliff and put it out of its misery. But the last time she had offered to do the deed for him, he had thrown what Gran would call a "hissy fit" and pouted for three days.

The car belched to a stop across the street; he got out and walked over to hers.

"Been waiting long?" he asked, looking only a bit sheepish.

"Darlin,' " she drawled, "I've spent the better part of my life waiting for you." She screwed the top onto the nail polish bottle and slipped it into her purse. "Well, have you got it?"

Reaching into his shirt pocket, he pulled out a pale yellow

document that bore the seal of the Great State of California in the upper left corner and Judge Harrington's signature at the bottom.

"Right here," he said, opening her door in a rare display of not-so-common courtesy. "And how about *you?* Have you got it?"

She sighed—she felt like they were a couple of worn-out drug dealers—and handed him the sack with the sandwich and the soggy milkshake container which had sweated a pool of condensation onto her dash. "Here, your favorite kind of food . . . free."

His haggard face split with a delighted grin as he peeked into the bag. He looked like an overgrown kid, checking out his Halloween treats. "Great! Come on." He nodded toward the lockers. "Let's go snooping around and see if we can find us some dirty laundry."

"If not," she mumbled, climbing out of the car, "we could always go back to your apartment."

The naked fifty-watt bulb that hung from the ceiling did little to illuminate the eight-by-eight-foot cement cubicle. But Savannah didn't need a lot of light to determine that the contents of the locker were a man's and not Lisa Mallock's.

A monster stereo system, sports equipment, and a big-screen television took up most of the space. A few duffel bags containing clothes were tossed on top of some boxes of magazines. Savannah bent to examine the boxes, while Dirk checked out the duffel bags.

"Hey, I'm not the only one with crunchy socks," he said, holding up some examples.

"Yeah, but you're wearing yours," she muttered. "At least he gives his a vacation."

Dirk ignored the insult. "Whatcha got there?"

"Mostly adolescent male stuff: mainstream porn, sports, mechanics, and . . . oh, yes, these. . . ."

She lifted out an interesting assortment of survivalist propaganda, everything from *The Armageddon Conspiracy* to *Mercenary Soldier*.

"Looks like our boy has anarchist tendencies," she said with another drop in her morale level.

"And that probably explains this." Dirk had lifted back a tarp in the corner, uncovering a strange contraption, that was bolted to a workbench. The equipment looked like an Erector set or a mad scientist's laboratory gone wrong, a clear plastic tube pointing upward, a canister filled with powder on one side. Instantly, Savannah recognized the mechanism as a bullet reloader.

"How quaint." She shook her head. "Earl rolls his own."

Dirk opened a small, dark green, brass-cornered chest and peered inside. "Mallock's ex-army, just like his daddy-in-law. An MP . . . in 'Nam." Dirk pointed to an assortment of dog tags, uniform patches, and other military paraphernalia. "Hm-m-mm . . . looks like he was in the same battalion as Colonel Neilson, but Neilson wouldn't have been a colonel back then."

"A combat-experienced, former army military police, wife stalker, with anarchist tendencies, who makes his own bullets. Not a particularly comforting profile."

"Especially since we don't even know where he is, or where he's been living for the past few months."

Savannah thumbed through the remaining magazines in

the box and one of the last ones caught her eye. "Look at this," she said, holding it up for his inspection.

"Vacations International?" Dirk frowned. "So what? It's a travel mag."

"It's more than that. My sister Vidalia gets this. She and her husband bought one of those condo time-shares a few years ago. This is the directory for other participating resorts across the country, in case you want to trade your week for another location."

Dirk was suddenly interested. "You think Mallock owns something like that?"

"It was sent to him and Lisa at their house last year," she said, studying the mailing address label. "You don't get these directories unless you're a paying member."

Quickly, Savannah began to scan the magazine, looking for the Southern California locations. "If there's anything local, he could be staying . . ." She found what she was looking for. "Three. There are three of them within easy driving distance of San Carmelita. One at a hot springs up in Los Padres, another on the beach at the marina, and . . . some cabins on Lake Arroyo."

They both glanced at the fishing paraphernalia propped in the corner: rods, tackle boxes, nets, and hip boots.

"Isn't Lake Arroyo famous for its bass," she asked, tossing the magazines back into the box.

"Yep, I caught a couple of nice ones there last fall."

"Let's go."

When Savannah and Dirk arrived at the Whispering Pines Lodge on Lake Arroyo, Savannah wasn't surprised—though she was a bit uneasy—to see Tammy Hart's hot pink Volkswagen sitting in the rear of the parking lot with the blonde inside. Earlier, Savannah had called her office to check for messages and had made the mistake of mentioning the latest development to Tammy.

"I want to come along," she had insisted. "I want to be there when you catch that creep."

"Nothing says we're going to catch him, Tammy," Savannah had replied.

"But you might. And I feel really bad about all this, like it was my fault and—"

"Okay, okay, it wasn't your fault any more than it was mine, but you can meet us there. Park in the back of the lot and *stay in your car* until Dirk and I arrive. Don't you dare make a move on your own. You could get yourself hurt or cause us to lose him."

Tammy had promised, and Savannah was relieved to see that she had been sensible, resisting the temptation to play Annie Oakley and charge in alone. Or, maybe, she had been just plain scared; but that, too, would be sensible under the circumstances.

Savannah climbed out of the Camaro just as Dirk was parking the Skylark next to Tammy. As Savannah had suspected, Dirk didn't look very happy to see her.

"What are you doin' here?" he asked as Tammy hurried up to them, an eager, flushed look on her pretty face.

"Savannah said I could come along."

"Oh, yeah?" Dirk turned his scowl on Savannah. "And who died and made you Mama Bear around here?"

With a start, Savannah realized that, for the first time, she and Dirk were not partners anymore, homicide detectives with the same rank and authority. He was the law enforcement officer in charge of the situation; she was merely a civilian along for the ride.

On the other hand, he was still plain old Dirk, and she would only let him take this "head honcho" stuff so far.

"She wanted to come, and I said she could. That's it, that's all." Savannah crossed her arms over her chest and stuck out her chin. She and Dirk had been together too long for him to mistake the stance.

"All right, all right. We're wasting precious time here. You . . . stay back and out of the way," he told Tammy. "And if anything funny starts to go down, eat some dirt."

Tammy looked at Savannah and raised one delicate, arched eyebrow questioningly.

"He's speaking Macho Ass-lish again," Savannah explained. "Translation: Any problem—take cover."

"Got it."

Savannah glanced around the parking lot, but saw only two other cars. "Mallock was driving a late model Ford sedan when he came to my office," she told Dirk. "I don't see it or the Jeep that he's registered to at the DMV."

"Not too surprising that he'd change cars," Dirk added. "If he was smart enough to pull the wool over your eyes, he's no dumbbell."

"Thanks, I guess," she muttered as they headed up the walkway toward the door marked "Office."

"Do you really think he's here?" Tammy asked, darting uneasy glances right and left at the quaint log cabins that were tucked among fragrant pines in a semicircle around the lake's edge.

Savannah breathed in the moist, rich scent of forest loam and sighed. "Somehow, I doubt it. But we'll know soon."

"He isn't here."

The lean, mean, overworked, and underfed secretary behind the counter stared at the two photos, shaking her head. From the combined smells of the office, Savannah surmised that the woman subsisted on strong coffee and menthol cigarettes. Like a Vegas blackjack dealer, she snapped both pictures onto the counter and pushed them in Savannah's direction. One was the DMV photo of Earl Mallock, the second the department artist's sketch of the same picture, minus the excess poundage, plus red hair and brown eyes.

"Are you sure?" Dirk sounded thoroughly aggravated, but the secretary didn't flinch. She gave him a cold stare, adjusted a twig of hair that had strayed from the French twist at the back of her head and said, "I'm sure. We only have three guests here now, so they're pretty easy to keep track of."

"Have you ever seen him?" Savannah asked. Hoping. It never hurt to hope.

"Oh, yeah. He rents here all the time. Was here for a couple of weeks, left just last night."

"Well, hell, why didn't you say so in the first place?" Dirk asked, shoving his omnipresent toothpick to the right corner of his mouth.

"You asked if he *is* a guest, not if he *was*."

Savannah could tell the secretary was enjoying baiting

Dirk. Everyone did. His surly attitude seemed to bring out the worst in nearly everyone around him.

"Can you tell us what cabin he was staying in?" Tammy asked sweetly, batting long lashes like a Mississippi coquette. "And we'd like to look at it, if you don't mind."

Dirk shot Tammy a warning glance. "I told you to keep back. I'm the one with the badge here. I'm doing the asking." He turned back to the secretary. "Which cabin?"

She ignored Dirk and pressed a key into Tammy's palm. "Number Fourteen. There's no one there now, so look around if you want. I haven't had a chance to clean it up yet . . . was going to get to that later this afternoon. Just be sure to lock it up tight after you leave."

"Give me that damned key," Dirk growled as the threesome left the office and hurried down the well-worn path to the cabin in question.

With great ceremony Tammy dropped it into his outstretched hand. "You're welcome."

Before he could close his fingers around it, Savannah snatched it away. "Enough of this crap," she said, sobering as they neared the log cottage with the numbers painted in red on the green door. "We're all a bit on edge," she admitted. "But we've gottta look sharp now. There's no telling what we'll find in there."

Savannah knew the moment she cracked the door. She could smell it. The stench of death.

Her heart sank to her shoes, and for a moment she couldn't move.

"You'd better wait out here, Tammy," she said finally, pushing the door open.

"But—"

"No buts. Stay out here and keep your eyes peeled for Mallock. If you see anything, just let out a holler."

Savannah gave Dirk a telling look and he returned it as he, too, entered the tiny cabin.

"Shit," he said under his breath.

"Yeah."

A quick glance told her the room was empty . . . if rotten smells, residual horror, and all-around dark, creepy vibes didn't count.

The cabin consisted of three small rooms, the main living area which had a threadbare, floral sofa, a tiny refrigerator, and a sink. Through one door to the left, Savannah could see a primitive bathroom, and through another, a bed.

"Hello?" Dirk said.

Only the eerie, heavy silence replied.

Savannah started to call out for Lisa or Christy, but couldn't bring herself to utter their names.

"What do you see?" Tammy's frightened voice drifted in from the front porch.

"Nothing yet," Savannah replied.

"That's good, huh?"

Savannah didn't answer.

On the sofa lay a Pocahontas coloring book and some spilled crayons.

"What's that?" Dirk asked.

Again, Savannah couldn't bring herself to reply as she bent

over the book and saw some words childishly scrawled in red across the top margin.

She read the four words:

Pleez help my mom

"Oh, God . . ." she whispered, feeling sick at heart and stomach. She turned and walked toward the bedroom. The odors became overpowering.

Dear Lord in heaven, please not Lisa, she prayed silently. *Please, not Lisa or Christy . . . please, please. . . .*

The bedroom was empty, too.

Except for the body lying on the floor, wedged between the double bed with its faded, pink chenille spread and the log and plaster wall.

"Don't let it be the kid," she heard Dirk whisper. "It's not the kid, is it?" he asked, crowding into the tiny room beside Savannah. Her own fear echoed in his shaky voice.

"No," she said. "Thank God it isn't."

Half of Savannah's heart rejoiced, as the other half broke. Tears flooded her eyes and sorrow choked her throat as she added, "But it's her mother. It's Lisa."

The details of what she was seeing rushed over her, a suffocating tsunami of crushing reality. The lifeless, staring eyes. The wrists and ankles bound tightly with thin wire. The neat round gunshot hole in the forehead. The blood and tissue spilling from the massive exit wound in the back.

"Dead?" Dirk asked.

"Yes," she whispered. "Very dead."

CHAPTER SEVEN

"Oh, my God! What happened? Is she . . . ?" Tammy Hart stood in the doorway of the bedroom, her hazel eyes wide with shock as she stared down at the body on the floor.

"Yes, honey, she is." Savannah walked over to Tammy and placed one hand on her shoulder. She could feel the younger woman shaking violently as the color drained from her cheeks.

"You two should get the hell outta here," Dirk said, his tone far more gentle than his words.

Transfixed on the corpse, Tammy ignored him and took a few halting steps toward the victim. Savannah watched with misgivings as Tammy knelt beside Lisa Mallock's remains.

"An entry wound to the front of the head," Tammy murmured in a strangely flat monotone . . . a student reciting a hard learned lesson. "Exit wound in the back. Close range powder burns. Looks like a large caliber—"

Her voice broke with a sob and she began to gag. Savannah reached for her and turned her around, forcing her to look away. "It's okay, sweetheart," she said, pressing a big-sisterly kiss to Tammy's forehead. "Dirk can take it from here."

"But it's our fault." Tammy looked up at Savannah and the misery and guilt Savannah saw registered on her pretty face went straight to her heart. It wasn't as though Tammy was saying anything new . . . anything that wasn't already slicing like a dull razor through Savannah's own mind and conscience.

"It's not anybody's fault," Dirk said, "except for the son of a bitch that pulled the trigger."

"And we know who that was." Tammy tried to turn and take another look, but Savannah's hands tightened on her shoulders, preventing her.

"No, we don't. At least, not for sure," Savannah told her, wishing she could believe her own words.

"That's right," Dirk agreed. "You never really know who done it, 'til you know for sure who done it."

"What?" Now Tammy looked confused as well as upset.

"The point is . . ." Savannah took her by the hand and pulled her out of the cramped bedroom and into the main living area. ". . . that Dirk has work to do, and we're only keeping him from doing it."

"But we could help him," Tammy protested. "That's what we do for a living, right?"

Savannah looked back at Dirk and gave him a sad, sick smile. More than anything in the world, she wanted to stay, to work this case through with him. They had been partners for so many years, it was almost impossible to walk away.

"We shouldn't be here," she told Tammy. "Dirk is already going to be in trouble for bringing us—me, in particular—with him to a crime scene. We don't want to make things any harder for him."

Savannah turned back to Dirk and mouthed the words, "I'm sorry."

He growled and shrugged his broad shoulders. "Just get goin', both of you. I'll give you a ring later, when I know what's what." Pulling a small, cellular phone—his only capitulation to advanced technology—from his inside coat pocket, he punched in some numbers.

"Coulter here," Savannah heard him say as she hurried out the door of the cabin and down the dirt path with a weeping Tammy in tow. "I got a stiff at the Whispering Pines Resort on Lake Arroyo. Yeah, that's right. Better get a wagon rollin' and call Dr. Liu."

"Are you dreading it?"

Tammy sat on the end of Savannah's living room sofa, a box of tissues in one hand, the other arm wrapped tightly around a floral, satin-fringed pillow, which she was hugging to her chest.

"What?" Turning from the front window, where she was keeping watch, Savannah tried to concentrate on what her distraught assistant was saying. "Am I dreading what?"

"Telling Brian O'Donnell that his sister is dead."

Savannah placed one hand on the windowsill for support

and resumed her vigil. Any minute now, Brian was due to arrive. He didn't know yet. And she felt she should be the one to tell him.

"Of course I'm dreading it," she replied, her voice husky. "Informing the next of kin was one of the worst things I had to do on the police force, and it looks like I can't get away from it even now."

"Are you going to tell him it's our fault?" Sniffing loudly, Tammy tossed the used tissue into a nearby wastebasket and reached for a fresh one.

He'll probably figure that one out on his own, Savannah thought, but she kept it to herself.

"No," she said, "and neither are you, because it isn't our fault. Dirk was right, Tammy; the only person responsible for this murder is the one who committed it."

"Do you really believe that? I mean, completely, truly?"

Savannah opened her mouth to deliver the routine reassurances, but they caught in her throat. "My head believes it," she said, when she finally found the words. "My heart is going to need some time. The truth is like that; it takes a while to filter down from the mind and through the emotions."

"How did you get to be so wise?" Tammy asked. Savannah could hear the sincerity in her voice. It both flattered her and made her ashamed.

If I were all that damned smart, Lisa Mallock would be alive right now and her little girl would be safe, her lacerated conscience whispered. But she didn't need to place any of her own guilt on Tammy. Judging from the kid's hunched shoulders and bowed head, she was toting more than a full load already.

"I'm not wise. Just old," Savannah replied. "Let's say, I've been around the Monopoly board a few times more than you."

For several long moments, neither woman said anything. At last, Savannah was pleased to hear Tammy take a sip of the cognac-laced, whipped cream–topped, hot chocolate she had made for her earlier. A little hedonism, once in a while, was good for everyone.

"What are you going to do now?" Tammy asked. "I mean, what's next?"

"I'll talk to Brian O'Donnell and make sure he doesn't hear about his sister on the news. Then I'm going to find Earl Mallock." Again, she gripped the windowsill, but this time the gesture wasn't one of weakness, but anger. "And when I get my hands on him, I'm going to send him directly to hell."

Brian took it better than Savannah had hoped. Much better. In fact, he was so calm and matter-of-fact about the whole thing that she entertained a few doubts about his own agenda.

"Are you absolutely sure that her ex-husband did it?" he asked.

"At this point, I would say it's likely. But you never know until a case is closed," she replied.

"I think I'll stay in town until then . . . until you know for sure."

"We'll stay in touch."

Other than the usual "hello" and "good-bye" pleasantries, that was the extent of their conversation, and Brian O'Donnell was on his way.

As Savannah watched his rental car pull out of her drive and disappear around the corner, Tammy appeared, a bunch of computer printouts in her hand and the glint of a smile showing on her tear-swollen face.

"I decided I was wasting time and energy feeling rotten about what happened to Mrs. Mallock," she said, pulling Savannah over to the sofa and forcing her to sit. "So, I got busy. You'd be surprised what you can find out about a person with just a computer and a modem . . . when you put your mind to it and stop feeling sorry for yourself, that is."

Savannah glanced over the papers and was duly impressed. "Good work, Ms. Hart. Don't let anyone call you a blond bimbo. You are extremely talented and intelligent. Don't ever forget it."

"Thanks."

"So, Earl Mallock held a city business license?"

"That's right. An antique shop, downtown on Harrington Boulevard. And he had a partner named Alan Logan. It went kaput a few months ago."

"We'll have to get Mr. Logan's address and have a talk with him."

Tammy grabbed the papers, sorted through them, and proudly produced a sheet with the information. "Here you go. Alan Logan's home address, new business address, *and* unlisted telephone number. By the way, his credit rating is the pits . . . filed bankruptcy six months ago, after the business bit it. Got a divorce two months ago."

"Is that all you have?"

Tammy jumped up from the sofa and headed toward the office. "You just go talk to him," she said over her shoulder. "I'm on a roll here. By the time you get back, I'll know if he wears briefs or boxers."

Savannah drove past the high school, with its hordes of loitering teenagers that made her homesick for her Georgia siblings, and turned left on Lester.

Less-than-picturesque Lester Street ran parallel to the prestigious Harrington Boulevard from one end of the downtown area to the other. But only geographically speaking. Both thoroughfares were located in the quaint, Los Angeles tourist trap part of San Carmelita, the area that surrounded the old mission. The only difference was: Harrington Boulevard had been renovated back in the eighties—palm trees planted, sidewalks widened, wrought-iron streetlamps installed—and Lester Street hadn't been touched.

The fact that Alan Logan's antique shop had once been located on Harrington, but was now situated on Lester, told Savannah that he had been forced to slide down a peg on the business ladder. Intuition told her that he probably wasn't too happy about it.

Glancing at her watch, she decided to give Dirk another call to find out what, if anything, was happening on his end. Punching in his car phone number on her own mobile phone, she watched the street signs, looking for Alan Logan's shop.

Dirk didn't answer. Well, that wasn't so unusual. He had a way of ignoring almost everything in life that he considered a nuisance, and his phone was certainly one.

She tried the next most plausible possibility.

"San Carmelita Police Station." Bette, with the fake French accent, was on the board. Somewhere on the distant shores of her gene pool, Bette boasted a Parisian *grand-mère*, and she seemed to think this lineage gave her additional sex appeal.

No one else seemed to hold the same opinion . . . but Bette didn't seem to notice.

"Sergeant Coulter, please." Savannah tried to douse her Southern accent and sound official, so she wouldn't be recognized. The last thing she needed right now was to have a long, boring chat with Bette.

"Savannah? Is that you?"

Savannah stifled a groan. "Yes. Oh . . . is this Bette?"

"Yes! Where are you?"

That was a funny thing to ask, Savannah thought. Usually Bette would launch into some nonsense about her latest boyfriend, her annoying neighbor, or some other equally less-than-fascinating topic.

"Just running some errands," Savannah replied curtly.

"Yeah, but *where?*"

"Here and there. Does it matter?"

"Ah . . . so, what's it like, being a lady of leisure, your own boss and all that?"

Savannah bit her lower lip. "I really wouldn't know. Is Dirk in?"

"I wouldn't know either." Suddenly, Bette sounded a little icy around the edges. "Hold on."

"Reid, is that you?"

When Savannah heard the grating, nasal voice of Captain Bloss, she almost wished she could transfer back to Bette.

"Yes, I think Bette got her lines switched. I need to talk to Dirk."

"I'll just bet you do. But *I* want to talk to *you.*"

"Why? I don't want to talk to you." She was past pretending to be polite with this jackass. Their mutual hatred had been openly declared long ago.

"This ain't social, Reid. This is business."

Warning bells went off in her head, like her smoke detectors at home the last time she had burnt a skilletful of liver and onions. The prospect of "talking" to Bloss was about as distasteful as that entrée had been.

"We don't have any business," she said.

"How about a nice little chat about you being charged with 'accessory to homicide'?"

She could hear the glee in his voice, and it made her want to slap him hard enough to make his ponderous jowls flap. It also made her pulse race, because she knew he wasn't bluffing. That son of a bitch would do it, if for no other reason than to make her life miserable for a while.

"That's ridiculous," she said, trying to sound nonchalant.

"So, come in and tell me to my face how ridiculous I am. And while you're at it, tell me what you were doing at the murder scene."

"Murder scene? What murder scene?"

"Come in."

"Why?"

"Come in, Reid, or we'll bring you in."

"All right, all right. I'm coming."

"When?"

Savannah glanced at her watch again. It was a quarter to five. Bloss liked to charge out the door at a minute to five and absolutely no later. But she knew he would wait for her. He wouldn't miss the opportunity to grill her for the world.

"I'm in . . . ah . . . LA right now. I can be there in . . . oh, say . . . an hour, maybe an hour and a half."

She grinned as she heard him mutter something under his breath. "One hour," he said. "I'll wait until fifteen to six, but you damned well better show."

"See you then," she said sweetly.

Switching off the phone, she pulled the Camaro into the parking lot behind a modest shop, bearing the sign: Logan's Collectibles.

"Yeah, right," she said, climbing out of the car. "I'll see you, Captain Bloss, when assholes like you can toot 'Yankee Doodle Dandy.' "

The moment Savannah walked into Alan Logan's antique store, she instantly wished she had ten thousand dollars in pocket change. Maybe more. This was exactly her kind of stuff: Victorian velvet settees, Tiffany lamps, wing chairs with diamond-tucked hunter green leather, rolltop desks, and ornately carved French beds with matching armoires.

Dirk had once accused her of having decorating taste that was "more gaudy than a whore's drawers." She had reminded him that not everyone had his distinctive flair for furnishing a house trailer with cardboard boxes and rusted TV trays.

"Mr. Alan Logan, please," she told the young woman who accosted her before she had gone ten feet.

"Al is busy right now. Perhaps I can help you." The guarded look in the saleswoman's eyes told Savannah that either commissions were a rare and coveted commodity in this establishment, or the lady had a thing for "Al" and didn't want to share him with another female. Not even a female customer.

"I'll wait," Savannah replied, then turned to study the deliciously secret cubbyholes in a nearby rolltop, oak desk.

"Suit yourself."

Savannah watched in her peripheral vision to see if the woman would go alert Logan to her presence. She didn't, so Savannah decided to do it herself.

Ignoring the woman's raised eyebrow, she marched past her and into the back room, where a fortyish, well-built man in stained jeans and a pleasantly tight tee shirt was scraping layers of paint off a piecrust table.

The fumes from the remover hit her with a wallop, and she decided to breathe through her ears for a while.

"How could anybody have done that to such a pretty piece of furniture?" she said as his blade curled up the layers of green paint with gold accents, revealing a rich mahogany woodgrain underneath.

"It's a crime," he replied, pausing to pull a red shop cloth from his back pocket and swipe it across his wet brow. The sweat was causing his dark chestnut waves to curl in a manner that she could only describe as "cute." "But then, I love peeling it off and seeing what I've got."

"My gran back in Georgia has a table just like that one," she said, dropping to one knee to examine the item more closely.

"So, maybe I can sell you this one . . . ?"

She smiled, giving him the full benefit of the famous Reid dimples. "Naw, Gran said she'd leave it to me in her will. Although I'm in no rush to get it," she added quickly. She wasn't exactly superstitious about such things, but with Granny Reid being eighty-three, you had to be careful what you said.

"I'm Alan Logan, owner of this place." He waved a stained

hand, the gesture proudly sweeping his domain. "What *can* I do for you?"

"Actually, I'm not exactly furniture shopping today," she admitted.

"I see."

Of course, he didn't see, but his hazel eyes looked vaguely interested behind his paint speckled, wire-framed glasses, and that was a start.

"You used to be over on Harrington Boulevard," she began, then reconsidered the wisdom of her opening gambit when she saw him scowl.

"Yeah, so?"

"And when you were, you had a partner named Earl Mallock."

"Unfortunately."

"Mmmm . . . well, I need to speak to him, very badly, and I was wondering if you might know how I could reach him."

Logan returned to his furniture stripping, and Savannah noticed that his hand was gripping the scraper far harder than necessary. His knuckles were literally turning white.

The excess blood seemed to have flowed to his face, which was bright crimson.

"I'll do you a favor," Logan said through a tight jaw, "I'll give you the best advice I can. Stay away from that bastard, and save yourself a lot of grief."

"Believe me, my intentions aren't romantic or even social in nature."

He perked up immediately. "Oh, really? Are you a bill collector or something?"

"An 'or something.' I'm a private investigator." She pulled

her identification from her pocket and flipped it open so he could read it.

"You're a P.I.?" He glanced her up and down with renewed interest. "I thought those were all ugly guys with gum on their shoes."

She lifted her loafer and showed him some residue which she had collected on her way in from the parking lot. "One out of three?"

He chuckled, and it occurred to her that he was rather attractive when he smiled.

"I don't know where Earl is," he said. "Haven't seen him since the day I dragged him into court. I won, too. But I can give you the name of somebody who does know where he is . . . whether she'll admit it or not."

"And who's that?"

"Not so fast. First you have to promise that when you find ol' Earl, you'll give him a message from me."

"A *verbal* message?"

He laughed, but he didn't sound amused. "Yeah, no lead or steel involved."

Savannah considered the deal. A few words delivered in exchange for a valuable tip. It seemed acceptable. Reaching into her purse, she pulled out a pad and paper. "Okay, I promise."

"There's a crazy bartender, six feet one inch, with purple hair who—"

"Purple?" Savannah just wanted to make sure she had heard correctly.

"That's right. Bright purple. She works at the Shoreline Club at the bottom of El Camino Boulevard on the beach. Her name's Vanessa. For some reason I could never figure, she's nuts about Earl. And Earl . . . well . . . he's just plain nuts. I'm pretty sure that she won't tell you, but she'll know where he is."

"Okay, thanks a lot." She scribbled on the notepad. "And what's the message?"

His friendly, hazel eyes went suddenly cold; the transformation was startling. "You tell him that he and Alan Logan still aren't even. Not by a lo-o-ong shot."

When Savannah got back into her car, she decided to give Dirk's mobile phone another try. This time he answered.

"Yo."

She sighed and shook her head. "Have I ever told you that your particular telephone salutation makes you sound like a cracker?"

He chuckled. "Yeah, several times. But considering you eat stale cornbread crumbled up in buttermilk with a dash of salt and pepper, I'm not going to lose any sleep over what you think of me."

"It's good in regular milk, too . . . without the pepper."

"Yuck. What do you want?"

She headed the Camaro homeward. A hot cup of coffee and a piece of raspberry cheesecake would give her some fuel to run on for the rest of the day. Maybe a bit of chocolate sauce drizzled across the top.

"I want to know what's going on," she said.

"Body's at the morgue. Dr. Liu is finished with her."

Savannah winced, having seen Jennifer Liu perform more than a few autopsies. More than anything else, Savannah had never gotten over the shock of seeing how a brutal act committed by one person could turn another living, breathing, human being into a piece of dead meat.

If it were the result of an accident or disease, one could more easily chalk it up to Divine Will, karma, or simple destiny. But murder went against the rules. There was no way to believe it was good or a natural occurrence.

"What did she find?" Savannah asked.

"Cause of death was the gunshot to the head."

In spite of herself, Savannah recalled the grisly details of the wound. "Yeah, no shit. We didn't need Dr. Jennifer to tell us that."

"Her wrists and ankles had been wired like that for at least six to eight hours before she died."

Savannah's stomach twisted a few notches tighter, and she nearly drove through a red light. "Great. I'm sure I'll dream about that one. Any hair or fibers?"

"The victim's. Some longer red ones that might be the kid's."

There was more; she could hear it in his voice. "And?"

"And a couple of medium length dark brown . . . almost black . . . and curly."

Unconsciously, Savannah reached up to her own head and fingered the thick, dark locks that she had tied back with a scrunchy. Distinctly, she remembered bending over the body. It was amazing how easy it was to transfer material from one source to another. "Oh, joy," she said without enthusiasm. "What else?"

"Bloss decided to get involved in this one personally . . . it being the daughter of a friend of the chief's and all."

"Yeah, he never misses an opportunity to kiss the back of Hillquist's trousers."

"The secretary at the resort gave us up, told him there were three of us there this morning. Of course, he recognized your description right away."

"Of course. Did you know that he told me to come in and 'talk.'"

Dirk took too long to answer. "Ah . . . yeah, Van. I heard."

"How serious is he?"

Again, too much silence. "He . . . um . . . he told me to bring you in."

"*You?*" Her south-of-the-Mason-Dixon-line, rebel temper flared. "That son of a bitch. Of all the others he could have sent, he had to rub salt in the wound by picking you."

"Not exactly."

"What do you mean?"

"I volunteered."

"You what?"

"Damn it, Van, if anybody's gotta do it, I thought it should be me."

"Thanks, I reckon." Tears of rage flooded her eyes and she could hardly see the road. "So, are you going to do it?" she said, "Are you going to take me in?"

She heard him clear his throat. "Would you rather come on in . . . on your own?"

"Sure."

"Good, I'm relieved to hear that. When?"

"After I run some errands."

"Oh." He sounded less relieved. "And how long will that take?"

"Look, Dirk," she said, trying to sound patient and as strong as she wished she were. "I know your hindquarters are dangling over a hot skillet here, and I don't want to make things any worse for you than they need to be. But I've got work to do. And I'm not going to find Earl Mallock if I'm sitting in that damned station house, getting the third degree from Bloss."

He didn't say anything for so long that she thought they might have been disconnected. Finally: "Okay, Van, I haven't heard from you, and at least for the moment, I can't find you. All right?"

"I love you."

She knew that would get his goat. Dirk could handle street violence, criminal brutality, public controversy, and the occasional whack upside the head, but he couldn't cope with affection.

"Yeah, right. Talk to you later. Good luck."

"You, too."

She made a U-turn at the next light and headed back toward the beach and the Shoreline Club. No going home. No raspberry cheesecake. Not now.

Not until she had some more answers . . . or at least fewer questions.

CHAPTER EIGHT

Savannah had been in worse dives than the Shoreline Club, but it had been a long time. Just walking into the place made her feel like a full-fledged yuppie. She appeared to be the only one wearing anything other than torn denim, black leather, and enough chain and assorted metal to rebuild the fleet of classic Harleys that were parked outside.

One sniff of the stale booze and rancid smoke mixed with pungent human sweat told her she was probably the only individual in the joint who had recently bathed.

The Shoreline had a definite "nautical" motif: a couple of stuffed fish on the wall, nets strung across the ceiling that were embellished with an intricate lacing of cobwebs. The bar was covered with a thick layer of clear resin coating which sported an assortment of hooks, sinkers, bobbers, and lures.

On the barstool nearest the door sat a couple of scrungy Hell's Angels rejects. The chubby one had a bright red scar that bisected his face diagonally. Apparently, the doctor who had stitched him hadn't bothered to line everything up first. He gave her a lopsided grin as she walked by and whispered something to his skinny, hunchbacked buddy about, "Fresh tuna swimmin' upstream."

Savannah resisted the instinctive urge to give him a swift karate kick to the groin. That would require bodily contact, and the thought made her shudder.

Not seeing anyone attending the bar, she walked to the opposite end and sat down on a stool, as far away as possible from Humpty and Dumpty. The wide, ragged cracks in the stool's vinyl pinched her rear, and when she leaned her elbows on the bar, she found it sticky.

A speaker, mounted on an "L" bracket over her head, crackled and spit out a "cryin' in my beer over you" country song.

Starving, Savannah grabbed the nearest bowl of peanuts and began munching on them. She would have preferred the chocolate-covered cashews in her crystal candy dish at home, but a calorie was a calorie.

At the other end of the bar, Dumpty hitched his belt up over his tractor tire–sized stomach and waggled his tongue obscenely at her. Opening her own mouth wide, she showed him her half-chewed peanuts.

"Gross," he said, his libido bubble apparently pricked. Picking up his beer and his change off the bar, he retired to the back corner of the room.

Reliable old "see" food . . . works every time, she thought. Experience had taught her that a lot of perverts had weak stomachs. She had often told the women in her self-defense classes that one of the most effective ways to interrupt a rape was to barf on your attacker.

"Good move," said a female voice beside her. "I'll have to remember that one."

Turning on her stool, Savannah saw she was no longer alone at this end of the bar. Alan Logan's description hadn't been exaggerated at all. She truly was over six feet tall, broad-shouldered, and street-rugged.

From what Alan had said, Savannah had been expecting one of those questionable red shades of hair that was too blue to be real. But Vanessa Whatever-her-name-was had hair the color of a grape-flavored soft drink.

Savannah might have thought it was a wig, but it was only an inch and a half long and stuck straight out from her scalp. Savannah considered the possibility that she was a platinum blonde who had been dipped, headfirst, in Easter egg dye.

She wore equally purple jeans that bristled with metal studs and a tee shirt.

Savannah offered her hand. "Hi, are you Vanessa?" she asked.

"Yep." She returned the handshake only briefly across the bar. Her skin was cold, damp, and a little pruned. An occupational hazard, Savannah decided, for someone who spent most of her day handling ice and cold drinks. "What can I get for you?" she asked.

"A minute of your time?"

Vanessa's dark eyes narrowed. Apparently, trust wasn't one of her greatest personality traits.

"Time for what?"

"A girl to girl talk."

Vanessa crossed her multibangled arms over the front of her black "Shoreline" tee shirt with its fluorescent purple lettering. "Are you a cop?"

"Not anymore."

"Why not?"

"They kicked me out."

Vanessa's frown instantly melted, replaced by a grin. That seemed to be all the personal recommendation she needed.

"If the cops got rid of you, you must be all right," she said with a conviction that Savannah found a bit frightening. "Who are you looking for?"

"Earl. Earl Mallock."

The arms went back over the front of the tee shirt, the grimace back on the face. "Why?"

"I just want to talk to him."

Vanessa studied her thoughtfully for a moment, then Savannah thought she saw a light of realization switch on in her eyes. "Hey . . . what's your name, anyway?"

"Savannah Reid."

That did it. Vanessa recognized the name instantly, and Savannah could practically see the purple fuzz bristling on her head.

"I think you better get outta here. Fast." Vanessa didn't bother to lower her voice, and several of the nearby customers stopped talking and perked their ears to listen.

"Why should I? After all, your boyfriend came to *me*. He contacted me first, but then, I guess you know all about that."

"I don't know anything."

She was flat-ass lying. Savannah could see it in her eyes.

She knew at least as much as Savannah knew, and probably a lot more. But she wasn't going to give up a thing.

"Earl's in a lot of trouble," Savannah said, knowing there was no way to pull this one out of the fire, but she had to try. "You could help him if you'd just tell me how to get in touch with him."

"*Help* him? You want me to *help* him by turning him over to you. Yeah, right, lady. Now get the hell outta my place before I have you thrown out."

"*Your* place? You own this club?"

"That's right, and you're trespassing." Vanessa turned to the corner where Savannah's previous admirer was sitting. "Hey, Joe, you want to show this gal the parking lot?"

Whoop-de-do, she thought. This was just what she needed . . . to get up close and personal with Joe Dumpty.

"I'm leaving. I'm leaving." She held up both hands in surrender as she slid off the stool and headed for the door. "But . . . next time you see Earl, you tell him that there's a whole heap of people who want to see him right now. We know what he did, and we aren't going to stop until we've got him."

She paused for a breath and to let her words sink in. Apparently, Vanessa was listening, because she was getting a bit pale around the gills, like the cobwebby, stuffed fish on the wall.

"It's not a question of whether anybody finds him," Savannah continued, "just of who nabs him first. And you tell him that, so far, the odds are on me, 'cause I'm the maddest."

On the way back to her car, Savannah glanced around the parking lot and spotted a bright purple Trans Am sitting near the rear entrance. The color was startlingly vivid, even in the dim light of the setting sun.

Gee, wonder whose that might be? she told herself.

She memorized the plates, then got into her Camaro. As she was jotting down the number, her phone rang.

With some misgivings, she answered it. "Yes?"

"Hi, Savannah, it's Tammy."

"Thank the stars." She wasn't up for another round with Bloss or even Dirk. "What's up?"

"Alan Logan sued Earl Mallock . . . for illegal bookkeeping practices that led to the demise of their business. Logan won."

"Mmmm . . . so that's what Alan was talking about. Interesting, though I don't know what that might have to do with Lisa's death."

"Sorry. I thought it might help."

Tammy sounded so disappointed that Savannah could have bitten her tongue. The kid needed to stay busy; it was the only way to heal her heart.

"*Everything* helps, honey. Good work. I have something else for you, if you don't mind."

"Of course not." She perked up instantly. "What is it?"

"Call Denise Harmon at the station. She should be on the desk by now. Ask her to run this plate for us." She read her the Trans Am's letters and numbers. "If we're lucky, we'll come up with the address where Earl may be staying."

"Really?" Her voice sounded thick, desperately hopeful. "Do you think that's where the little girl is now?"

Savannah thought of Christy's message, frantically scribbled with a red crayon in the Pocahontas coloring book. "Ah,

Tammy," she said, feeling the ever-increasing sense of urgency that was twisting her nerves into knots. "From your mouth to the good Lord's ears."

Savannah was relieved to see that Captain More Gun's didn't close at six o'clock, along with most of the other downtown stores. Apparently, survivalist/gun enthusiast types shopped later than the usual boutique/cappucino bar patrons.

Hurrying through the door, she mentally rehearsed her string of white lies that would hopefully garner some information about Earl Mallock. Something told her he spent a lot of time here.

Reeking of cordite and excessive testosterone, the store contained everything any self-respecting anarchist could want: guns, knives, flak jackets, camouflage, and K rations. And, of course, powder, primers, brass casings, and lead slugs—all the ingredients necessary to make your own bullets from scratch.

On the wall to her left hung a large poster of a Rambo–wanna-be, bristling with guns, knives, grenades, and rocket launchers. He was covered with sweat and grime, his fatigues ripped, veins popping on exaggerated muscles. No doubt, some males' idea of sex appeal.

A large Confederate flag nearly covered the back wall, and the sight of it gave her a little twang of homesickness. Good ol' Dixie. Magnolia trees gently draped with Spanish moss, tall glasses of iced tea with sprigs of fresh mint, and sultry summer nights.

But after seeing the two yahoos behind the counter the sweetness of nostalgia faded, and she decided that the rebel flag might have different significance for the store's owners.

"Yo, darlin, what can we do you for?" said the guy who was wiping down a Sig Sauer. The second one guffawed at his partner's attempt at humor, and Savannah thought of every Jeff Foxworthy redneck joke she had ever heard. Certain scenes from *Deliverance* came to mind, too.

Gee, that was a real knee-slapper, she thought, but she plastered a smile on her face and sauntered over to the counter.

"Actually, I'm looking for a fellow, who—"

"Hey, got one for you right here! His name's J.T." He gave the other guy a gouge in the ribs with the barrel of the pistol he was cleaning. Savannah cringed, amazed at some people's lack of common sense when handling firearms. "Course, if you want somebody more prettier," he said, "you'll have to settle for me. I'm Bobbie."

"Thank you, Bobbie. But it's a particular gentleman I have in mind," she said, slathering on the Southern charm. "I met him at a gun show down at the fairgrounds last month. His first name is Earl, I believe, and his last might be something like . . . Bullock or . . ."

"Mallock?"

"Yeah, that's it."

The twosome exchanged knowing looks and giggled like a couple of adolescent boys over a *Penthouse*.

"What you want with Earl Mallock?" J.T. asked.

"Yeah," Bobbie added. "What's he got that we don't got?"

"A Colt Sportster. He said he might sell it to me if the offer was right. I've been saving my pennies, and I'm ready to take it off his hands."

"What does a lady like yourself need with a high-powered carbine?" J.T. wanted to know.

She smiled and deepened her dimples. "Home protection."

"Where do you live, sugar, Fort Knox?"

Rather than disappoint him, she chuckled, then leaned across the counter, ignoring the cigar that smoldered in a tray under her nose. "Seriously, do you know where I might find him?"

"You don't need Earl. We got Sportsters." Bobbie—whom she had dubbed Yahoo Number One—lifted a rifle from the wall rack behind the counter and laid it in front of her.

"I'd need extra magazines." She picked up the Sportster and checked the breech, finding it empty.

"Got 'em," he said.

She slammed the block home, swung the gun to her shoulder, expertly sighted at the poster boy's crotch, and squeezed off a dry shot. "And steel-jacketed ammo?"

His eyes widened, and she could see that he was quickly falling deeply in lust with her. "I'll get you some," he said, far too eagerly. He lowered his voice and leaned into her face. "I'll get you anything you want, sweet thing. Anything at all."

"Why . . . thank you so much, kind sir," she said, batting her lashes. Abruptly, she dropped the rifle onto the counter, along with her demure act, and fixed him with blue lasers. "But my mind is made up. I want *Earl's* gun. Do you know where I can find him, or not?"

"Well, I . . . I don't know. . . ." He turned to his friend. "What do you think, J.T.? Should we—?"

"Get her phone number, Bobbie. Yeah, that's it. Get her number and we'll have Earl call her. How's that?"

Bobbie gave him a look of deep appreciation. "That's

good." He turned back to Savannah. "Leave your number, honey bunch, and we'll tell Earl you're looking for him."

Tired and disgusted, Savannah left a few minutes later. She was no closer to finding Earl Mallock or Christy. Her head ached, she was weak with hunger, and her spirits were dragging the pavement.

But she could take satisfaction in imagining the look on J.T.'s and Bobbie's faces when they called the number she had given them and spoke to the no-nonsense, not-so-benevolent despot, Sister Mary Theresa, who ran the local rescue mission. Best case scenario: They might even be dumb enough to ask Sister for a date. . . .

The moment Savannah heard Tammy's voice on her car phone, she knew something was wrong.

"Savannah, could you come home, right away? Please!"

Immediately, Savannah did a U-turn on Harrington and headed the car toward home. "Tammy, what is it? Are you crying?"

"A little. It's just that . . . well . . . someone is here and . . ."

Savannah's heart leapt as she imagined the worst. "Mallock?"

"No, the colonel. He's here in the office, and he wants to talk to you, and he says it's all our fault that something's happened to his daughter and—"

"Tammy, listen to me." She gripped the wheel, fighting her temper. Sure, the man must be worried out of his mind, but that was no excuse for . . . "You take the colonel into my sitting room and tell him to '*Sit*', then get him a cup of coffee. Stick it in his hand, leave the room, and close the door firmly behind you. Lock it if necessary to keep him in there, but don't put up with any more guff off him. Got that?"

"Yeah. And Savannah . . . thanks."

"No sweat, kiddo. I'll be there in four minutes, five tops."

She put the Camaro's pedal to the metal. Maybe three and a half.

CHAPTER NINE

Savannah stood in the middle of her living room, staring up into the angriest eyes she had seen in ages. "Colonel Neilson," she said, keeping her voice low and even, "I'm going to assume that you are, at heart, a gentleman, and this momentary lapse in your manners is due to the fact that you are overwrought with grief."

The moment she had walked through the front door, he had verbally attacked her, calling her names that—as Granny Reid would put it—"No man should say and no lady should hear."

In the corner of the room stood Tammy, still quietly crying. Apparently, the colonel had not accepted her offer of refreshments or obeyed the command to "sit."

"You're damned right, I'm overwrought," he said. "You saw

what he did to my baby. That bastard had her trussed up like an animal. And he shot her in the head like a . . ."

His voice broke and she thought he was going to start sobbing, but he seemed to rally. She could see the war of emotions in his eyes, the grief versus the fury. It was a battle she had seen every day when she had patrolled the streets.

Rage won.

"And you led him straight to her." Neilson's fists were tight balls at his sides. "For all I know, you helped him do it."

"Surely, you don't believe that, Colonel."

She could smell the heavy odor of liquor on his breath as he leaned close to her. For a moment he swayed on his feet and she thought he might go down.

"The police believe it," he said. "At least, they're considering the possibility."

"The brass of the San Carmelita Police Department and I have an old vendetta going," she said, feeling about 107 years old with another birthday pending. "They hate me. I swear, they would be plumb giddy if they could prove I was Jack the Ripper, but that doesn't make it so."

Again he weaved, unsteady on his feet.

"Colonel, why don't you have a seat before you fall down."

"I told her—" He jabbed a thumb in Tammy's direction. She cringed as though it had been a loaded pistol. "I don't *want* to sit down. I'm all right."

"Tammy," Savannah said, sensing that the young woman was near the end of her emotional tether, "why don't you run along home. It's been a long day."

"But . . . shouldn't I stay . . . I . . . ?"

"No. Everything is fine here. You run along."

With an expression that contained a mixture of misgivings and intense relief, Tammy seized the opportunity, grabbed her purse and jacket, and bolted out the door.

"Colonel," Savannah said gently, turning back to Neilson, "I know that you *aren't* all right. In your circumstances no one would be. You're exhausted, you're terribly upset, and I suspect you've had a bit too much to drink. Please sit for a spell and let's talk. Just the two of us."

She saw the momentary flicker of vulnerability in his eyes and knew he needed understanding and sympathy from someone. She would have been honored to give it, but right now, for reasons she could certainly understand, he considered her the enemy.

"We're on the same side, really, Colonel," she told him as she gingerly took his arm and led him over to the sofa. "We need to find your granddaughter and bring your daughter's killer to justice. I know that's what you want, too."

He jerked his arm out of her grasp and refused to sit. "You caused my only daughter to be killed, my little granddaughter to be stolen from me. What kind of fool do you think I am? I'm not going to sit here in your house and drink coffee as if we were best buddies. You're not going to get off that easily, Miss Reid."

"Colonel, please, I—"

He headed for the door with a purposeful, if unsteady, stride and jerked it open. Outside, the night was dark and a soft rain was beginning to fall. "I've said what I came to say."

She rushed to him. "Colonel Neilson, don't go yet. Stay for at least one cup of coffee. Really, you're in no condition to drive."

Again, she grasped his arm, but more firmly than before.

"Get your hands off me, before I forget you're a woman, and knock you on your ass."

Savannah's face hardened. Grieving father or not, she was getting her can full. "You could try," she said, lifting her chin a couple of notches, "but I'm not sure you would succeed."

Slowly, she released his arm, knowing there was no way to hold him if he was determined to leave.

"I really need your input, Colonel, if I'm going to help your granddaughter," she called as she followed him out of the house. "Later, when you've thought things over, we need to talk. Please, stay in touch."

Ignoring her, he staggered down her sidewalk toward his car, which was parked at the curb. The rain was falling more heavily by the moment, dripping on her from the bougainvillea that draped the porch. A cold wet trickle slid down the back of her collar, causing her to shiver.

When was this rotten day ever going to end?

Through the wet haze, she saw the outline of a yellow car . . . a taxi . . . pulling up behind his Lincoln.

Who was . . . ?

No one she knew ever took a cab, not in San Carmelita. To her knowledge, the local service only had two cars, one for the senior citizens' retirement home, one for Friday night drunks.

The cabbie rushed out of the car and around to the rear door. He opened it with flourish and offered his hand to his passenger.

Savannah watched, holding her breath as a woman unfolded herself from the taxi. A beautiful head of silver hair that glowed like moonlight beneath the streetlamp. A more-than-ample female figure in a long, flowing caftan, covered with a brilliant floral print. Sparkling, youthful eyes set in an aged, lined face.

The beloved face of her grandmother.

"Gran?" she whispered, her heart hopping up into her throat between her tonsils. "Granny Reid?"

Savannah was only dimly aware that her grandmother's attention was fully on the colonel, who didn't seem to notice anyone or anything as he climbed into his own car and pulled away from the curb.

"Gran?" Savannah called, finding her voice at last. "Gran, is it you? Of course it's you."

"Savannah?" She squinted, nearsighted as always, but still unwilling to admit that she needed glasses. "Is that you, baby?"

"Oh, Gran!" Savannah sailed across the space that separated them and threw her arms around the person she loved most in the world. Warm, salty tears of joy mixed with the cold rain on her face. "How did you . . . when did you . . . ?"

"Just now. Flew all the way from Atlanta, I did, into Los Angeles." Her Southern accent was as sweet and poignant as the rose perfume she had worn for as long as Savannah could remember.

Gran shoved some cash at the driver, then cast a lingering look at the colonel's car as it disappeared down the street. "Guess I shoulda showed up a few minutes earlier. Then, maybe I could have made the acquaintance of your gentleman caller. He looks more my age than yours."

"It's probably just as well," Savannah said under her breath.

The cabbie handed Savannah a suitcase, nodded respectfully, wished Gran a wonderful vacation, and dismissed himself.

Savannah had always been fascinated by the amount of adoration a woman in her eighties could receive from members of the opposite sex.

"This is such a wonderful surprise," Savannah said. "When did you arrive in California?"

"About an hour ago. I flew on a red nose. It was cheaper."

"A red nose?" Strange visions of reindeer danced through Savannah's head until she had completed a quick, mental translation from Gran-ish to English. "Oh, you mean a red *eye*."

"Don't you go correcting your elders, young lady. I know what the hell I flew on." She stood on tiptoe to plant a bright scarlet, lipstick kiss on each of Savannah's cheeks.

Savannah returned the kisses.

"Now, are you going to invite me in for a nip of something to warm these stiff old bones," Gran said as the taxi drove away, "or are we going to stand out here in the rain 'til we catch our death o' cold?"

Savannah had to hug her one more time; she couldn't remember when she had been so happy to see someone. She couldn't remember when she had needed anyone so much. Gran had a way of showing up just when Savannah expected her least and needed her most.

With the suitcase in one hand and her other arm wrapped around her grandmother's shoulders, she walked her up the sidewalk toward the house. "I'm tickled to death to see you, Gran," she said. "Whatever made you decide to come out now?"

"I'm going to die soon, Savannah."

Savannah felt a seismic tremor run through her soul. She dropped the suitcase, grabbed Gran's shoulders and whirled her around to face her. "Oh, God . . . Granny! What is it? Is it your heart? Oh, no . . . it's not ca . . . canc—" She couldn't bear to say it, couldn't even think it.

"What? Oh, pooh, you're such a silly girl. It's nothing like that."

"But you just said—"

"That I'm going to die soon. Well, for heaven's sake, Savannah, it's true. Let's face facts; I'm eighty-three years old. I'm bound to kick off before too long, and I figured I'd better do some of those things I've always been intendin' to do, but never got around to."

Savannah felt her knees go weak with relief. "Then, you aren't sick, or—?"

"Hell no. What an imagination you have. I came out here because I want to go to Disneyland."

"Disneyland? You want me to take you to Disneyland?"

"No. I'm going to take *you*. Tomorrow morning, bright and early."

"Tomorrow?" Reality returned in a nauseous wave. She retrieved the suitcase and searched for the appropriate words, that didn't seem to be anywhere near the tip of her tongue. "Ah . . . Gran, I've got some things going on here that . . . well . . . oh, shoot . . . just come inside and I'll fix you a hot toddy."

Looking up, her grandmother blinked at the drops falling onto her face. "I thought they said it never rains out here in California."

Savannah started to reply, when she saw a familiar, battered old Skylark lumbering down the street in their direction. Dirk was behind the wheel. He pulled up in front of the house and cut the engine.

"Great . . ." Savannah muttered, "that's all I need now. Un-

fortunately, Gran, that bit about the perfect climate isn't alto-
gether true," she added with a sigh. "And sometimes, when it
rains, it really pours."

"What do you mean, you're going to arrest my granddaughter
for murder?" Gran stood in the middle of Savannah's living
room, her hands on her waist, her feet spread in a battle stance,
her face looking like a Mississippi River lightning storm. She was
glaring at Dirk, who sat on the sofa, squirming miserably beneath
her scrutiny.

"I wasn't exactly here to *arrest* her, ma'am, I just . . ."

"Gran, please." Savannah sat on the edge of her easy chair,
clutching both cats to her sides for comfort.

"You're that Dirk guy she's written me letters about,"
Granny continued. "You used to be her partner, and now you're
supposed to be her friend. You know damned well she wouldn't
kill an innocent person."

Gran shrugged and seemed to briefly reconsider. "Oh, well,
she did shoot a couple of fellows, way back when," she conceded,
"you know, her being a peace officer and all that, she had to.
And she's knocked the snot out of quite a few when they were
askin' for it. She knows that fancy black belt stuff and she does
have a bit of a temper, but she wouldn't—"

"Really, Gran," Savannah interrupted. "Please don't 'help'
me."

"Well, somebody sure needs to. It sounds like you've got
yourself in a heap of trouble this time. Worse than usual, even
for you."

"They just want to talk to you for a while, Van. That's all."
Dirk turned pleading eyes to Savannah.

"Talk? Bloss and Hillquist want to grill me like a porter-house—rare and bloody—and you know it."

"Who's Bloss? Who's Hillquist?" Gran demanded. "Do you want me to go down there for you, sugar? I could set things straight."

"No, really!" Savannah spoke so loudly that the cats both ejected themselves from her lap. "You don't need to do that."

"I don't mind at all."

Memories flashed across the back screen of Savannah's mind: Gran literally tossing a vacuum salesman and his wares off her back porch, Gran telling Savannah's grade school principal to "Sit on a fence post and spin" because he had kept Savannah for an hour after school, Gran threatening one of Savannah's dates that she would "Jerk a knot in his tail" if he "got out of the way" with her granddaughter.

"Yes, Granny, I'm sure you could settle everything for me," she said. "But it's your vacation, and I think I should take care of this."

Dirk brightened.

Savannah knew she had to let him off the hook by going in and facing whatever music Bloss and Hillquist wanted to subject her to, even if it were the last thing on earth she wanted to do.

"Will you feed the cats for me, Gran?"

"Is that all?" She looked genuinely disappointed. Her cheeks were flushed pink with excitement and her eyes alight with mischief.

"Yes, that's all. And don't wait up for me. I have a wonderful Black Forest cake in the refrigerator," she said wistfully.

"Feel free to dig in. The guest room has clean sheets. Make yourself at home."

She stood and lifted her purse from a nearby table. Dirk hurried to get her raincoat from the hall closet. The perfect gentleman, he held it as she slipped it on. Like most males, his manners were always at their best when he was overwhelmed with guilt.

"When will you be back?" Granny asked her as she followed them to the door, her long caftan skirt swishing gracefully. Her steps were slower, but as always, the picture of Southern elegance.

Savannah gave her a hug, inhaling the lovely scent of roses and basking in the momentary comfort of maternal love. She thought of the long night ahead and wished she could just ask Granny to "Go talk to the principal" for her. It would be so lovely to let another person be strong in her stead.

There were definite disadvantages to growing up.

"Not in time to go to Disneyland bright and early tomorrow morning," she said. "I'm sorry, Gran."

"Awk, that's all right. Mickey and Donald have been waiting for me all these years; I suppose they can hang on a bit longer."

CHAPTER TEN

"How much did you tell them?" Savannah asked as she and Dirk walked down the hallway at the rear of the station which led to Hillquist's office.

"They asked me what happened. I told 'em. No more, no less," Dirk replied. He was staring down at the gray, industrial-dull tiles as though expecting the floor to open and swallow them whole. Maybe he was hoping.

"You know, you don't have to beat yourself up about this," Savannah said, lacing her arm companionably through his. "In spite of what my granny said, you aren't really a good-for-nothing, backstabbing, double-crossing tallywhacker. She just has a special way with words."

Dirk chuckled and his mood seemed to lighten a tad. "Appears to run in the family."

"Here we are." She paused before the door to the chief's office. "Tell me again, just how mad was Bloss?"

"He waited here for you for three hours. How mad do you think he'd be? Whatever possessed you to do a thing like that . . . as if you weren't in deep enough shit as it was."

She grinned sheepishly and shrugged. "Seemed like a good idea at the time. Wish me luck."

"No way. I'm coming in with you."

"They won't let you stay."

Dirk stuck out his lower lip and banged the door open. "They'll let me stay."

If pecking order were signified by creature comforts and chair assignments, Savannah didn't have to think long to figure out where she stood . . . or sat . . . at the moment.

The chief lounged graciously behind his modern, blond oak desk in an executive, high-backed, leather chair. At his side, Bloss sprawled across an upholstered tweed, cushy affair, while she and Dirk were perched on folding, metal contraptions. Hers was rusty.

"Unless you're her lawyer, leave," Bloss told Dirk, snuffing out his cigar in the chief's ashtray and pulling another from his shirt pocket.

"I'd like to stay," Dirk replied as he stared at the scuffed tips of his loafers.

"I'd like to have left five hours ago." Bloss made a ceremony of consulting his wristwatch. "But we don't always get what we want, thanks to certain individuals." He gave Savannah a dirty look.

The chief said nothing, but sat with his hands folded gracefully on the desk in front of him. At first glance, he seemed a more highly evolved specimen than the one sitting beside him. But his eyes reminded her of a few dead fish she had seen in the seafood section of her local supermarket.

"Good-bye," Bloss told Dirk.

"With all due respect, sir . . ." Dirk slurred the "sir" and his facial expression was anything but respectful. ". . . I'm staying."

Bloss looked to Hillquist for reinforcement.

"Let's get on with it," Hillquist said.

"Yes, please," Savannah said, sitting back in her miserably uncomfortable chair and trying not to look as nervous as she felt. "I'm tired, I'm in the middle of PMS, I haven't had my dinner yet, and I'm starting to get cranky."

"None of us have had our dinners yet," Bloss growled. "After that little stunt you pulled earlier this—"

Hillquist held up one hand to silence Bloss then turned to Savannah. "Did you kill Lisa Mallock?"

"No."

"Did you help someone do it?"

"No."

"Do you know who did?"

"I have a pretty good idea."

"Who?"

"I think it was her ex-husband, Earl Mallock."

"How do you know that?"

Savannah winced as the wound went a notch deeper into her conscience. "I don't *know* it, but I suspect it's true. Mallock lied to me, claiming to be her long-lost brother, and used my agency to find her."

Neither Hillquist nor Bloss registered any emotion at all.

Hillquist didn't appear to even have any brain waves. Savannah wondered why they were going over this, when it was obvious she wasn't telling them anything they didn't know already.

Hillquist picked up a gold Cross pen from his desk top and began to write on a piece of paper. At first, she thought he was taking notes, but another look told her he was merely doodling.

She couldn't help wondering what he was drawing. Probably a hangman's noose.

Without looking his way, Savannah knew that Dirk was watching her closely. She didn't dare even glance at him for fear of intercepting some sweet, schmaltzy look that would twang her heartstrings. She had to keep her head clear; this definitely wasn't the time to give in to emotions.

"Are you aware that trace evidence has been found that links you to the scene of the murder?" Hillquist continued to doodle, his eyes still as flat as his monotone.

"I'm not surprised," Savannah replied. "I was there in the cabin the morning following the murder. I stood over the body. I touched it."

"How do you know that was the morning after?" Bloss had been quiet as long as he could. He had to interject his nickel's worth. "How come you're so sure that she was killed the night before?"

"I've seen quite a few stiffs in my day . . . sir. The body exhibited total rigidity, cloudy corneas, and fixed lividity. No insect infestation to speak of, but she was indoors . . . windows and doors closed. My best guess would be that she had died around midnight. Am I close?"

"Dr. Liu says one," Dirk said quietly.

"What was your relationship with Earl Mallock?" Hillquist

said. He looked bored, but Savannah noticed his hand had tightened around the gold pen.

"The man was my client. That's it, that's all. And he wasn't a very good one at that, since he lied to me and paid me only half of what he owed me."

"And what if we can prove that he was far more to you than simply your client?"

Savannah laced her fingers together and could feel her pulse pounding out to their tips. "Since it isn't true, it would require a lot of fabrication on your part. But, I suppose if you really wanted to, you could. It all depends on how far you'll go to settle old scores."

She heard Dirk's slight intake of breath and watched as a flicker of hate lit the chief's dull eyes.

"I'd watch what you say, Miss Reid," he said carefully. "We're just about to charge you with accessory to murder."

"I don't think so, or I would have brought an attorney with me."

"We've checked your financial standing. Since you've left the department, you can't afford an attorney."

That was much closer to the truth than Savannah cared to admit, even to herself. She was in the rotten, middle-class bracket of individuals who couldn't afford the services of professionals: doctors, lawyers, plumbers, or automobile mechanics, but weren't sufficiently poverty-stricken to warrant public assistance.

Her blood sugar level dipped to an all-time low. She stood and tucked her purse under her arm. "Are you going to charge me or not?"

"I haven't decided yet," Hillquist replied.

"Well, you better make up your mind. I've got a Black Forest cake in my refrigerator and an eighty-three-year-old grandmother in my house."

"You aren't going anywhere, Ms. Reid," Hillquist said. He had stopped doodling and was giving her his full attention. "I'm not finished with you yet."

"Yes, you are," said a deep voice from the door. "This has gone far enough."

Savannah turned and was astonished to see that her new advocate was the venerable Colonel Neilson himself.

"I called your home to apologize for my behavior earlier this evening, Ms. Reid," he explained. "A pleasant houseguest of yours said you had been arrested for my daughter's murder. Is that true?"

"I'm afraid I don't know yet." She glanced at Hillquist, Bloss, and her watch. "You'll have to tune in later. Film at eleven."

The colonel turned his intense, blue-eyed scrutiny on Hillquist. "I know you're trying to help, Norman," he said. "For old time's sake and all that. But you and I both know this woman didn't kill Lisa. Earl did it. And the four of you are sitting here in this office, playing mental chess, while he gets away. There has to be a better way."

He gave Savannah a kind, sad half smile that gave her spirits a better boost than an intravenous drip of Black Forest chocolate. "I was . . . shall we say, 'in my cups' when I visited you earlier, Savannah, but I recall something you said about us being on the same team, about us needing to work together."

Savannah held out her hand to him, and he shook it. For once, neither Hillquist nor Bloss seemed to have anything to say.

"I'd like that very much, sir," she told him.

"Do you need a ride home?" His hand, arthritic though it was, felt warm and strong wrapped around hers.

She thought of Granny Reid and the attention she had paid him earlier in the evening. Gran, at least, would be quite pleased to see him again.

But she could feel Dirk standing beside her, tense and waiting for her reply. Good ol' Dirk . . . still a faithful partner.

"Why, thank you, kind sir." She batted her eyelashes and deepened her dimples. "But my grandmother taught me that a lady always leaves with the gentleman who brought her."

She gave the chief and her ex-captain her best "Kiss My Ass" look, took Dirk's arm and said, "Let's go, Beauregard. You can walk me home in the moonlight by way of the river . . . but only if you promise not to take liberties."

Savannah's bravado failed her the moment she stepped across her threshold and into the sanctity of her own home. For the past twenty-four hours, she had been running on raw nerves, and she had reached her limit.

Most of the lights in the house were off. Only one lamp glowed, turned down low, in the living room. She was relieved—and a wee disappointed—that Granny hadn't met her at the door. Good, she had taken Savannah's advice and gone to bed. After all, an octogenarian needed her beauty rest.

However, her arrival hadn't gone unnoticed. Cleopatra and Diamante came running to her and twined their sleek black bodies around her ankles. Their pale green eyes and rhinestone collars glimmered in the lamplight.

"Hi, girls," she said, feeling a tenderness for the two animals well up inside her. Dropping her purse onto the foyer table, she scooped one up in each arm and gave them kisses. Their bellies were pudgy; Granny had always boasted the reputation of overfeeding every living creature within her domain.

As she passed through the living room, she was surprised to see that Gran hadn't gone to bed after all. She was curled against the end of the sofa, her reading glasses nearly sliding off the tip of her nose, her open Bible across her lap, and her eyes closed. She was snoring softly.

Savannah thought of all the times she had come home late from dates and found her grandmother in exactly this position. Gran had always been a better mom than Savannah's own mother, the most positive maternal influence in her upbringing.

"Gran . . ." After setting the cats on the floor, she placed one hand on the older woman's shoulder and shook her gently. "Granny, it's Savannah. I'm home now, and you should go along to bed."

"Huh? Oh, it's you, sugar." She stirred and pulled out the antique, locket-watch she wore around her neck. Flipping it open, she squinted down at its mother-of-pearl face. "High time you got back, too."

Savannah chuckled. "Well, it's not like I was out kicking up my heels, you know. I wasn't exactly making out with Tommy Stafford up at Lovers' Peak."

Closing her Bible, Gran set it aside and rose from the sofa. "How did it go? Did you give 'em hell?"

"I'd like to think I held my own. That's about as good as it got."

"Fair enough."

Arms around each other's waists, they walked toward the kitchen.

"Are you hungry?" Gran asked. "Can I make you some fried liver and onions, or I could bake you some corn bread, if you've got some buttermilk to go with it."

Savannah felt her stomach roil at the mention of food. "Thank you, but I've waited so long to eat, and I'm so tired that I feel sort of nauseous. I think I'll just hold out until breakfast."

"Then why don't you go on up to bed, and I'll bring you a nice cup of peppermint tea in a few minutes."

"Are you sure? You're my guest; I feel like I should be serving you."

"Aw, I'm not a guest. I'm family. Hightail it outta here and get yourself into bed before you fall apart at the seams."

After pressing a kiss to her grandmother's forehead and making one more feeble complaint, Savannah allowed herself to be shooed upstairs.

When she walked into her bedroom and flipped on the light, she found another lovely surprise. Gran had folded the comforter down, then pulled the blanket and sheet back in a neat triangle. Across her pillow, her grandmother had laid one of her prettiest nightgowns, a slip of peach silk, embellished with lace and seed pearls.

"Oh, Gran," she whispered as she stripped out of her street clothes and pulled the gown over her head. As she allowed the satiny waves to trickle down her body, she smelled the slight fragrance of roses. Gran had even remembered to spray the gown with cologne.

She had only been in bed a few minutes when her grandmother arrived, bearing a china teacup filled with aromatic mint tea.

Taking the delicate porcelain from her, Savannah breathed in the scented steam and instantly felt better.

"I was just lying here thinking about you," Savannah said as Gran sat on the bed beside her. "About my thirteenth birthday. Do you remember what we did?"

"Of course I do. But then, I don't have any problem remembering things that happened forty years ago, just yesterday."

"Gran, it wasn't forty years ago, for heaven's sake."

Her grandmother laughed and tweaked her nose. "Of course not. It was only yesterday, right?"

"It seems like it." Savannah closed her eyes and snuggled deeper into the sheets, savoring the memory. "You told me that, because I was turning thirteen, I was a young lady."

"That's right. And we went shopping together, because I told you that a lady must always have two things—"

"Beautiful lingerie and her own special perfume."

"It's true. You never know when you're going to be in a car wreck . . . or something much nicer . . . and you'll need to be looking your best, all the way down to your skin."

To emphasize her point, Gran demurely lifted the hem of her caftan and revealed the exquisite bit of lace that edged her slip. "Besides, even if no one else ever sees what a person is wearing beneath her clothes, a lady knows, and it has a lot to do with how she feels about herself as a woman."

"Thank you, Gran . . . for the tea, for coming to see me . . . for teaching me about the good things in life."

"You were a delightful and eager student, Savannah. I learned a lot from you in the process." Gran's eyes searched hers.

"How are you, really, child? How is your life here in California?"

Savannah thought for a moment, deciding whether to give a pat answer or an honest one. With Granny Reid, there was only one choice. No matter what she said, her grandmother could always sense the truth.

"Most of the time, I love my life. I have good friends, a comfortable home, work that is fulfilling and worthwhile. But . . ."

"There's always a 'but.' That's the bitter and sweet of it."

"It's just that right now, things are tough. I've had cases that disturbed me, angered me, frustrated me. But this one has to be the worst so far."

"Even worse than when you lost your job?"

"Yes, much worse. There's much more at stake here. A woman's life has been lost. And a beautiful little girl—"

Savannah couldn't hold it in any longer. The emotions turned to hot liquid and spilled down her face. Her grandmother handed her a box of tissues from the nightstand.

"I'm sorry," Savannah said between sniffles. "I don't want to ruin your visit by crying on your shoulder like this. It's just that so much has happened, and . . ."

She hiccuped and sobbed harder. Gran climbed into bed beside her and gathered her in her arms as though she were still ten years old.

"And you know how I am just before my period," Savannah continued, unable to stop the torrent. "Sometimes I cry over the darnedest things . . . the national anthem . . . an inspiring margarine commercial on TV. I mean, that crown appears on the kid's head and I . . . I just lose it."

"There, there . . ." Granny Reid stroked her granddaughter's hair and kissed her forehead. "This time I think it's a lot more than a margarine commercial."

"Of course it is. Oh, Gran, you should have seen what that son of a bitch did to her. And now he has Christy, and I have to find him. I have to undo what I've done."

"Shhh-hhh, sweetheart. My dear, brave girl. You *will* find him. You'll do everything you need to do to set things right. Because that's the kind of person you've always been."

Savannah could feel the words sinking into her heart like a healing balm. She snuggled closer into her grandmother's arms, allowing herself the rare and wonderful luxury of absorbing the other woman's strength.

"But the day is over and done," Gran continued. "And you can't do a single thing tonight, except sleep, and gather strength for tomorrow."

Gran wiped the tears from Savannah's cheeks with her fingertips, and Savannah wondered at how soft human skin was, at both the beginning and the end of life.

Granny Reid began to sing quietly. Her voice wasn't as strong as it had once been, and it quivered with an old lady's vibrato. But to Savannah, her grandmother's singing was, and always would be, a gift of love.

Savannah could feel herself drifting off into a sweet sleep. "Gran . . ." she whispered, "why did you really come to California? Did you know I needed you?"

"Shush. Of course not. I told you, I want to go to Disneyland."

CHAPTER ELEVEN

"I heard that yesterday was pretty awful for you, Savannah. I'd like to make it up to you with a champagne breakfast."

Ryan Stone's deep bass voice was like velvet caressing her skin first thing in the morning. She wasn't even out of bed yet. All the better to lie here in her silk nightgown and imagine, just for a moment, that the big, gorgeous hunk was lying beside her, not just on the other end of the telephone.

"I'd love to, Ryan, believe me. I'm half-starved. But I have work to do." She glanced at the clock and groaned. Eight-thirty.

"You don't have to feel lazy; this will be work. I've uncovered some very interesting facts for you. I can fill you in over strawberry cheese blintzes. How about it?"

"My grandmother is visiting me and . . ."

"I know. How do you think I found out about your terrible day?"

Savannah sighed. "If I want something broadcast, I don't need to telegraph or telephone. Tell-a-Gran is much more efficient. When did she bore you with all the gory details?"

"When I called last night. But she didn't bore me at all. She kept me entertained for half an hour. What a colorful turn of phrase . . . reminds me of a certain, charming relative of hers. Why don't you bring her along for breakfast, and I'll invite Gibson."

Warning bells went off in Savannah's brain. "Ahhh . . . I'm not sure that's such a good idea."

"Why not? She and Gibson will get along famously."

"Exactly. John Gibson is a very attractive older man, and Granny can be a bit of a vixen. She might even hit on him."

"It's just as well. Then Gibson will understand the torment I've had to endure for his sake, resisting the allure of a beautiful, deliciously available Reid female."

Savannah dared to hope . . . but only for a couple of accelerated heartbeats. Then she came back to earth with a thud. "Why . . . Mr. Ryan Stone, I do believe you're toyin' with my affections."

"But you know that I love you, Savannah, and I do want to buy you breakfast. Fredrico's. Half an hour."

"We'll be there."

Savannah hung up the phone, sprang out of bed, and ran to her bedroom door.

"Rise and shine, Gran!" she called down the hallway. "We've got a double date for breakfast . . . kinda sorta."

Polished teak furnishings, classy maritime decor, a magnificent view of the harbor, and the best cheese blintzes in town. Ah . . . Fredrico's was one of Savannah's favorite bits of real estate on earth.

As Ryan had predicted, John Gibson and Gran appeared to be extremely impressed with one another. Toasting with mimosa and nibbling each other's San Francisco Benedict and crêpes Suzette, they seemed a likely twosome. Except that Gran was probably twenty-five years his senior and, of course, John Gibson was already committed, life and heart, to Ryan.

And who wouldn't be? Savannah thought as she tried to ignore his thick dark hair, his green eyes with their long black lashes, and the strong jaw that would have been a perfect model for an electric shaver commercial.

"What is this?" she asked, when he passed her a manila envelope.

"Good stuff. But I can't take complete credit. Gibson came up with the information on Earl Mallock's court-martial."

"Court-martial? You're kidding."

"Not at all. Take a look."

Savannah thumbed through the documents, which had apparently been faxed to Ryan from numerous government agencies during the past twenty-four hours.

"Earl Mallock was in the army. Dirk and I found evidence of that in his storage locker," she said, staring down at his service photo. Young, dark hair cut short, looking heavier than when she had last seen him, Mallock was standing in front of an American flag, wearing a staff sergeant's uniform and a military police armband.

"That's a grim grimace," she remarked.

"I think it's standard military issue."

Her eyes scanned the first paper. "He served in Vietnam . . . we knew that, too. He received a medical discharge."

"Hospitalized. That was how he and Lisa Neilson met. She was a nurse on staff at the VA Hospital; Earl was a patient."

"Physical injuries?"

"Psychological."

Savannah glanced over at Gran, aware that a certain amount of discretion might be in order. But Gibson was keeping her occupied with some yarn about having served as a guard at Buckingham Palace. Or, at least, she assumed it was a yarn. With Gibson, one could never tell. He seemed to have lived at least a dozen lives already this time around.

Locating the documents concerning the court-martial, Savannah read, "Charged with . . . using excessive force while performing his duties . . . assigned to guard duty . . . prisoners of war . . . accused of . . ." Savannah dropped the paper and stared at Ryan.

He nodded. "That's right. He bound some of his prisoners' wrists and ankles with piano wire, then tortured them by twisting it tighter and tighter."

Crime scene photos that her eyes and brain had already processed flashed through Savannah's mind. Suddenly, she had no appetite, not even for Fredrico's cuisine.

"Dear God," she whispered. "He's done it before."

"And he got away with it."

"How? The military tribunal didn't believe he did it?"

"Oh, they know he did it. He never denied that fact. They found him 'not guilty' by reason of temporary insanity. It seems he snapped under the accumulated stress and strain of combat."

"So, his atrocities were 'justified'?"

"Supposedly, or at least understandable. In their opinion, that is."

Savannah felt the old rage growing, the fury that those who had committed horrible crimes against their fellow human beings were set free to do it again and again. It was an old story, and she was sick to death of hearing the same, tired ending.

"How do you suppose he got away with it?" she mused.

Ryan reached across the table and handed her another document that was several pages thick. "Here is a segment of the trial transcript. The testimony of Earl Mallock's commanding officer. It's quite a moving account, a powerful argument on behalf of the accused. Besides, Mallock's advocate was a Congressional Medal of Honor recipient. I'd say it had a lot to do with Mallock's acquittal."

"What kind of man would defend someone who had done something like that?"

"Someone with a code of honor that might be different from yours or mine. Someone who felt it was his duty to stand beside his men . . . no matter what they had done." Ryan lifted his glass, watched the tiny bubbles racing up the sides of the flute in iridescent threads, then took a sip. "That someone was a Captain Forrest Neilson."

Savannah sat at her dining room table. Gran to her right, Dirk to her left, and Tammy at the other end, typing furiously into her laptop computer.

"I already knew about Mallock serving in 'Nam," Dirk said, pouting as he wolfed down a plateful of tuna sandwiches which Savannah had thrown together for him.

"But you didn't know about the court-martial, or the fact that Mallock had served under Neilson." Savannah never passed over an opportunity to humble Dirk. It was a rotten job, but she felt she was the only one who loved him enough to do it.

"So, no big deal." He chomped off a quarter of a sandwich and chewed noisily. "Any moron could have come up with that."

"*You* didn't." Tammy gave him a nasty look over the rim of her glassful of mineral water.

"You know, Dirk, I think you're jealous." Savannah refreshed her grandmother's root beer float with another generous scoop of Dreyer's vanilla and then her own.

"You must admit," Gran said, stirring the ice cream until it made caramel-colored swirls in the amber liquid, "those two are extremely handsome and charming fellows. And smart, too. That John Gibson used to guard the palace of the queen of England, you know. I feel so honored just to have met him."

"I suppose they aren't too bad," Dirk said sarcastically, "if you don't mind the fact that they are a couple of quee—"

"Gays," Savannah interjected, giving Dirk a sound smack on the side of the head. "And very dear friends of mine, so watch your mouth."

She jerked the plate of sandwiches out from under his nose. Leaning down to his ear, she lowered her voice and said, "Try not to make an ass of yourself, Coulter, if you can help it."

"Gays?" Granny suddenly became all ears. "Are you telling me that John and Ryan are homosexuals?"

Savannah sighed and returned to her chair and her ice cream float. "Yes, Gran, they are . . . among many other things . . . qualities too numerous to mention. Now could we please—?"

"Well, I'll be." Granny shook her head in amazement. "Who would have guessed it? They didn't *look* like homosexuals. I mean, they were so masculine and all."

Savannah shot Dirk a look that told him how she felt about him having started all of this.

"Ah . . . Gran. . . ." Savannah paused, choosing her words carefully, reminding herself that people could only be held accountable for the amount of enlightenment they had been given. Her grandmother's upbringing and social discipline hadn't exactly been progressive. Dirk, on the other hand, had no excuse.

"Gran . . . not all gay men act effeminate. In fact, none that I've ever known. Just as not all elderly ladies are sticks in the mud, who sit around and knit all day." She turned to Dirk. "And, thankfully, not all cops are homophobic jerks."

Granny didn't seem to be offended by Savannah's observations, only fascinated, as she mulled over this new revelation.

"Could we get back to business now?" Savannah said, looking at Tammy, who nodded in agreement, and then at Dirk, who was still sulking.

"What's next?" Tammy asked, helping herself to one of Dirk's sandwiches.

"I think Ryan and I should go visit the colonel. At the station last night, he seemed far more likely to cooperate than before. And judging from what we know about his long-standing relationship with Earl, he might be able to point us in the right direction."

"I'm going along," Dirk said with an indignant sniff. "After all, I'm the only one around here who's got a badge."

"Oooo, low blow." Savannah winced.

"At least I didn't whack you on the head. That's the twenty-seventh time you've hit me. I know, I've been counting."

"Only twenty-seven times in how many years?" Tammy asked. "That must be some sort of record for patience and forebearing, Savannah."

"Tammy, call the colonel and tell him we want to drop over," she said. "Ask him to feed Beowulf a big meal and put him on a sturdy leash. Then let Ryan know what's happening. Let's get going; time's a wastin'."

Savannah gulped down the last of her float and grimaced as it froze her sinuses. "I'll see you later, Gran, just as soon as I can. You stay out of trouble now, hear?"

When Savannah, Ryan, and Dirk arrived at the colonel's home an hour later, Beowulf wasn't on a leash, but apparently he had been fed recently. He was lying peacefully on a rag rug beside the fireplace, asleep, his great muzzle tucked beneath his paws. He had opened one eye as they entered the room, dismissed them, and resumed his nap.

"Do you want some coffee?" the colonel asked, once he had them seated around the living room.

"I wouldn't want to put you out," Savannah said. Judging from the black bags under his eyes and the sallow cast to his complexion, she thought he would be better off lying in a hospital bed, rather than serving guests.

"It's already made." He left the room slowly, his arthritic shuffle far more pronounced than she remembered. Colonel Forrest Neilson seemed to have aged ten years in the past twelve hours.

While they waited for his return, the threesome took the

opportunity to scrutinize the contents of the room. On a small, round table against the far wall was an ornately carved, ebony inlaid box, which was propped at a forty-five-degree angle to better display its contents.

Leaving her seat, Savannah studied the object through the glass top. "It's his Congressional Medal of Honor," she told them, keeping her voice low. "Wonder what he did to get that?"

"Sacrificed a bit of his soul, I'd say," was Ryan's quiet reply.

She continued to walk around the room, taking in the other interesting aspects. The most distinctive features were the clocks, dozens of exquisite antique clocks hanging on walls, cluttering every horizontal surface. Three towering grandfather clocks, glass-domed anniversary clocks, Bavarian cuckoo clocks, mantel clocks, music box clocks. All were running and all were set at the precise time.

"I collect and repair them," the colonel explained as he arrived with a tray, laden with mugs of strong, black coffee, cream, and sugar. "Normally, I would make corny jokes about having a lot of time on my hands, but I just finished making funeral arrangements for my daughter. I guess I'm not in a joking mood."

Savannah returned to her seat and opened her mouth to say, once again, how sorry she was. But, thankfully, Ryan did it for them all.

"We can't express how sorry we are for your loss," he said in his deep, gracious voice. "And that's why we're here today. We're all working very hard to bring some closure to this tragedy. But we need your help."

The colonel sank wearily into a well-worn recliner and leaned back. He shut his eyes briefly, then opened them and said, "What do you want from me?"

"Information," Dirk replied, wearing his most "sensitive cop" face. "I understand you and Earl Mallock go back a long ways."

The colonel seemed mildly surprised that they would know this. "Yes. That's true."

When he didn't elaborate, Savannah added, "And we know about what happened in Vietnam."

Neilson's face hardened. "Young lady, I sincerely doubt that you know anything at all of what happened in Vietnam. You couldn't. You weren't there."

"I was," Ryan said softly. "Special forces."

"Me, too." Dirk picked up a mug of coffee and took a slurp. "Umm . . . infantry," he added reluctantly, upstaged by Ryan.

"Then you'll understand why I'm not inclined to drag up the past right now. God knows, the present is hard enough to handle."

"Yes, we do understand, sir," Ryan said. "But we need to discuss the similarities in the charges that were brought against him then and . . . forgive me . . . what happened to your daughter."

"The similarities are there." Neilson rubbed his eyes; Savannah could only imagine how much his head must be aching. "Earl committed the atrocities in Vietnam, just like they said he did. I was a fool to defend him. What can I say? It seemed the honorable thing to do at the time."

His voice caught in his throat, and Savannah thought he was going to lose the battle with his emotions. But he rallied. "Staff Sergeant Earl Mallock . . . he was my soldier. He had been on a trip through hell and back, a trip I had sent him on. What he did was horribly wrong, but I thought it was a once-in-a-lifetime act, the result of all he'd gone through. How was I to know that, years later, he would wind up doing the same thing to my daughter?"

"There was no way anyone could know, Colonel," Savannah said. "You mustn't blame yourself."

"Thank you." His expression was sincere, his eyes compassionate when he added, "You either."

"Colonel, you've known this guy for years, he was your son-in-law," Dirk said. "What can you tell us about him that might help us figure out where he's taken your granddaughter?"

"If I knew the answer to that, I would have told you long ago."

"Does he have any friends or relatives that he may have turned to for help?" Savannah asked.

"Earl is a loner. He doesn't like people, doesn't trust them. And not many people like him. He has a girlfriend named Vanessa, but I've talked to her already, and I don't think she knows anything. In fact, I think she's put out because she thinks he's run away and left her."

"And what do *you* think?"

"I think he's hiding out somewhere, waiting for things to calm down before he tries to leave the state. With his picture and Christy's all over the evening news and the front page of the papers, he'd have a hard time traveling with her now."

"That's what I figure, too." Dirk helped himself to Savannah's untouched mug of coffee. "But we've checked all the motels, hotels, flophouses, and fleabags. Can't find hide nor hair of them."

Ryan had stood and was walking slowly around the room, examining the clocks, the Congressional Medal, and miscellaneous memorabilia. He seemed particularly interested in a collection of framed photos on top of the baby grand piano in the corner.

"Excuse me, sir," he said, "do you play?"

"Yes, a little."

"Classical?"

"Jazz, but not as much as I used to . . . with the arthritis and all."

Ryan picked up one of the pictures and brought it to Neilson. "Can you tell me where this was taken?"

The colonel glanced at the photo, then handed it back. "I'm not sure. It was a long time ago."

Savannah craned her neck to get a glimpse. It appeared to be a shot of two men, standing in a wooded area.

"The reason I was asking," Ryan continued, "is because it looks like a place where a friend of mine camped a few years ago, up in the hills beyond Turner Canyon. About an hour's drive from here. I think it was called Montega Ranch, Montoya . . . something like that."

"I don't think that's where it was taken, but I don't remember for sure. It might have been. Earl and I used to go out for a week at a time, and he'd choose the locations. He was really into that survivalist routine, getting back to nature and all that. I got too old, too many aches and pains in the joints; we hadn't been for years."

"Do you think he might have taken Christy out into the wilderness?" Savannah asked. "That might explain why they haven't been seen in the city."

"I don't know." The colonel was becoming agitated. "If I

knew where my granddaughter was, don't you think I would tell you?"

"Of course you would, sir. I'm sorry. It's just that we're—"

"We're obviously imposing on you at a difficult time," Ryan said, returning the photo to its original place. "We should get going."

"If you think of anything, you let us know right away," Dirk said, finishing off Savannah's coffee.

As the three of them left the house and walked down the sidewalk, Savannah said, "Well, that was a waste of time."

"Yeah, we don't know any more than we did," Dirk agreed.

"Speak for yourselves." Ryan looked excited, pleased, eager.

"You got something?" Savannah said hopefully.

"Let's drop into Mort's Bait and Tackle shop, and I'll be able to tell you for sure."

Fifteen minutes later, Savannah and Dirk were sitting in Dirk's Buick in front of Mort's store, waiting for Ryan.

"I don't know what you see in that guy," Dirk said with a self-righteous sniff. "It's obvious you've got the hots for him, and he's not the least bit interested in you."

"Jealousy does not become you, my friend."

"Jealous? Of him? Why, I—"

"I think we'd better change the subject fast," she said, giving him the evil eye, "before I have the overpowering urge to snatch you bald." She turned her face toward the passenger window and added under her breath, "*Both* hairs, that is."

"What did you say?"

"Nothing. Shut up; here he comes now."

Ryan opened the back door, shoved some fast-food garbage

off the seat, and slid in behind Savannah. "We're in luck," he said, an eager smile on his handsome face.

"Oh, goody . . ." Dirk muttered.

Savannah pinched his ribs hard, twisting the ample flesh between her finger and thumb. He jumped, but didn't yell.

If Ryan saw or heard the exchange, he ignored it. "Earl was in here about a week ago," he said.

"Are you sure?" Dirk perked up visibly.

"The owner is a friend of mine, and he identified the photo I showed him."

"And . . ." Savannah held her breath, hoping, hoping.

"And he bought two rooster tails."

"I beg your pardon?" Dirk asked sarcastically.

"Rooster tails. A special kind of spinner bait used for trout fishing."

"Oh, yeah . . . I knew that." Dirk cleared his throat. "So, what does that prove?"

"It doesn't prove a thing. But most of the fishermen in this area use rooster tails for creek fishing, and almost all of the creeks are dried up. That one little shower we had the other night was the first one we've had in months."

"Okay, okay. We don't need a weather report," Dirk growled. "Everybody knows about the drought." He jumped as Savannah pinched him again.

"The creek that runs along the edge of the Montoya Ranch almost always has water," Ryan continued, "and trout. And everybody who fishes around here knows that it's the best place to use a rooster tail."

Savannah looked at Dirk, Dirk looked at her, and they both

looked at Ryan. A contagious smile spread across all three faces in unison.

"How long will it take us to drive there?" Dirk asked.

"Less than an hour. But we can only drive as far as Turner Canyon." Ryan chuckled; he seemed to delight in giving this information. "From there on in, we have to hike."

"How far?" Savannah asked.

"Six or seven miles. Maybe a couple more. But it'll be fun."

Savannah turned to Dirk and saw her own lack of enthusiasm registered on his scowl. "Sure," she said, trying not to sound sick at the thought of hiking anywhere, anytime, for seven miles, and maybe a couple more. "Great fun."

Dirk rolled his eyes. "Yeah . . . who-o-pee."

CHAPTER TWELVE

The first two miles of the hike, Savannah had reveled in the joys of the great outdoors: the tantalizing smell of the sage, the marguerites growing in wild profusion with their yellow-and-white faces lifted toward the sun, the gentle breeze stirring her hair, and the occasional shade offered by a fragrant cedar or pine.

The third mile, the romance began to fade. The breezes were too damned gentle—hardly even there at all. The pines and the cedars were too few and far between. And she had decided that the wild sage and daisies stank.

Four miles in, she consoled her aching feet and back that this was some sort of spiritual excursion, a discipline that would enrich her soul. Hell, she might even lose a few pounds.

The fifth mile she began to curse Ryan Stone silently for bringing them into this godforsaken place.

The sixth, she let him have it.

"They'd better be out here, Stone, 'cause if we've gone through all this for nothing, you're dead meat," she said, huffing and puffing as the sweat dripped down her forehead and into her eyes. "I'm going to bop you over the head and leave you out here to rot."

"I'm more convinced than ever that we're on the right track," Ryan said, dropping to one knee to examine the ground.

Savannah was grateful for the chance to pause and catch her breath. Turning to look back down the trail they had come, she saw Dirk, trudging along. His face was a deep, sun-scorched red, but the top of his head was even worse. He refused to put sunblock on his bald spot; to do so would be to admit it existed.

Pulling the canteen—which Ryan had bought for them at Mort's—from her back, she unscrewed the lid and took a long drink.

Instantly, she spit it onto the ground. "Yuck! What the hell did you put in my water after I filled it up at that last stream? This tastes like crap."

"Actually, it tastes like iodine," Ryan replied good-naturedly. "Those little tablets that I dropped into your canteen kill the bacteria in the water. Believe me, you don't want to catch beaver fever. John and I caught it once and it nearly killed us."

She gave him a searching look to see if he was serious or making some sort of silly, obscene joke. But his eyes were wide and almost innocent.

He chuckled. "Seriously, Savannah . . . just swallow fast and you won't taste a thing."

"Yeah, yeah," she muttered. "I've heard that one before. When do we eat?"

"Why didn't you ask sooner? I bought some wonderful, nutritious treats to keep our spirits and energy up."

He took off his newly acquired backpack, reached inside, and pulled out a couple of packets. "Here you go. Trail mix . . . or would you prefer beef jerky?"

"You wouldn't happen to have a pint of Ben and Jerry's Chunky Monkey in there? Or maybe a Dove bar?"

"Sorry. This is it."

Trying to appear grateful, she accepted the trail mix. After a couple of bites, she was finally able to discern most of the ingredients: sawdust, Styrofoam, balsa wood and—What was that slightly pungent accent flavor?—oh, yes . . . mothballs.

"Is it lunchtime yet?" Dirk asked, catching up to them.

"Yeah. Here, you can have mine." She discreetly slipped the bag to Dirk, while Ryan continued on ahead.

"Thanks."

"Wait until you taste it before you thank me."

"What is it?"

"A little treat to keep our spirits up."

Dirk downed the bagful in four bites and didn't seem to mind the lack of flavor. Maybe there was something to this "swallowing fast" thing.

A few minutes later, they caught up with Ryan. He was standing silently by the side of the path, motionless, staring at the ground.

"What is it?" Savannah asked, afraid that she knew.

Slowly, he took a step backward in their direction. Then another, and another.

Savannah heard it. The telltale rattle.

"Oh, shit!" she whispered, reaching inside her shirt for her Beretta. "It's a snake. A rattlesnake. Damn, I hate snakes."

Dirk pulled out his Colt and they waited as Ryan crept back toward them.

"He was sunning himself right there in the middle of the path," he said when he reached them. "I almost stepped on him."

"So, what do we do?" Savannah asked.

"He was there first," Ryan replied. "We go around him."

"Are there a lot of rattlers out here?" Dirk asked.

She could tell he was trying to be macho, but his voice sounded a little shaky.

"This time of year there are zillions of them," Ryan replied as he forged a circuitous route, leading them on. "But not to worry, they're all friendly."

"Friendly rattlesnakes?" Savannah didn't believe she had ever heard of a sociable rattler.

"Yeah. Like that one back there," Ryan replied. "He was a friendly sort of guy. Didn't you see him wagging his tail? Just a great big puppy dog."

Farther along, they drifted back onto the trail. "Not that I'm nervous or anything," Dirk said, "but we *do* have a . . . um . . . puppy dog bite kit along, don't we?"

Ryan patted the side of his backpack. "Right here."

"Remind me never to go hiking with you again," Savannah said, realizing that, sooner or later, she was going to have to drink some of that stuff in her canteen that tasted like frog pee. "This is *not* my idea of a good time."

"It'll be worth it," Ryan said. "They're up here."

Savannah's heart leapt and suddenly she didn't feel so tired. "Are you sure?"

He nodded.

"How do you know?" Dirk asked. Even he sounded encouraged.

"Footprints. I thought I saw some farther back . . . a man's and a child's. Now, here they are again, and they're fresh. This time I'm certain."

Savannah and Dirk squatted to examine the faint prints Ryan pointed out to them on the hard-packed earth.

"Well, hell . . . what are we waiting for?" Dirk said with a determined sniff. "Let's get going and hope Tonto's right."

"They aren't here." Savannah wanted to cry, but her eyes were already irritated by the dust and her own dripping sweat, and she didn't want to make them worse.

"So, we dragged our candy asses all the way out here for nothing," Dirk added, giving Ryan a look that was half aggravation and half I-told-you-so satisfaction. "Nice goin', Stone."

Ryan had led them to the old, abandoned cattle ranch, the focal point of their search being the decrepit ranch house. His best guess had been that Mallock would have sought shelter for his daughter inside the condemned building. Even in its deteriorating condition, it would have been more serviceable than a tent and wouldn't have to be carried in.

But the house was empty. A family of squirrels, some bats, a plethora of spiders, and a gopher snake were the only residents. From the even layer of dust and the curtains of undisturbed cobwebs, it appeared the three were the only human visitors for a long time.

Ryan was unfazed by his companions' criticism. Standing on the porch, he leaned against a post and assumed a contemplative pose.

"Actually, it makes sense, if you think about it," he said. "If you were Mallock, would you stay right here in the house? If I know about this place, that would mean others do, too. It was an alternative lifestyle commune in the sixties and—"

"Alternative lifestyles, oh, you mean a hippie joint," Dirk said, sinking down onto the steps and dropping his canteen onto the dirt.

"As I was saying," Ryan continued, ignoring him, "the house itself is too obvious. Besides, I believe the well that once served the residence has dried up. That would mean he would have to carry water from the stream."

"The stream? What stream?" Savannah said, her own mental wheels churning.

"The one that borders the property on the north and west. The one I told you about earlier that seldom dries up, even when the others do."

"Where you can catch trout with a rooster tail."

"Exactly."

"Are there other buildings that might be closer to the water source?" she asked.

"That's what I was thinking." Ryan drummed his fingertips on the post. "If I remember correctly, there are a couple of outbuildings, small feed sheds, right beside the stream. The ranchers probably stored hay and grain for the animals there in the winter."

"Let's go check them out," Savannah said.

"Yeah, let's." Still full of energy, Ryan bounded off the porch.

Dirk dragged himself to his feet. "Oh, joy. We get to walk again. I can hardly wait."

As they approached the third outbuilding—a tiny, tar-papered shack with a corrugated tin roof—Savannah knew they had scored.

"Look at that," she said, pointing to the canvas bag that hung on the end of a rope, draped over an oak limb. "Isn't that a camper sort of thing to do?"

"Yes. It's to keep the animals away from your food stash," Ryan agreed.

To their left, an expert campfire had been laid with lots of wood stacked nearby. On some rocks near the stream some clothing had been spread: a large pair of jeans, a towel, and a small Beauty and the Beast tee shirt.

"At least Christy's still okay," Savannah said, greatly relieved.

"Maybe," Dirk added, always Mr. Negativity.

They crouched behind a clump of sage and surveyed the surrounding area. Their hiding spot was the only one around. The brush appeared to have been recently cleared away and, other than the oak, there were no trees nearby.

"Good choice," Ryan said.

"Yeah, he can see us comin' a mile off," Dirk added, wiping the sweat off his face with his sleeve.

"We probably shouldn't just march up to the door and knock a 'shave and a haircut,' huh?" Savannah's legs were seizing into a cramp from squatting, so she knelt in the dust. It didn't help much.

"I wouldn't recommend it," Ryan said.

"Mallock's probably not even in there," Dirk suggested. "It's just some old codger who got sick of civilization and moved up here to get some peace." Other people thought dark, pessimistic thoughts; but Dirk Coulter was always the first to utter them aloud. "It's still daylight. Even if Mallock and the kid are here, they could be anywhere, doing anything. Choppin' wood, skinnin' a bear."

"Do you want to wait until dark?" Ryan asked.

"Not really." Savannah thought of how it would be to have to navigate the path they had just taken or spend the night out here in the sticks with nothing but mountain lions, coyotes, and friendly rattlesnakes for company. "I'd just as soon get it over with," she said. "But there's no point in all of us exposing ourselves. I'll sneak up and take a peek in the window. Then I'll come back here and let you know what's up."

"I really think I should go," Ryan said. "I know the two of you are exhausted, not being accustomed to hiking so far and—"

"I'll go," Dirk snapped. "I'm the cop around here, even if everybody does keep forgetting that little fact. You two are just along for the ride."

"Are you sure?" Savannah asked. "We could all go together."

"Yeah, right," Dirk said irritably. "We'd look like the Three Stooges marching up there, three abreast." He looked across at Savannah's generous chest. "Okay, you definitely count for two . . . *four* abreast." He pulled his Colt and checked his ammo.

"I'm going. You two are staying. I'll take a look and then give you the high sign."

Cautiously, he left the meager shelter of the scrub and scurried toward the house, keeping low to the ground and out of view of the one small window.

"What's the high sign?" Ryan asked. "I've always wondered exactly what that was."

"I don't know what it is officially," Savannah admitted. "But Dirk usually just flips you the bird."

They watched closely as Dirk approached the shed, all the time keeping a sharp eye for any other movement in the surrounding area. But only the trees swayed from time to time, the dry oak leaves rustling like a starched Southern petticoat in the breeze.

Nearby a dove cooed, and they could hear the burbling sound of the stream. It was a natural, peaceful sound that seemed out of context, considering their mission.

Savannah held her own gun tightly in her sweat-slick palm, waiting for anything as Dirk plastered his back to the shed and slowly made his way around to the window.

The casement held four panels. Three of the glass panes were filthy and obscure, but the lower left corner one was broken, with only jagged edges. Dirk squatted below it, bobbed up for a quick look, then back down.

He repeated the move, then again, pausing a bit longer each time.

Finally, he stood and stared through the window for a long, tense moment. Ryan and Savannah held their breaths. Without turning toward them, Dirk beckoned with one hand, the movement slow and wooden.

They left their hiding spots and hurried toward the shed.

Dirk walked away from the window and made his way slowly toward the door. When they reached him, Savannah whispered, "What is it? Is anyone inside?"

He didn't reply. Instead, he pushed the door open and stepped into the semidarkness.

"Shit," he said softly. He moved aside to make room in the tiny shed for the other two to join him.

By the sound of his tone and the horrible, distinctive odor that filled the structure, Savannah braced herself, knowing that she wasn't going to like what she was going to see. But she still wasn't prepared.

"No," she said, her mind rebelling at the sight of yet another body sprawled on the floor. It felt like an instant replay of Lisa's murder scene.

In the darkness she couldn't see details, and the corpse was already beginning to distort from the natural process of decomposition. The stench was overpowering, and Savannah tasted her stomach juices rising.

The victim lay in a fetal position, and at first glance it appeared the wrists and ankles were bound with wire. The person appeared to have died from a gunshot to the head . . . just like Lisa Mallock.

This time the room hadn't been closed; the open window had allowed the flies access. The larvae were busy, doing what they did best.

Ryan was the last to squeeze into the crowded space. "A body," he said, identifying the smell even before he saw the corpse.

"Yeah," Dirk said. "Another dead one. I guess we were too late again."

"Not the little girl?" Ryan stared over Savannah's shoulder, as all three allowed their eyes to adjust to the darkness.

"No, thank God," Savannah said. "I think it's Earl Mallock."

"Yeah . . ." Dirk shook his head in bewilderment. ". . . go figure."

CHAPTER THIRTEEN

Savannah sat beneath the shade of the one oak tree and watched despondently as Deputy Coroner Jennifer Liu and her team processed the murder scene. Dirk had called out on his cell phone and delivered the bad news once again. The forensic gang had cheated—as far as Savannah was concerned—and had ridden a helicopter into the area, landing in a fairly smooth field of prairie grasses several hundred feet from the ranch house.

Back in the olden days, when Savannah had carried a gold detective's shield on a chain around her neck, she would have been in the thick of things at the scene, helping, asking a hundred questions, supplying answers when she had them.

But now she was a civilian . . . and not a particularly popular one at that.

She and Ryan had just finished an exhaustive search of the surrounding region, looking for any sign of the missing child. But, other than several items of clothing inside the shed and the tee shirt outside, there had been nothing. Savannah didn't know whether to be relieved or even more worried than before. She supposed she was both.

"Now I don't know what to think," she told Ryan. He offered her a sip of water from his canteen, but she declined. Intending to hitch a ride back on the chopper, she had decided just to wait until she reached civilization and Sparkletts.

"I know what you mean," he agreed. "Seems like we're back to square one."

They watched silently for a minute or so as Dr. Jennifer's two assistants carried the blue-bagged body of Earl Mallock out of the shed on a stretcher. The blue bags were for homicides; their zippers had locks.

"It sure looks like the same MO as Lisa. The wire around the wrists and ankles, the shot to the head." She thought she had never felt so tired, so completely wrung dry. "And I was sure Earl had killed her. Somebody out there has been laughing up his sleeve while I've been running around like a decapitated chicken, chasing the wrong person."

"Do you have any ideas who?"

"Sure, several. And as soon as I get back, I'll get to work on them. But for right now, I just want to know where that little girl is. My God, I can't imagine what she must be going through, what shape she must be in. She's probably witnessed both of her parents being murdered."

Savannah shuddered, and Ryan reached over to put his arm around her shoulders. "There's no way a kid could ever get over something like that," she said. "Even if she's alive and physically healthy, that is."

"One thing at a time, Savannah. You've got enough to handle mentally and emotionally, just with what you know. Don't let your imagination torture you . . . if you can help yourself."

"Can you?" She searched his green eyes for an honest answer. "Can you control your imagination at a time like this?"

He sighed and pressed a kiss to her cheek. "No, I can't. But be a good girl and do as I say, not as I do."

"Okay, Dad. I'll try."

Fat chance, she thought, returning his kiss.

Savannah saw Dirk standing by the door of the shed, giving her and Ryan a jealous, pissy look. She wondered how he could be so petty as to even think of such foolishness under the circumstances.

Reluctantly, he returned to his job at hand, scribbling notes and diagrams on a yellow legal pad that Dr. Liu had provided.

The team was carrying bag after bag of evidence from the shed. Apparently, Earl Mallock had stashed a lot of equipment and supplies. One assistant had even shinnied up the oak tree and untied the pack of provisions. Someone had disappeared inside the shed with a fingerprint kit.

"I wish Dr. Jennifer would hurry up and get this mess over and done with," she said, tucking her knees up under her chin and leaning on them. "I've got to get back to town, back to my car, back to a phone, back to work . . . like you said, back to square one."

"Well, if it helps at all, you won't be standing there all alone." Ryan squeezed her hand.

Her eyes misted, and for a moment harsh reality went out of focus. A pleasant relief. "It helps," she said. "A lot."

In the middle of her living room floor, Savannah sat with her "suspect board" in her lap, moving the bits of sticky-backed papers from one corner to the other.

"What do you have there, sugar?" Granny Reid asked as she entered the room and slipped a cup of hot chocolate into Savannah's hand.

Savannah looked at the mug and smiled up at her grandmother. "Whipped cream and chocolate sprinkles on top . . . just like you used to make it for me when I was a girl."

Gran chuckled. "Not exactly. You're a *big* girl now. It's got a good stiff shot of Bailey's in it, too."

Savannah never had to wonder from where she had inherited her hedonistic tendencies. The almost-black hair, the blue eyes, and the sweet tooth had definitely come from her father's side, because Gran still had hers. Except for the dark hair, which had turned silver some years ago.

"This . . ." Savannah pointed to her piece of red poster board with its tiny notes. ". . . is where I keep all my information, once it becomes too much for my brain. It keeps me from overloading the circuits between my ears."

Gran pulled the footstool over beside Savannah and sat down. "How does it work?"

"Up here at the top I put possible suspects, beneath each name I put the motive, opportunity, and physical evidence—if I have some. Down here at the bottom are individuals who are involved in the case, but, if I don't have enough information yet to establish a motive, opportunity, or incriminating evidence, I can't consider them actual suspects."

"Ummmm . . . I see. And over there in the lower right-hand corner?"

Savannah cleared her throat and swallowed hard. "That's where I stick the dead ones."

Gran studied the board for a long time. "Well," she said at last, "you've got nobody at the top . . . that means no suspects. You got a whole bunch of people at the bottom, but that doesn't help you much, if you don't know how or why they might have done it. And you got two stuck over there in the dead corner."

She shook her head and gave Savannah a sympathetic look. "I hate to say it, sugarplum, but so far . . . you ain't doin' too good."

Dirk had told Savannah on the phone that he had already informed Colonel Neilson of his former son-in-law's death, so she wasn't sure what to expect when she arrived at Neilson's home the following morning.

The two men had history, positive and negative, and she wondered how the colonel had taken the news.

Badly.

That was the thought that ran through her mind when she entered his backyard and found him bent over a bed of impatiens, looking even more exhausted and bedraggled than he had the day before.

"Good morning, Colonel," she said, glancing around the yard for the ubiquitous black beast. For once, he didn't seem to be around. "I knocked on the front door, but I guess you didn't hear me."

"I heard you."

He refused to look up at her and continued to dig in the flower bed with his hand shovel.

"Oh. Then I guess you didn't want to talk to me."

"Don't take it personally, Miss Reid. Right now, I don't want to talk to anybody."

"I can certainly understand that. And I wouldn't be here if I didn't feel it was important."

He stabbed the shovel into the soil, brushed off his hands, and stood. Obviously, the simple act caused him tremendous pain and his face registered the misery.

Strange, she thought . . . he was twenty years or so younger than Gran, but far less flexible. Maybe it was—as she had always suspected—not the years but the mileage.

As many times before, she wondered if physical disabilities mirrored the condition of the soul. Of all the colonel's personality attributes, she didn't think that flexibility was likely to be at the top of the list.

"What do you want from me?" he asked as he led her back toward the house. "I've told you everything I can think of."

"You haven't told me who might have a motive to kill your daughter *and* your son-in-law."

"Are you sure the same person killed them both?" He opened the kitchen door and ushered her inside.

"I haven't spoken to the coroner yet, but I've seen both murder scenes, and it appears so."

After taking two glasses from the cupboard, he walked to the refrigerator and poured them each an iced tea. He handed Savannah's to her, then sat at the kitchen table. "No," he said. "I can't think of anyone other than Earl who would kill Lisa. To my knowledge, other than him, she didn't have an enemy in the world."

"Was she seeing any other men after she separated from Earl?"

"I don't know. She kept that side of her life private. I didn't always approve of the men she chose, and I never minded saying so. I think she decided it was easier just not to discuss her dating practices with her father."

Savannah took a drink of the tea and found it strong and bitter. "I noticed that she didn't have much in her home, not many belongings."

"Thanks to Earl, she had to travel light. Besides, his lawyer screwed her in the divorce settlement."

"I was wondering if, perhaps, she kept some things here. Personal letters, memorabilia. . . ."

He thought for a moment. "I have a couple of boxes up in the attic that were hers. I'm not sure what's in them."

"Would you mind if I borrowed them, just for a few days? I'll take good care of them and return everything intact."

He shrugged. "I suppose so, as long as I get them back. What do you think you'll find in them?"

"I don't know. Over half of an investigation is looking for something and not knowing what you're looking for, until you find it."

"Sounds frustrating."

"Believe me, it can be."

The Capri Inn held several fond memories for Savannah, and those recollections stirred accompanying feelings of excitement and sensuality as she walked into the lobby. Long ago—far *too* long ago, she decided—she had enjoyed several romantic encounters within these mirrored walls.

The glittering, crystal chandeliers, the lush atrium with its rock waterfall, the plush dark plum carpeting, all made her wonder why she hadn't taken much time the past few years to indulge herself in some of the more physical pleasures of life. Other than food, that was.

She wouldn't be here now if it weren't for business.

"Brian O'Donnell?" she inquired at the desk.

The clerk called his room, and she was sent upstairs to the fourth floor.

"Savannah, how good to see you," he said, practically pulling her inside the room. "Come on in."

Glancing around, she noted how neat and tidy the room was, considering he was a man away from home. Books and magazines were neatly stacked on the bed stand, clothes hung, drawers closed, suitcases stashed in the closet.

"Any news?" he asked.

"About Lisa or Christy . . . no."

He waved her into a chair and sat tensely on the edge of the bed near her.

"Oh." He appeared genuinely disappointed. "I was hoping that was why you were here."

"I'm sorry. But I did think I should keep you apprised of the new developments."

His eyes searched hers. "From the look on your face, I'm almost afraid to ask. Is it bad?"

"I suppose that depends on how you look at it. But, yes, I would say so. We found Earl Mallock."

"Really? That's great! Where is he?"

"Ah . . . well . . . at the moment, he's in the city morgue. I'm afraid he's dead, too."

"Mallock dead?" She watched his reaction closely; he didn't seem to be any more surprised or alarmed than when he had been told that Lisa was dead. If anything, he simply appeared confused.

"Yes, murdered. In the same manner as Lisa."

"But, I thought he was the one who killed Lisa. How could—?"

"We don't know. But we're trying to find out."

"Do you think the same person killed them both?"

"We'll know more after the autopsy. It looks that way."

He sat quietly for a long time, as though absorbing the information. Savannah had to admit it was a lot to swallow; Brian had received more than his share of bad news since arriving in California.

Standing, he shoved his hands into his slacks pockets and walked over to the window. He stood with his back to her, staring down on the freeway that whizzed by below—an infinite line of red lights going one direction and white going the opposite.

"It's such a weird feeling," he said. "Knowing that someone I just spoke with not that long ago is now dead. And murdered, too. It's just . . . weird."

"When did you last speak to Mallock?"

"On the telephone just before I left Orlando. That was when he told me where I could find Lisa. Or, at least, he gave me an address. But as I told you before, it turned out to be fake."

He returned to his seat on the bed. "Oh, did I offer you something to drink? I have some juices, some ice, and—"

"No, thanks. I can't stay long, I just . . ."

The sliding door to the closet was open and something inside caught Savannah's eye. It was a bag that appeared to be filled with children's clothes and a stuffed animal. Instantly, she thought of Christy and the abandoned toys in her empty bedroom, her small shirt that had been left to dry on the rocks on the Montoya Ranch.

Brian saw that she had noticed the bag and colored slightly. "For my kids at home," he explained. "I miss my boys. I've never been away from them this long. I'd better head back home soon, or I'll go broke, buying out the gift shop downstairs."

"I know how you feel. I love children myself."

"Do you have any?"

"No."

Suddenly, Savannah wanted to leave the room, leave this man whose presence reminded her of the part she had played in his loss. Besides, his love for his own family reminded her of what she had never had.

She stood abruptly and headed for the door. "I have to get going," she said. "I just wanted to tell you what's been happening so far. As soon as I have other news, I'll let you know."

"Maybe it'll be good next time," he said, offering her an encouraging smile as he walked her out the door and into the hallway.

"One can always hope."

CHAPTER FOURTEEN

The state of Dirk's living conditions had ceased to shock Savannah years ago. She had grown accustomed to the ten-by-forty-foot house trailer that sat off the road in a wooded area, called Casitas Maria, about fifteen miles east of San Carmelita. Besides, over time she had come to realize that the place wasn't really as filthy or disorganized as it appeared on first glance.

Although a thick layer of dust covered all surfaces and no attempts at decorating had ever been made, the trailer was free of dirty dishes, vermin, and human and animal wastes. In Dirk's mind, that constituted "basically sanitary."

He had pushed his collection of periodicals and videotapes onto the floor, clearing the coffee table, for her visit. She had been deeply flattered.

Side by side, they sat on the antique gold, threadbare carpet, leaning against the sofa, examining the materials spread out before them.

"Look what I found," she said, pointing to some articles of interest she had garnered from the boxes taken from the colonel's home.

She grabbed a black high school yearbook with silver lettering that said "Wolverines" and opened it to a page she had marked with the preaddressed envelope from her overdue electric bill. What the heck, this was just the yellow notice, and she knew she wasn't going to pay it until the red one came. It would have its own envelope.

"Here is Lisa's high school graduation picture," she said, tapping her fingertip on the photo of a softer, sweeter version of the face she had seen over the plate of M&M cookies. Before Earl Mallock. Before the abuse and the heartaches.

"Looks like a nice kid."

"I'm sure she was." Savannah flipped back to the section reserved for the junior class. "And *this* is Vanessa Pearce . . . without the purple hair."

Dirk studied the face of the pretty blonde who, even back then, wore too much makeup for her delicate good looks. "Hmmm, that was Earl's girlfriend."

"*Was*, being the operative term. She and Lisa Neilson went to the same school, one year apart."

"Okay . . . so?"

"They were more than just schoolmates." She pulled out some snapshots of the two girls playing in a swimming pool, on the beach, at a school basketball game, at a birthday party where Lisa was blowing out candles on a cake. "Lisa Neilson and

Vanessa Pearce were best friends all through high school and for years afterward."

"And both of them wound up having the same guy?"

Savannah nodded. "Even back then. I found some letters . . . right here . . . that were written when the women were in their thirties." She pulled the rainbow-striped stationery from her tote bag and spread the letters on the table. "These are from Vanessa to Lisa. It seems that at one point, Earl was dating them both."

"Busy guy."

"Extremely busy." She pushed one particular letter into Dirk's hand. "He got both women pregnant within a few months of each other. Lisa first, then Vanessa. In that letter, Vanessa is begging Lisa to give him up so that she can have him."

"Whoa, now *that's* messy."

"Positively sca-a-andalous. If such a thing had happened in Georgia, some of the male relatives would have run Mr. Mallock out of town on a rail, wearing a fine ensemble of pitch and turkey feathers."

"I wonder what the colonel had to say about it all?" Dirk took a long swig of beer and wiped his lips with the back of his hand.

"Well . . . Earl married Lisa, didn't he? I'd say the colonel might have had something to say about that."

Dirk checked the dates on the letters. "We know what happened to Lisa's baby; that would have been Christy. But what about Vanessa's kid?"

Savannah shrugged. "Don't know yet. But at least now I have somebody to move to the top of my board."

"You mean Vanessa Pearce . . . that she had a motive?"

"Why not?"

"Because, if she was going to knock somebody off, it seems like she would have done it ten years ago, when all this was going down."

"But what if she didn't do it back then? What if she finally got Earl—prize that he was—away from Lisa? What if, after she thought she had him all to herself for good, he started to obsess about Lisa again? What if Vanessa found out about it, and it was just one rejection too many?"

Dirk considered the possibilities for a while and sipped some more beer. "Well, you've talked to her. Does she strike you as the type of person who could kill two people?"

"No." She sighed. "But I've been wrong before."

When Savannah dropped by the house later to check in with Tammy, she opened the front door and received quite a shock.

Granny Reid was standing in the middle of the living room, wearing a bright red, one-piece bathing suit. Part of the shock was that she looked much better in it than Savannah would have expected.

"I never had one before . . . not in my whole life," she told Savannah as she twirled around the room, showing the suit from all its best angles. "I thought it was high time."

Savannah began to laugh as she ran to her grandmother and grabbed her around the waist. "Just look at you! You look like Esther Williams!"

"That's what I thought when I tried it on at Wal-Mart today. I just had to have it. After all, I can't go wading in the big Pacific Ocean in one of my caftans or nightgowns."

"You're absolutely right. There's a wonderful little lagoon

over by the marina. I'll have to take you there as soon as I get a chance."

Tammy walked into the living room, just in time to hear Savannah's last words.

"Don't wait until you 'get a chance,' Savannah," she said quietly, "or you'll never do it."

"Tammy, I can't. You know what's going on around here, and—"

"Yes, I do. And I know that you aren't the only one working on this case. You have Ryan and John running their buns off for you, Dirk is busting his, and I'm doing everything I possibly can every waking moment."

She nodded toward Granny and smiled a sweet, knowing smile that was wise beyond her years. "You can take two hours, Savannah. Even the president could take two hours under these circumstances."

Savannah thought of Lisa, of Earl . . . and, of course, of Christy.

Then she looked at her grandmother, so eager, a child eighty-three years young, who had never set foot in the Pacific Ocean, who, until today, had never worn a bathing suit.

"The temperature in that lagoon is really lovely this time of day, Gran," she said. "But you'll have to wear a robe or something as a coverup on the way there and back. That red suit is just too-o-o-o risqué for public!"

"Oh, you're right! I'll go get one." Granny Reid giggled as she hurried up the stairs. In record time she reappeared with her Victoria's Secret's terry-lined, satin robe over her arm.

Savannah barely had time to grab her own gear.

"I've made a very important decision, Savannah," her

grandmother told her as they walked to the car, arm in arm.

"And what is that, Gran?"

"I've made up my mind that I'm going to do something out-rageous every year for the rest of my life. Last year I got my ear-lobes pierced . . . *both* of them. This year it's the bathing suit and wading in the Pacific Ocean." She lifted her chin a few notches. "And *next* year . . . oh, hell . . . there's no tellin' what I might do!"

Savannah laughed and made a decision of her own: With every passing year of her own life, to become more like her grandmother.

Lying on her back on the sun-warmed sand, Savannah allowed herself to enjoy the rare delight of doing absolutely nothing for a moment. The healing heat penetrated the stiff muscles of her shoulders and down her spine, loosening the knots, easing the tension. At least a little.

A few feet away, Gran was playing tag with the waves and some children who had recognized a kindred spirit and had lin-gered to wonder at the joy she radiated.

"How old are you?" asked the little boy. "Are you older than my mom?"

"I'll betcha I'm older than your mom's mom," she replied.

"How come you have so many wrinkles on your face?" his sister inquired.

"Those are from laughing so much," was the ready answer.

The girl considered her words, but still looked puzzled. "You laugh on your *neck?*"

Savannah winced, but she heard her grandmother roar, far too highly evolved a soul to be hampered by mere vanity. Humor was, and always had been, far more important to Granny Reid.

"Oh, my Lordy, Savannah, did you hear that?" She plopped down onto the beach towel beside her and wriggled her toes into the sand. "Have you ever heard anything so funny in all your days?"

"Children do have a way of putting things."

"Yes, they're wonderful. They're just the way the good Lord made them: pure and sweet and honest as the day's long . . . the way we all were before the world messed us up."

Savannah rolled over toward her and shaded her eyes with one hand so that she could clearly see her grandmother's face.

"Gran," she said thoughtfully, "can you always tell, ahead of time, if a person is bad or not?"

Granny stretched out on her side, facing Savannah, and contemplated her answer carefully before speaking. "No, I can't say as I can. Because I don't really believe there's any such thing as a bad person."

"But how can you say that? You've lived long enough to see people do horrible things to each other."

"Sure I have. But I don't think there's anybody that hasn't got a smidgen of good in 'em. Course, with some folks, the good is as hard to find as teeth in a hen's beak. But that doesn't mean it ain't there. Just means you ain't looked hard enough to find it."

Savannah shook her head and began to draw nonsensical lines in the sand to express her anger and frustration. "I guess you haven't seen the sort of things that I have, Gran. When you're a cop, you—"

"Now, don't go givin' me that bunch of hooey. A body

doesn't have to be a police officer to see meanness. You think I haven't seen wickedness in my day, girl? I lived through two world wars, not to mention those messes in Korea and Vietnam. I was in the thick of the Civil Rights Movement, marchin' right there with the best of 'em. With my own eyes I saw horrors perpetrated on African-Americans and their little children by cowards wearing bed sheets. And I tell you now, I'll never forget it."

She took a deep breath and rolled over onto her back. "I've seen evil and I've seen the suffering it caused. But I still don't think people are 'good' or 'bad.' We're all a combination of both. It's just that some are more one than the other."

A couple of seagulls floated overhead, while sandpipers pranced on skinny legs along the lacy edges of the waves. Savannah watched, feeling mildly chastised as she considered her grandmother's wisdom. It was always so easy to assume that you knew more than your elders, she thought. So easy, and so foolish.

"That's why people are so surprised," Gran continued, "when a 'good' person does a 'bad' thing. We go around thinking there are the heroes and there are the villains, and that everybody is either one or the other. But even the best of us and the worst of us play both roles from time to time. A person is capable of doing loving and noble deeds, and he's capable of doing hateful, hurtful things. He makes the decision every minute of every day which he's gonna do."

Savannah thought of the trials she had attended, where the defense attorneys had presented evidence that their clients had given generous donations to orphanages, lovingly cared for aged parents, and supported the local Little League teams. But the prosecution had proved, beyond a reasonable doubt, that those same individuals had committed heinous crimes with cold calculation and a complete lack of remorse.

"I guess," Savannah said, "that in the course of a lifetime, we all do plenty of both."

"That's right, sugar."

"But that's a lot more complicated, Gran. It's so much easier to just think 'we' are the good guys, and 'they' are the bad ones."

"*Easy* ain't always *right*."

"That's true, Gran. And right ain't always easy."

When the petite, conservative brunette behind the bar at the Shoreline told Savannah, "No, Vanessa isn't working today," Savannah could almost swear she looked relieved.

Past experience had taught her that it could be very enlightening and worthwhile to talk to your suspect's enemies. Their motives for spilling what they knew might be less than honorable, and you had to take what they said with a barrel of salt pork. But often they were more truthful than friends.

"I'm Zelda. What can I get you to drink?"

Savannah knew better than not to order anything. Bartenders didn't trust anyone who wasn't holding a glass in their hand.

"A Coke will be fine."

Slender, physically fit Zelda looked Savannah up and down. "Diet?"

"No way."

She drew her a cola and set it on the bar in front of her. "What do you want Vanessa for?" she asked, trying to sound casual, but not succeeding.

Aha, Savannah thought, *Zelda is nosy, too. All the better.*

"I wanted to ask her some questions about her boyfriend, Earl."

"He's dead. Murdered, they say."

"Who says?"

"The police. Some half-bald guy in a trench coat and dirty sneakers came in this morning and told her."

"That would have been Dirk Coulter. The sneakers aren't really all that dirty, just ancient. He really does toss them into the washer once in a while."

"You know him?"

Savannah nodded.

"Are you a cop, too?"

"No, a private detective."

Zelda looked up and down the bar, but the place was empty and they were alone. She pulled up a stool and an ashtray and settled down to talk to her only customer.

"You're a P.I., huh? Who are you working for?"

"At this point, I suppose I'm working for Christy, Lisa Mallock's little girl."

"Oh, yeah. Earl has brought her in here a few times; Vanessa has, too. Vanessa is crazy about that kid . . . about all kids, for that matter."

"Really? She didn't seem like the maternal type."

"Aw . . . she just likes to show off with the purple hair and the chains and black leather and all. She's a pain in the neck, it's true, but she's not as bad as she thinks she is. I've known a lot rougher."

"How were she and Earl getting along lately?"

Zelda stubbed out her cigarette butt and promptly lit another. "Funny you should ask. They had a big, hairy fight in here about a week ago."

"Do you know what it was about?"

"Sure. Everybody in the joint with two ears knew what it was about. Vanessa isn't exactly subtle when she's mad. She was accusing him of wanting Lisa back. She's always been pretty insecure about that."

"Do you think he gave her a reason to feel insecure?"

"Oh, yeah. Earl never got over losing Lisa and Christy. He was always scheming about how he could get Lisa to come back to him."

"How bad was the fight?"

"Well, there weren't any beer bottles thrown, or shots fired, nobody got stabbed. So, for this place, I guess it wasn't too bad."

"Did Earl threaten Vanessa, or—"

"Oh, no. Vanessa was the one doing all the yelling. Poor old Earl looked like he wanted to crawl under a booth somewhere. She told him that, if he dumped her to take off after Lisa again, she'd kill him. I guess that's a threat, huh?"

"Do you think she meant it?"

"I'm sure she did at the time."

"Yep, then I would definitely call that a threat." Savannah nodded thoughtfully. "When the cop told her that Earl had been killed, how did she take it?"

"Really hard. She had a fit, crying, screaming, and all that."

"What happened then?"

"After the cop left, she calmed right down and said she wanted to take the day off."

"Do you have any idea where she may have gone? Home or—?"

"No, she said she was going downtown to the Fiesta Del Mar, the big beach party down by the fairgrounds."

"Yes, I know the place." Savannah studied Zelda's plain, seemingly honest face to see if she was telling her the truth. She seemed guileless, but you couldn't tell these days.

"Vanessa helps out at the booth there for the Boys' and Girls' Club every year, no matter what," Zelda said. "It's a big deal to her. She wouldn't miss it . . . not even for Earl."

"But you say, as soon as the cop left, she cheered up?" Savannah asked again, just to make sure she had it straight.

"The minute he walked out the door. The difference was night and day. Judging from the way she was acting when she left, I'd say she's down at the beach, partying hard."

CHAPTER FIFTEEN

Like the other ninety percent of San Carmelita's population, Savannah had to park about a thousand blocks from the beach and walk to the city-sponsored fiesta. Los Angeles tourist bucks were a big boon in the summer, and the town council wasn't above throwing these little shindigs to lure hot, stressed-out city dwellers to the cooler, less smog-choked coast.

And there were *never* enough parking spots. A few more mercenary downtown citizens were allowing cars to park on their lawns for five bucks. Savannah declined on principle alone. Where she came from, only white trash parked vehicles on grass.

Four blocks of city beach were cordoned off for the party. Families milled up and down the sidewalks, viewing local art displays, eating cotton candy and ice slushies, riding skateboards, tandem bikes, and, occasionally, dads' backs.

The scent of barbecued chicken and ribs filled the air, along with the sounds of merrymaking.

A local radio station blared "Surfin' U.S.A." and other selections by the Beach Boys, while the disc jockey interviewed the "man on the street" or the "kid on the beach," whoever walked by between songs.

Booths, distinguished by bright banners that flew and snapped in the sea breeze, advertised various businesses and charitable organizations.

It didn't take long to find the Boys' and Girls' Club of San Carmelita setup. The display was quite impressive. They had erected a huge pavilion that was filled with tables full of children doing crafts: finger painting, clay modeling, and miscellaneous projects with popsicle sticks, cotton balls, and Elmer's glue.

Vanessa was equally easy to locate. With her purple hair and exceptional height, she was distinctive. Although, this time it wasn't the color of her hair that Savannah noticed first. It was the expression on her face.

She sat on a stool in the corner of the tent, a paintbrush and palette in hand. A line of children waited for her to decorate their faces with stars, moons, green cheeks, red noses, or a rainbow across their forehead.

Savannah couldn't remember seeing anyone more happy, more completely content.

Vanessa was laughing and chatting with the kids, who complained of the brush "tickling." Wearing a simple white tee shirt and jeans, she bore little resemblance to the black leather, chain-toting motorcycle mama at the Shoreline.

The boy she had been working on was finished, and the

next in line was a young girl who looked very much like Christy in fair complexion, long red hair, and dainty demeanor. She wore a pink-and-lavender crown of sparkling glitter and ribbon streamers.

Savannah recalled what Zelda had said about Vanessa adoring Earl's daughter. She waited, wondering if Vanessa would notice the similarity.

"And what do you want me to paint on *your* face, little princess?" Vanessa asked. "How about a nice fat toad with warts and everything?"

"No! I want something pretty!"

"You do? How boring. How about a unicorn?"

"That would be great! I want a white unicorn."

Savannah watched, staying well out of sight, as Vanessa created something resembling a unicorn with only a few strokes of the paintbrush.

But as she worked, tears flooded Vanessa's eyes. One spilled down her cheek.

"Are you crying?" the little girl asked, very concerned.

"No," Vanessa replied, ruffling the girl's hair. "What reason would I have to cry? I'm having fun. I just have some sand in my eye."

Savannah turned and walked away without disturbing Vanessa or her afternoon, surrounded by the love and rejuvenating innocence of children. Of course she had noticed the similarity between the two girls, Savannah thought. And she had shed tears accordingly.

Did those tears mean that she had loved Earl, that she loved his daughter? Did her acts of kindness toward the children mean that she was incapable of doing anything so hideous as two murders?

Or, as Granny Reid had observed, was it simply a case of someone being a complex mixture of good and evil?

With a bit of computer digging, Tammy had uncovered Alan Logan's home address: a slip number in the marina . . . a fifty-foot-long sailing yacht with two masts, named *The Big Bust*. When the unfriendly female clerk at the antique store on Lester had told Savannah that Al had "split an hour ago," she had hoped she would find him in the marina.

From what little she knew about boats, she knew that owning one meant you had no time for other hobbies. Anytime she had extended a weekend invitation to a friend/boat owner, she had been refused because they were sanding, polishing, mending sails, working on the engine, or plugging leaks—*when* they weren't simply trying to find out what the hell was leaking.

Bingo, she thought as she approached the slip and saw a decidedly male figure kneeling on the deck, sanding.

She watched his face carefully as she approached, to see if he was happy to see her, or apprehensive.

Of course, she told herself that her interest was purely professional. It had nothing whatsoever to do with the fact that he was a very attractive man with well-defined muscles, nicely curled chestnut hair, and hazel eyes. Nope, nothing at all.

But when he did spot her walking in his direction, she couldn't read his expression behind his wire-rimmed glasses.

Enigmatic, was the best word she could think of to file away in her ever-increasing mental cabinet.

"Permission to come aboard, Captain?" she asked.

She had plenty of time to listen to the seagulls squawk and contemplate the meaning of life before he finally answered. "Permission granted, Ms. Private Investigator Reid."

He rose from his knees, walked over to the side of the craft, and offered her a hand. "Watch your step, unless you're a good swimmer."

She tried not to cling desperately to his hand, but it wasn't easy. Like shaky ladders and other things that bobbed beneath her feet, boats weren't her favorite things. She was definitely a "landlubber."

"Who told you I was here?" he asked, sounding just a tad put-out.

"Your saleslady said you were gone for a while. My personal assistant found the 'address.' "

"A good agency," he mumbled. "I'll have to remember that if I ever need you."

She pointed to the name painted on the hull. *The Big Bust?* I don't think I should ask."

"Why not? Everyone else does. Number one: No, I'm more of a leg man, myself. Number two: I went broke after the divorce. She got the house, the cars, the bank accounts, and a face-lift. I got this. But enough about me. Why are you here?"

"The weather was great and I like the marina. I like boats and all that nautical stuff, so I thought I'd drop by."

"You like the marina? Maybe. But I don't think you're being completely honest with me." He grinned at her, watching her wobble on unsteady legs. "You can't fool an old sailor like me; I can tell. You don't like boats."

"Does it show that much?"

"Oh, yes. You look like you could get seasick right here in the slip."

"That's highly likely."

"So, have a seat, but if you feel like you're going to barf, do it over the edge."

"Thanks." This wasn't turning out to be the semiromantic encounter she might have hoped for. She looked around, but there was nothing resembling a chair in sight. "Where?" she asked.

"There." He pointed to an unsanded spot near where he had been working. Once she was seated, he tossed her a block of wood covered with sandpaper and pointed to the deck. "Don't take it personally. I make everyone I know work if they drop by. It keeps me from having a lot of unwanted guests—a built-in hazard when you own a boat."

"Yes, I suppose that would take care of the problem," she admitted gruffly as she began to sand. Not a good day to be wearing a white denim skirt.

He continued to work at a feverish pace. It occurred to Savannah that this man probably couldn't stop working and relax if his health and happiness depended on it.

"Well . . ." he said, ". . . did you find Earl?"

So, he didn't know, or he didn't want her to know he knew. As usual, she wasn't sure which.

"Yeah, I found him."

"Did you deliver my message?"

"The bit about you not being even with him yet, not by a long shot?"

"That was it. Don't tell me, you forgot."

"You're right. I forgot."

"We had a deal. See if I help *you* out again."

"You honestly don't know yet?" she asked, wondering that Dirk hadn't made it out here already.

"Know what?"

His hazel eyes were guarded; a muscle bunched in his jaw.

"Earl is dead."

"Dead?" He dropped his wooden block and sat down hard on the deck. She could have sworn he turned a bit pale beneath his sea tan. "My God," he said, "are you sure about this?"

"Very. I saw the body."

He covered his face with both hands and a shudder ran through him.

"Oh, man . . . this is too weird," he said. "I mean, you wish a guy dead for so long and then it happens and you . . . it's just too strange."

She didn't reply but watched him closely. Although she had informed many people of many terrible things over the years, she had decided long ago that no two reacted in exactly the same way.

"You wished Earl dead?"

"Of course I did. That bastard cost me everything I had: my business, my life's savings, my home, even my wife and kids. I wanted him to suffer, big time."

He drew his knees up to his chest and hugged them tightly, rocking slowly back and forth. "Did he?" he asked.

"Did he what?"

"Did Earl suffer?"

Unbidden, mental pictures of twisted wire appeared in technicolor across the movie screen in her head. Pictures of thin wire cutting into flesh. "Yes," she said, "I think it's pretty safe to say that Earl suffered a lot before he died."

"What a surprise. That actually makes me feel worse, not better. I wouldn't have bet on that a week ago. You never know how you're going to react to a situation, until you're in it."

"That's true."

Savannah waited for him to collect himself, waited for the obvious question that didn't seem to be forthcoming.

"He had it coming, you know," Alan said, rubbing his eyes as though they stung. "He's hurt so many people for so long. It's a wonder somebody didn't knock him off long ago. Hell, I've even threatened to do it myself."

"Did you?"

His eyes locked with hers, and she could see he had switched to "red alert." She remembered how cold he had gone that day when he had asked her to deliver his message to Earl.

"Did I threaten him? Yes. Did I murder him? No. Thinking about it and talking about it, are a long way from doing it."

"If you don't mind me asking, do you have an alibi for Wednesday night?"

"Am I going to need one?"

She shrugged. "I don't know. I'm not a cop anymore. But it never hurts to remember where you were when something like that happens. Especially considering your past history with Earl and your public threats against him. Sooner or later, somebody besides me is gonna ask you."

"Yeah, I've got an alibi." He shook his head as though disgusted with himself, or perhaps with Fate. "See that spot right there . . ." He pointed to a four-by-four-foot square on the deck near the bow, where the surface was dull. ". . . I was sanding that. Do you suppose anybody would believe it?"

A few minutes later as Savannah was wiping the dust from her white skirt and climbing back into the Camaro, she was thinking of how she would describe the conversation to Dirk.

Sitting in the car, she reached into her purse and pulled out her tiny, personal recorder.

"Overall, he seemed sincerely upset," she dictated into the minuscule machine. "Important to note, though . . . I didn't tell him Earl had been murdered. I only said that he was dead, and he never asked how he got that way. Mr. Alan Logan, captain of *The Big Bust*, seemed to know that all by his lonesome."

Savannah checked out the station house parking lot, before going inside. Not seeing the chief's BMW or Bloss's generic, beige, "Fed" sedan, she decided the coast was clear. Dirk's grungy Skylark was a welcome sight. These days, she missed him more than she wanted to admit.

It was around seven, and most of the "brass" had gone home—at least the ones she was openly feuding with. Bette the Blabbermouth was at the front desk; Savannah wasn't pleased.

"Oh, hi there, Savannah. Nice to see you again." At least Bette had the decency to look a little embarrassed.

"Uh-huh," Savannah replied without enthusiasm. "Where's Denise?"

"Vacation. Aren't you happy to see me?"

"That depends. Are you going to put me on hold so that Bloss can shove my backside through a wringer?"

"Oh, come on, Savannah. I was just doing my job." Bette toyed with one of the bleached, frosted, and permed locks that curled over each ear. The rest were piled on top of her head and haphazardly held with a butterfly clip.

A quaint, Southern phrase drifted through Savannah's mind. Something about: Snatching her bald . . .

Bette held out her hand. "Sisters?"

Savannah grunted and gave it a brief, limp shake. "Cousins . . . maybe," she mumbled. "Twice removed."

She found Dirk, as always, rooted to his desk chair, staring bleary-eyed at a mountainous stack of papers in front of him, an assortment of burnt-out cigarette butts bristling from a nearby ashtray.

His tired face lit up when he saw her, and she felt special. Maybe, as Granny said, absence did make the heart grow fonder.

"What's shakin', sugar?" she asked, dragging up a chair to sit beside him.

"I've had better days, maybe better lifetimes," he growled.

She reached over and pinched his arm. "If I ever ask you how you are, and you say, 'Fine, thanks,' I'll faint."

"If you're unconscious, does that mean your mouth won't be runnin'?"

She grinned. "No guarantees. I've been known to hold entire conversations under general anesthetic."

"Why do I find that completely believable?"

Leaning over, she rested her head briefly on his shoulder. "Miss me?" she asked in her best Dixie coquette impression.

"Nope."

"Not even a little?"

He cleared his throat and looked miserably uncomfortable. Dirk couldn't handle any "mushy" stuff at all.

"Maybe a bit," he admitted. "I'm going through nail polish fume withdrawal. Stakeouts are pretty boring without you pestering me."

She tickled his ribs, and he jumped, overly sensitive about the extra weight he had added around the middle lately.

"Seriously, what have you got?" she asked, looking down at the papers on his desk.

"A pain in the rump. Nothing makes sense."

"What's the problem?"

He lit up a Camel and blew out a long, frustrated stream of smoke. Away from Savannah. With great effort, she had finally taught him some of the finer points of smoking etiquette.

"The problem," he said, "is that everybody hated Earl Mallock and wanted to kill him, but, other than her ex, nobody would have killed Lisa Mallock. She was a really nice person, and everyone loved her. Even Earl, in his own sick way."

Considering Vanessa, Savannah didn't necessarily agree about Lisa being loved by everyone, but she decided to keep her observations to herself for the moment. Dirk was exhausted, and when he was tired, he wasn't known for being receptive to new ideas.

"So, I'm figuring it was somebody who didn't really know them all that well," he said. "I think it's the brother."

"Brian? What reason would he have to hurt his sister and her ex?"

"The oldest reason in the world: Money. He just inherited pretty big bucks from his dad, and he has to split it down the middle with a sister that he hardly knows."

He pointed to the avalanche of papers on his desk. "I've been doing some checking, and Daddy Dearest was a real bastard for the last five years of his life. Brian and his wife took the old guy in, nursed him, put up with a lot of grief off him."

"Brian seems like the sort of guy who would do that without complaining."

"I would, too, if I thought I was going to get a nice inheritance at the end of it all. But by the time he divides it with sissy and pays Uncle Sam, he's not going to have much left. That would tick *me* off, and I'll bet it did him, too."

Savannah silently speculated that maybe Brian was a more generous and mature individual than Dirk. Ninety percent of the population probably was. But some things were better left unsaid.

"I checked the details of old man O'Donnell's will," he continued. "With the sister gone, the money would go to the kid. The kid is underage, so it would go to her legal guardian . . . which would be Earl if Lisa was out of the picture."

"So, you think Brian O'Donnell killed Lisa, then Earl, and the girl, too?" She shook her head. "He has children of his own. I can't imagine he would kill anybody, let alone a child."

"I don't know if he offed her, too." He blew a snort of smoke out both nostrils. His "dragon routine," as Savannah called it. "I guess we'll have to hope to God we find her, or else wait for her to turn up. She will sooner or later, alive or dead."

"Think *alive*, Dirk. Keep looking and thinking, *alive, alive, alive.*"

CHAPTER SIXTEEN

"Burning the midnight fluorescent?" Savannah asked as she entered the county morgue's examination room.

Dr. Jennifer Liu sat on a high stool at the counter, peering down into a microscope. A petite Asian woman with exotic eyes, a full, sensitive mouth, and lush black hair pulled back with a colorful scarf, Dr. Jenny didn't fit Savannah's preconceived notion of what a coroner should look like. She was far too pretty, much too sexy . . . and wasn't even a bit "crusty around the edges" as Savannah had once thought all forensic experts would have to be.

"It was a busy weekend here in San Carmelita County," Jennifer said, putting her hand to the back of her neck and rubbing the stiff muscles. "The bodies are starting to stack up around here, and Barry is on vacation. I'm getting behind."

"I'm getting quite a behind these days, too, but I'm not here to talk about *my* body." Savannah pulled a two-pound box of See's candies from her tote and handed them to Jennifer. "Here, assorted creams. You can apply those directly to your hips. I've always said, wear only the best."

"Ah, Savannah, you shouldn't have. But I'm thrilled you did." Instantly, she dug into the box and sampled one. A look of ecstasy crossed her face.

"Good?"

"Orgasmic."

The two women had often swapped war stories about the therapeutic qualities of chocolate on the PMS female human. Both were avid believers.

Savannah sat on a stool nearby. "Whatcha working on?"

"Lisa Neilson-Mallock. Such a sad case. Some of them get to you more than others. I had nightmares about this one last night."

"What have you found?"

"Mostly that she really suffered. That sadistic bastard sure put her through it before he killed her." She pointed to the microscope. "He had her bound with the wire for several hours. That's a tissue sample from the area around her wrists. Take a look."

Reluctantly, Savannah ventured a glance through Dr. Liu's scope, steeling herself, as always, for whatever horrors she might see.

But even after a second and third peek, she wasn't sure what she was looking at. Mostly, she saw a lot of blue-black dots.

"I give up," she said. "What are they?"

"Inflammation cells. They take a few hours to form. At least five or six."

"They couldn't have appeared postmortem?"

"No, only a living body produces those."

"Great." Savannah sighed and pushed away from the microscope, as though doing so would provide any emotional distance. "Now we can both have nightmares."

Dr. Jenny gave her a compassionate pat on the shoulder. "I can show you something that might make you feel a bit better about it all," she said.

"Please do."

The doctor walked to a file cabinet, opened a drawer and took out a manila envelope. After breaking the seal, she spread a dozen or more graphic, color photos across the counter.

"These are going to make me feel better?" Savannah asked, wincing at the documentation of the violence perpetrated on Lisa Mallock.

"This one will."

Jennifer chose one and held it up for Savannah's closer examination. The picture clearly showed abrasions on the knuckles.

"Defensive wounds?" Savannah asked.

"On the contrary, I'm fairly certain they're *offensive*. Of course, almost anything is possible. But in my experience, that sort of skinning of the knuckles is usually done when a person is punching someone else . . . and pretty effectively, too."

Savannah allowed that information to bubble in the mental pot for a few moments. "So, are you telling me that you think she got at least a few licks in before she bit the dust?"

"That's right. If it's any comfort to you, I think you can be fairly sure that Lisa Mallock went down fighting."

The thought of Lisa landing some painful blows on her attacker did help. A little. If she was fighting, she had hope, up until the moment she died.

Although Savannah couldn't exactly explain why, somehow, that made it better.

With Lisa Mallock weighing heavily on her mind, Savannah found herself drawn to the simple duplex. Sitting in her car on the opposite side of the street, Savannah wished she had woke Lisa that night and warned her that Earl was on her trail. If she had only . . .

Don't play "If," she warned herself. *It'll drive you crazy.*

The problem with the "If" game was that there was no end to it. "If" she had warned Lisa that night. "If" Lisa had never married Earl Mallock. "If" Earl had stepped in front of a truck and gotten flattened a year ago today. "If" Lisa's biological father hadn't given her away after his wife died.

The fact was: Lisa was dead, reduced from a human being to an autopsy on Dr. Jennifer Liu's examination table. Nothing could change that now.

Once, Savannah had asked Jennifer how she stood it, day after day, seeing the cruelty that one person could visit on another.

"I don't think I could bear to work in an emergency room," Jennifer had told her, "to see the misery and know it was my responsibility to try to stop it. But it isn't so bad, being a medical examiner. By the time they come to me, the suffering is over.

Nothing I can do will make it worse for the victim. But, if I can unravel the puzzle, I may be able to bring them justice . . . and closure to their loved ones."

And that's all you can do now, too, kid, she told herself as she studied the small house, the pink bicycle with training wheels chained to the side fence. *Just try to unravel the puzzle.*

An elderly lady in a red-and-white-striped shirt and blue shorts was watering a flower bed in front of the house. She was keeping a close eye on Savannah, and it occurred to Savannah that not much would get past her.

As she stepped out of the Camaro and strolled up the sidewalk toward the woman, she temporarily allowed her sadness to be set aside, supplanted by hope. Maybe she could find one more small piece of the puzzle.

"I already talked to a cop," Mrs. Abernathy said as she handed Savannah a can of generic store brand cola and a tall glass of ice. "He was kinda heavy without a lot of hair. He had on a wrinkled-up trench coat. I think his name was Dick or Kirk something."

Savannah accepted the seat she was offered in the living room, a multipatched, leatherette chair. Mrs. Abernathy sat in a rocker and picked up a piece of cross-stitch. She didn't appear to own a sofa . . . or much else for that matter, like her neighbor Lisa.

"Yeah, I know about the trench coat," Savannah admitted. "Detective Coulter is a friend of mine. Dirk doesn't mean to dress like a slob: he's just seen one too many episodes of 'Columbo.' "

"I didn't really mind. He was pretty nice . . . didn't have much of a sense of humor . . . but nice enough."

"I suppose he asked you a lot of questions already."

"Not that many. Mostly if I heard anything unusual the night Lisa and Christy were taken."

"Did you?"

She shook her head sadly. "Not a thing. The doctor gave me some new sleeping pills, 'cause I hadn't been able to get to sleep lately, and they worked really good that night."

Great time to break a streak of insomnia, Savannah thought. If only . . . no, she wasn't going down that road again.

"Mrs. Abernathy, how much did you know about Lisa Mallock's personal life?"

The woman's cheek twitched and she looked away quickly, as though Savannah had accused her of something. "Well, not that much really. Mostly, I just tend to my own business."

"I'm sure you're the soul of discretion," Savannah said soothingly, summoning as much false sincerity as she could muster under the circumstances. "I've no doubt that you always respect the privacy of others. I just thought maybe you might have seen or heard something, living so close to Lisa and all. These duplexes do have thin walls."

Mrs. A. cleared her throat and popped the top of her own can of cola. "I might of heard a thing or two." She lowered her voice. "Maybe a *fight*."

"Between Lisa and someone else?"

She nodded. "Yep. It was just hard words, loud voices, that's all. I didn't hear any fistfighting, you understand, or I would have called the police right away. I don't believe in that sort of business—a man hitting on a woman. My ex-husband tried that just once, and I kicked him out on his rear."

"Good for you. Now, Mrs. Abernathy . . . about this particular argument . . . do you know who the person was?"

"Well . . . let's see here." Savannah watched as Mrs. Abernathy began to warm to the situation, feeling the measure of her own importance. She knew Savannah was hanging on her every word. "The big argument I heard was about two weeks ago. It was on a Sunday afternoon. I remember that because I had just gotten back from church and was in a prayerful mood, but that sort of ruined it, listening to all that hoopla."

"What exactly did you overhear?"

"Lisa was telling some man to get out and not come back. Something about him not treating her little girl right. In fact . . ." She paused and glanced out the window as if expecting some sort of eavesdropper, but the coast was clear. Lowering her voice to a whisper, she continued, "Lisa told this man that if he showed his face around here again, she'd shoot him between the eyes."

"Are you sure you heard her say that exactly?"

"Between the eyes, that's what she said. I heard it clear as could be."

Savannah easily imagined the lady with her ear pressed to the wall, relishing every tidbit of potential gossip.

"To your knowledge, did Lisa own a gun?"

"She told me she did. Said she kept it around in case she had trouble with her ex-husband, said he was out to get her. Do you think he's the one who killed her? Or do you figure it was the man she was arguing with that day?"

"They weren't the same man?"

"No, not at all."

"How can you be sure?"

"That policeman friend of yours, the one in the wrinkled coat, he showed me a picture of her ex-husband. And the fellow I saw coming and going that Sunday afternoon didn't look anything like him."

Savannah coughed. "Well, Mr. Mallock had a way of altering his appearance, so—"

"Nope. Altered or not, it wasn't him, I tell you. This guy was real tall and had lots of curly blond hair, longer than yours. I saw him come over quite a few times. I'm pretty sure she was dating him . . . up until the day of the fight. He always wore jeans and long-sleeved shirts rolled up to his elbow, you know, to show off his muscles. He wasn't a bad-looking fellow."

Savannah had taken her pad and pen from her tote and was making notes as fast as she could. "Anything else that might help me locate him?"

"Well, let me see. Oh, yes, he drove a truck that said, 'Warner Electric' on the side. It was a white truck with red writing and a big, red lightning bolt. The license plate was one of those you choose yourself. It was HI VOLT. Cute, huh? And when Lisa yelled at him, she called him, 'Ian.' That's kind of a weird name, don't you think? Not everybody's got it."

Savannah was in shock. Puzzle pieces were raining on her from heaven, via Mrs. Abernathy.

"There," the older woman paused for a breath, "is that enough to help you?"

Savannah laughed. "Mrs. Abernathy, dear lady, consider yourself kissed."

————

"How come Abernathy didn't tell *me* all that?"

On the other end of the telephone line, Dirk sounded miffed. It was a sound that delighted Savannah. She still wasn't above trying to get his goat from time to time.

"Probably because you didn't ask her the right questions."

Turning the Camaro down her own street, she felt the warm tingle that often accompanied the idea of "going home" in the evening after a productive day's work. But it was much more pronounced, knowing that Granny Reid would be there, waiting for her.

"Are you intending to look this guy up, question him, and make some sort of citizen's arrest all by yourself, too?" he asked petulantly.

Not for the first time, Savannah asked herself how she could be so fond of such an old grump.

"No, sugar, I'll leave that up to you. The arrest part, that is. As far as who gets to question him first . . . I guess it's whoever gets down to Warner Electric tomorrow morning."

She chuckled, knowing that Dirk hated rolling out of bed early. It was right up there at the top of his list of Least Favorite Things, along with housecleaning, personal grooming, and being shot in the rear end during a bust gone wrong.

It had happened twice.

"What if we go together at about ten?" Dirk would do anything to grab a little sleep.

"Are you asking me out, darlin'?"

"Yeah, you can buy me an Egg McMuffin."

"Gee, how could a girl turn that down? By the way," she said, "if we're going to continue to be seen in public together, you should probably shed the trench coat and the sneakers. I've heard disparaging remarks about your apparel from the last two individuals I've questioned."

"So, what's your point?"

"If you want me to burn them and spread the ashes at sea, I'll do that for you. It would be my pleasure, and I would consider it a public service."

"Yeah, well, screw you, Reid. And just what are *you* wearing right now?"

"What am I wearing? Is this some sort of obscene phone call?"

"You wish."

"See you tomorrow."

"Yeah, thanks for the tip. I owe you one, kid."

As Savannah pulled up to her house, she felt good. Not magnificent, because she still hadn't found Christy Mallock. Not great, because she still didn't know who had killed Lisa and Earl, and no arrests had been made.

But it had been a good day. Several interesting interviews, some new leads, a spot of light at the end of the tunnel.

Then she saw the colonel's Lincoln parked directly across the street from her house.

What now? It could mean almost anything.

"Shit," she whispered to no one who cared. "That spot of light is probably an oncoming locomotive."

When Savannah walked into her living room, she was surprised at the sight that awaited her. Granny Reid sat on the sofa, the skirt of her best satin caftan spread demurely around her, a dainty cup of tea in her hand. Her gold hoop earrings sparkled in the light of the lamp, which was actually dimmed a few notches.

Beside her was the colonel, holding a hefty mug, looking every bit as masculine as Gran did feminine. There was plenty of room on the sofa, but he was sitting next to her. *Right next to her grandmother!*

And even if the closest thing to sex in Savannah's recent past had been the reference to an obscene phone call with Dirk, she recognized sexual tension when it was floating this thick in a room.

Savannah opened her mouth, intending to say something obnoxious like, "Well! It's a good thing I got home in time. God knows what might have happened in the next five minutes!"

But, just before she made a total fool of herself, she recalled when the situation had been reversed and Gran had walked in to find her sitting next to a gentleman caller on the sofa. She decided to do what Granny had done all those years ago.

She turned up the light until it was eyeball-searing bright, took a seat directly across from them, and pasted a plastic smile on her kisser.

"Hello, Grandmother, Colonel Neilson, and how are we this evening?"

"*We* are just fine, dear," Gran replied. "And obviously, *you* are too, since you're grinning like a goat eating briars."

"I have had a nice day, thank you."

"Does that mean you have some news about my granddaughter?" the colonel asked. When he turned to face her, Savannah saw that his eyes were swollen and red, his nose, too. In his hand he held a crumpled tissue. On the coffee table in front of them was the box.

She felt like an idiot.

He hadn't been making a move on her precious grand-mother; Gran had been comforting the poor man. The colonel didn't strike her as a person who would let down his guard easily with a stranger. But Granny seemed to quickly earn the trust of everyone she met.

"No, Colonel, not yet," Savannah told him. "I'm so sorry. But I just spoke to Detective Coulter on the telephone, and we have several new leads now that may help a great deal. Believe me, we're doing all we can."

"I'm sure you are, and I'm grateful. It's just that . . ."

"I understand." She settled back into her easy chair, and Diamante and Cleopatra appeared almost magically on her lap. "Since you're here, there is something I'd like to ask you about . . . if you don't mind."

He did seem to mind, but he said, "Go ahead."

"When I was looking through the boxes that I took from your house, I found pictures and letters that show Lisa and Vanessa Pearce had been friends for a long time."

The colonel wadded his tissue into a tight ball. "That's true. Vanessa's family lived across the street from us for years. She and Lisa were close."

"Until Earl came along?"

"Yes. Until Earl." From the look on his face, Savannah could see that it was an effort for the colonel to even speak the name, as though he found it distasteful.

"I also understand from the letters, that Earl was involved with both women at one time . . . about eleven years ago."

"Yes."

"And that both Vanessa and Lisa found themselves pregnant by him at approximately the same time."

"Yes."

"Lisa and Earl got married. Lisa had her child, and that was Christy, right?"

"Yes."

Savannah wondered if she was destined to receive only one-syllable answers in this conversation. A bit of elaboration might be helpful, but he seemed suddenly quite tight-lipped.

"Do you know what happened to Vanessa's baby?"

His breath came quick and hard, as though he had been running a race, rather than lounging on a sofa with a mug of tea in one hand. His coloring faded to an unhealthy gray. "Yes," he said.

"What happened to it?"

His hand started shaking so badly that he had to set the mug quickly on the table. "She had an abortion."

"Are you sure, Colonel?"

"Yes, dammit, I'm sure." He turned to Gran and gave her a look of deep embarrassment and apology. "Forgive me, Mrs. Reid, but . . ." When he returned his attention to Savannah, his eyes were so full of pain that Savannah felt it, running hot and cold through her own soul.

"I know she had an abortion," he said, "and because of complications, she can never have children of her own. I know what a hell that is, because I went through it with my own wife before we adopted Lisa."

He closed his eyes and leaned his head back on the sofa.

"And I'm sure, Miss Reid, because I was there through the whole unfortunate, tragic business, doing what I believed I had to do to protect my own daughter. I know because I paid for Vanessa's abortion. I paid, and I paid, and goddammit I'm still paying. . . ."

CHAPTER SEVENTEEN

Savannah entered her guest bedroom to find Gran sitting in bed, reading a romance novel which, judging from the amount of cleavage spilling over the woman's bodice on the cover, was of the "hot and steamy" genre.

"I decided it was your turn to be pampered," Savannah said as she set a tray on the nightstand and poured herself and Gran a cup of jasmine tea.

"Pampered, my hind end." Gran gave her a knowing smirk. "You're just feeling guilty about jumping to conclusions earlier this evening, and now you're trying to kiss up."

Savannah's mouth fell open. As always, she was taken aback by her grandmother's insight and candor. "So?"

Gran shook her head and sipped her tea. "Now, *there's* an intelligent response. How can I possibly argue with that?"

"Does that mean you don't want the tea?"

With a look of pure ecstasy, Gran took a long, deep smell of the steam that curled from the rim of the delicate china cup. Savoring the essence of the flowers, she said, "No. I'll keep it. I can be bribed. Sit yourself down."

Gran pulled her legs up, and Savannah stretched out across the foot of the bed. Lying on her side, she propped up on one elbow.

"What did the colonel have to say?" she asked, trying to sound casual.

"Who's asking? My granddaughter, whom I love and trust, or Savannah Reid, P.I.?"

Savannah thought for a moment and decided to be honest. After all, her interest was more professional than personal. "The P.I., I suppose."

"Then, in that case, it's none of your business. Colonel Neilson is my friend now, and I don't tell tales on friends . . . unless they're really good, juicy ones about sex," she added. "Then I might tell Florence."

Florence and Gran had been next-door neighbors and best friends for thirty-five years.

"I wouldn't want you to betray a confidence, Gran, you know that."

"I don't know that at all, so don't be all sweet and lightness with me. I know more about you than you know about yourself, young lady. And the truth is, you'd do most anything to solve a case."

"Well . . . I . . ."

"On the other hand, I understand how important it is to you to settle this one in particular. I know how bad you feel about your part in it, plus you're worried sick about that little girl."

"That's true, I am. And if the colonel were to mention anything to you that you thought might help me . . ."

"I'd tell you. Okay?"

Savannah relaxed, knowing she had no reason for concern. Gran was sensible, if nothing else.

"Mostly, the poor man is just grieving over losing his daughter, and I know how he feels." Gran's eyes momentarily lost their luster as she looked into the past. "I thought it would just about kill me, too, when I lost your Uncle Henry, your father's oldest brother. He died in the Korean War, you know."

"Yes, Gran, I know. Dad told me about it. I'm really sorry I never met Uncle Henry."

"I wish I never raised him in the first place. He was my first baby, you know, and real sickly. But I took good care of him and brought him up to be a fine young man. I remember askin' myself, 'What for?' Just so he could step on a mine and get blown to kingdom come?"

Savannah reached over and covered her grandmother's hand with her own. "I'm sure Henry was a blessing to the world for the time he was here."

"He was; it's true. But I know what the colonel is suffering. In some ways it's even worse than losing your mate. I hated losing your grandfather, but at least he had led a long, fulfilled life."

Stroking Gran's fingers, Savannah tried to return some of the support and comfort she had received over the years. It felt good to be on the giving end for a change.

"My great-great-grandma, Granny Shaw . . . she came over here on the boat from Ireland, you know, during the Great

Potato Famine," Gran continued, "and she used to say, 'It's un-natural for the lamb's fleece to hang from the rafter before the sheep's.' And that's the way it feels when one of your own children goes before you. It's not the way the good Lord intended it, and it hurts more. You ask any mother or father who's lost a young'un."

"I'm sure that's true, and I'm sure the colonel must be in terrible pain."

"He is, indeed. I have no doubt at all about that. Plus, his baby was taken away through an act of cruelty, not an accident, or illness, or war like my Henry. That has to be even worse."

"About the worst thing a person can endure, I have no doubt."

Gran set her romance novel aside and picked up her small, well-worn Bible from the nightstand. "We'll have to remember Colonel Neilson in our prayers tonight, Savannah. He needs all the comfort he can get."

Half an hour later, Savannah lay on her own bed, staring up at the antique ceiling fan she had installed last summer.

She liked to think of herself as a spiritual person, if not particularly religious. But it had been longer than she cared to remember since she had uttered a long, formal prayer. Most of her prayers were said on the run, hasty words muttered in the heat of battle. "Please, God, don't let so-and-so happen," or "Oh Lord, what should I do now?"

The last few times she had stepped into a church, it had been in the course of an investigation, not for worshiping purposes. So, she felt a little rusty around the edges.

"I'm not so good at this," she whispered. Her voice sounded

alien and strained to her in the dark quiet of her bedroom. "You haven't exactly heard from me in a while." She laughed at herself. "But I guess I don't need to tell You that. Gran says You keep pretty good tabs on things like that.

"I hope you're keeping track of Christy. Please don't let her be hurt any more than she already has. To be honest, I've always had a problem understanding why You let bad things happen to innocents like Christy and other kids. But I guess You have your reasons. Gran says You do. I hope You do."

She thought back on her childhood prayer format, looking for direction to continue.

"And God, bless Gran for being the wonderful person that she is, and thank You for sending her to me at a time like this. Bless the colonel and try to numb his pain, if You can. Keep Christy in the palm of Your hand and help me return her to the love and safety of her family.

"And while You're at it, could You make me a little smarter? Right now, it would really help. Amen."

She lay there, thinking about what she had done, feeling a bit like the Scarecrow asking the Wizard of Oz for a brain.

But a quiet voice inside—maybe the voice of Hope, that her grandmother sang of—whispered a word of comfort.

It told her that her prayer, rusty or polished, had been heard and received.

The last time Savannah had tried to speak to Vanessa Pearce, she had been eighty-sixed from the Shoreline. But Savannah experienced only a passing twinge of misgiving as she pulled up before the tiny, bread box of a house. Talking to people who didn't like her or want to talk to her was a part of life. Not the most pleasant part, to be sure, but an accepted one.

Earlier, Savannah had decided that she had some time to kill before meeting Dirk for the electrician's interview. So, she had called the Shoreline to see if Vanessa was working. She had been told that Vanessa was taking the day off to fix her motorcycle, its having "thrown a rod."

Not being especially knowledgeable about vehicle repair, Savannah hoped she would be finished "throwing" things by the time she arrived. A tussle with a six-one, purple-haired, bad-ass motorcycle chick wasn't her idea of a good time.

Apparently, automobile repair mechanics rated high on Vanessa's list of priorities, far above lawn and home maintenance. Half a dozen partially dismantled vehicles littered the lawn and an engine had been torn apart on the porch.

Savannah left the Camaro and waded across the sea of grass. In the rear, next to the alley, stood a two-car garage that was larger than the house. Its two doors were flung open, hanging loosely on their hinges, like a bird's broken wings. From inside came a long, colorful stream of verbal abuse.

Vanessa was making eloquent observations about someone or something's family pedigree, Oedipal tendencies, and probable eternal destination.

She walked through the open doors, just in time to see a wrench fly across the garage and smash into the far wall. It seemed Vanessa liked to throw her tools, too.

"What the hell do you want?" Vanessa squatted on the floor, a mess of greasy components spread out before her. The smell of gasoline was strong, emanating from a washtub filled with gas and more oily engine pieces. Savannah recalled that this practice was what her brother Macon called "soaking parts."

"To talk a few minutes. You can keep working though, if you want," she added, hoping to sound cordial.

Standing, Vanessa tossed her dirty shop towel onto the cement floor. "I'm warning you, I just found out that my Harley's engine has to be completely overhauled, so I'm not in a very good mood."

Mmmmm, Savannah thought. *Cordial doesn't seem to be working.*

She dropped the "nice" routine and allowed her expression to register her fatigue and annoyance. "My investigation isn't going very well, either," she said, "so that makes two of us."

"The cops say somebody blew Earl's brains out." Vanessa's tone was flat, but challenging. Savannah could tell that the statement was intended to shock her. But she wasn't easily shocked and didn't like being worked.

"Actually, when I saw the body, the brains were still inside. No exit wound," she replied evenly. Two could play that game.

"Did you kill him?"

"No. Did you?"

Both women stared at each other for a long, tense moment. In the end it was Vanessa who broke eye contact.

"Okay," Vanessa walked over to a cement block and sat down. She didn't offer Savannah a seat, but Savannah didn't want one. "What do you want to know?"

With most people Savannah tried to exercise a degree of decorum and common civility. But, even though Vanessa appeared to be wonderful with kids, she seemed less socially adept with adults. Maybe she just didn't like private detectives. Or perhaps it was more personal and she didn't like blue-eyed women with Southern accents who asked her obnoxious questions.

Whatever the case, Savannah decided to dive right in, head first.

"Did you hate Lisa?" she asked.

"She and I were best friends."

"Even after Earl Mallock married her instead of you?"

Vanessa's eyes blazed and she bit her lower lip hard enough to make it bleed as she struggled with her temper.

Yes, Savannah thought, *pay dirt.*

"Earl had to marry her. She was pregnant with his kid."

"So were you." Savannah's tone was gentle, but Vanessa looked as though she had been hit with a bull whip.

"How the hell do you know *that?* Who told you that?"

"I read it in some of Lisa's letters. I'm sorry, I don't mean to violate your privacy. I'm just trying to understand what—"

"You don't need to understand a damned thing about me or my past. It's none of your fucking business. You get the hell off my property, bitch, before I knock your goddamned head off. Do you hear me? Do you?"

Savannah assumed that everyone on the block could hear Vanessa; she was screaming the words. But tears were beginning to flow down the woman's grease-smeared cheeks, and Savannah knew she had taken the situation as far as was wise at the moment.

Quietly, she turned to leave, as Vanessa continued to hurl insults at her back.

There was no reason to tarry. She had the information she had come for. The answer was: Yes, Vanessa was capable of violence. Anyone listening to her now, or who had seen the wrench sailing across the garage, would have no doubt about that.

"Don't you ever come back here again! Never! I mean it!"

Savannah continued to walk without turning around. It was a dangerous gamble. She half expected to get a socket wrench thrown at her back.

"If you want to find out who killed Lisa and Earl," Vanessa shouted, "go after that child molester/pervert that Lisa was dating. She gave him the boot because of what he tried to do to Christy. He probably killed her . . . and Earl, too. Hassle *him* for a change. Don't go bothering people who didn't do anything wrong."

Savannah could hear Vanessa's voice breaking, and she knew that once she was gone, the hard-nosed motorcycle mama would fall to pieces.

In spite of herself, Savannah couldn't help feeling sorry for her and a bit guilty that she had caused her to be so upset.

But, on the other hand, Savannah rationalized as she climbed into the car, if Vanessa Pearce had anything to do with the murders, she deserved to feel rotten. And if she was innocent, the cry would do her good.

"Where is it?" Dirk asked, the moment Savannah got into his Buick.

She shoved the sack with the Egg McMuffin at him. "Why am *I* giving *you* bribes when this is *my* lead?" she asked as he quickly unwrapped it and chomped off an enormous bite.

"Because you love me?"

"Guess again."

"Because I'm not so grouchy when I've been recently fed?"

"That's more like it." She punched his shoulder and pointed to the ignition. "Let's get rollin', pal. We've got even more reason than ever to visit Mr. Ian 'High Volt' Warner."

"What's that?"

"I'll tell you on the way. Drive."

CHAPTER EIGHTEEN

"I just came from Vanessa Pearce's garage, and she says Ian Warner is a child molester." Savannah rolled down the Skylark's window to escape some of Dirk's secondhand smoke. For a refreshing change, he took the hint and hung his cigarette out his window as he drove. "But it might have just been a fanciful turn of phrase," she added.

"He *is*." Dirk flipped the butt away.

"He is?"

"Yeap. I ran a check on him and he's got a record. Three arrests, one conviction, ten-year sentence, six served."

"All molestation charges?"

"All."

"The conviction?"

"Forced oral copulation—an eight-year-old girl. One of his girlfriend's daughters."

"Oh, man . . . that fits what Vanessa told me. She said Lisa was dating the guy, but broke it off because of something he did, or tried to do, to Christy."

"Do you believe her?"

Savannah thought for a moment. "She was pretty peeved at the time . . . at me . . . but she seemed sincere enough. And it goes along with what Mrs. Abernathy, the neighbor, said about Lisa having a fight with Warner and telling him not to come around anymore."

Dirk pulled the Buick into a dirt parking area beside a windowless, cement building with a bright red lightning bolt on the side and a sign that said: Warner Electric.

Beside the building was parked the van which Lisa's neighbor had mentioned. The white one with the red lettering and the vanity plate.

Dirk turned to Savannah and smiled. "I'm gonna enjoy this," he said. "Nothing quite makes my day like rousting a child molester."

The moment Dirk and Savannah walked through the front door of Warner Electric, a small, dark man in blue coveralls darted out from behind the counter and greeted them.

"Hi, can I help you?"

"Yeah," Dirk said. "We need to have a word with Ian."

"He's busy, can I—?"

"So are we." Dirk flipped open his badge. "And we have to talk to Ian. Right away."

Savannah walked on into the room, picking her way between reels of coaxial cable, bundles of conduit, and shelves, bristling with strange-looking metal boxes that sprouted wires and exotic connectors. At the other end, standing between a couple of heavily loaded pallets, was a tall, good-looking man with a leonine mane of golden curls that any woman would have envied.

Savannah chuckled to herself. The hair was another reason why Dirk would enjoy hassling this guy. If there was anything on earth that Dirk hated more than a child molester, it was a child molester with more hair than he had. And that included a large slice of the pervert demagoguery.

As Mrs. Abernathy had noted, Ian Warner wore his long sleeves rolled up to the elbow to reveal muscular forearms. He was, indeed, a handsome man. Long ago, Savannah had stopped trying to figure out why a man who could so easily find a willing woman to warm his bed would turn to a helpless child for gratification.

Savannah turned back to Dirk and nodded in Warner's direction. Dirk caught the look and walked past her toward the back. Toward Warner.

When Dirk was only halfway across the room, Ian glanced his way and suddenly tensed. He seemed to lose all interest in the customer he had been speaking with. A knowing look crossed his face . . . a look that Savannah knew well.

Damn, he's gonna run, she thought.

A heartbeat later, he bolted for the back door.

"Police! Freeze!" Dirk shouted, running after him.

"Yeah, right." Savannah whirled around and headed back out the front door. "The day one of them does what Dirk tells them, he'll keel over with a heart attack."

She ran straight for the HI VOLT van in the parking lot,

and her hunch had been right. Warner was running straight to her with Dirk in his dust.

Holding her Beretta in both hands, she leaned over the hood of the van and braced her feet, pointing it straight at him.

"*Now* you're gonna freeze, Mr. Warner," she said as she sighted down the barrel, "just like the nice policeman told you to. Because if you don't, I'll plug you one right between the eyes."

Ian nearly tripped over his own feet as he skidded to a stop on the other side of the hood. He glanced back at a fuming Dirk, who was closing the distance, then at Savannah. He looked genuinely confused.

"Are you with him?" he asked her.

"Yeap."

"Are you a cop, too?"

"Not anymore," she replied. "But I'm still a damned good shot."

It didn't improve Savannah's mood any to have to leave Ian Warner in Dirk's hands and miss out on the questioning. But it was still business hours at the station, which upped her chances of running into Hillquist or Bloss. Besides, it would be stretching the rules considerably for Dirk to allow a civilian, such as herself, to hang around while he was conducting the interview.

And, having recently pointed a gun at Warner's head, she would be hard put to convince him she was a public defender.

So, she headed home, to talk to Tammy and regroup. Maybe grab a bite to eat and see Gran. The poor ol' dear was probably bored to death, sitting at home, waiting for her to show.

———

"Your grandmother caught a cab and took off to the beach in her red swimsuit," Tammy told her when she walked through the door. "Don't worry, I loaned her one of your coverups, so she's decent. Then she said she was going to check out the mall and some of the local Mexican food. Said she likes it spicy."

Savannah laughed. "I'm sure she does. Don't be surprised if she comes back plowed. She likes margueritas, too."

"She's so neat. I wish I had a grandmother like that," Tammy said wistfully as she led Savannah into the office.

"I just hope I'll *be* a grandmother like that."

"Oh, you will be. You two are a lot alike."

"I'll take that as a compliment. What have you got for me?"

Savannah could tell Tammy was proud of herself as she presented her with a sheet of paper.

"Another lead. Alan Logan's ex-wife. I called and asked her if she would be willing to talk to you. She was thrilled at the thought. I think she wants to dump on you about Alan. She sounds like she's still bitter."

"All right!" Savannah grabbed the paper. The address was nearby, only a few blocks away. "The more bitter the better, I always say."

"Do you always say that?"

Tammy was so gullible, and Savannah loved her for it.

"Naw. This was the first time. But I think it's going to be my new motto."

At first glance, it wasn't apparent that Jillian Logan had anything to be so bitter about. Alan hadn't been kidding when he had said that his ex-wife had taken him for everything. With a

Lexus and a Mercedes in the driveway of a rambling new ranch-style home, she didn't appear to be hurting too badly. At least, not financially.

But then, money wasn't everything, Savannah told herself as she walked up the brick driveway to the stained glass French doors.

"Hello, Ms. Reid, I've been expecting you," said the perfectly tanned, perfectly manicured, perfectly frosted blond woman who ushered her into the spacious foyer.

They passed the atrium full of expensive silk plants, and into a professionally decorated, chic, and overfurnished living room. Savannah was reminded of the covers of home decor magazines, where there was so much artistic clutter in the room that you couldn't see a thing.

But, beneath the jungle of knickknacks, Savannah saw a number of exquisite antiques . . . probably the fruits of Alan's labors in his business.

"Do have a seat. May I serve you a glass of sparkling water?" Jillian asked with a wave of red-white-and-blue-striped acrylic nails.

A rather patriotic gesture, Savannah thought. Worth remembering for the Fourth of July.

"Sparkling water . . . that would be very nice," Savannah replied. "If you don't have anything better," she whispered as Jillian wriggled her teeny-tiny butt out of the living room and into the kitchen.

"A private detective. How fascinating," she cooed when she returned, carrying a wineglass filled with water, ice, and a slice of lemon.

"Not really, but it pays the bills . . . sometimes. What do you do, Mrs. Logan?"

"At the moment I'm taking some classes at the community college. Home decorating, sculpture, flower arranging, and wok cooking. I'm still devastated over my divorce, you see, and I'm trying to find myself. I don't know how I'm going to live on the piddly amount my ex-husband left to me. He really is a horrible man. What do you want to know about him?"

Boy, howdy . . . she is eager. Too eager.

Savannah hauled out the mental bullshit shovel and slipped on her fantasy hip boots.

"Whatever you would like to tell me, Mrs. Logan," she replied, playing it safe.

"Well . . . I understand you're investigating the murder of my ex's business partner and his wife."

Savannah wondered who had told her. But she would get to that later. "That's right; I am," she said. "Is there anything you can tell me that might have to do with their deaths?"

"You mean like . . . that Alan wanted to have an affair with Lisa, and she turned him down and Alan was furious, and he never really got over it, and that he hated Earl because Alan blamed Earl for them losing their business, and then I left Alan, and Alan said that was Earl's fault, too, but it was really Alan's fault, not Earl's because Alan was never home and didn't pay me any attention at all, and that was why I left him, because I just couldn't—"

"Wait! Please!" Savannah held up one hand in surrender. "There isn't, like, a quiz on all this later, is there?"

Jillian Logan looked at her blankly. A couple of "blonde" jokes floated through Savannah's head, but she quickly dismissed them as being unworthy of a such a mature and sophisticated brunette as herself.

"A quiz? I don't know what you're talking about," Jillian continued. "I was just wondering if that was the sort of thing you wanted to know."

Savannah considered sticking her head in the wineglass of sparkling water . . . just drowning herself . . . ending it all. But the glass was too small, and her head too big. So, instead, she reached into her purse and pulled out her pad and paper.

"Certainly, Mrs. Logan," she said, trying her best to sound patient. "Now, if you could just start at the beginning."

"Oh, okay. No problem. It all began back in 1973. Alan—that rotten creep—and I met at a . . ."

CHAPTER NINETEEN

Savannah was getting ready to dash out of her house and hit the road again, when she opened her front door and nearly ran into Brian O'Donnell. He was standing on her doorstep, his fist raised, ready to knock.

"Oh, hi . . ." She wasn't exactly prepared to speak to him again so soon. She had hoped to have something more concrete to tell him the next time she needed to give a report.

After delivering so much bad news to the poor man, she was hoping to have something optimistic to relate.

Oh, well . . . so much for thinking positive. Usually, when she tried the upbeat, pull-only-good-things-to-you routine, things got worse. Or, maybe she had just been hanging around Dirk too long and had caught his infectious pessimism.

"Hello, Savannah," O'Donnell said. "I don't mean to be a

pest, but I'm sitting there, hour after hour, in my hotel room, worrying until I'm almost sick."

"I'm sure you are. I'm sorry."

"I feel so damned helpless. I had to do something, even if it was just to come over here and bug you."

"You aren't bugging me, Mr. O'Donnell. Why don't you come in for a minute, and I'll fill you in on what we have so far."

"Is that it?" Brian O'Donnell asked Savannah, after she had spent nearly half an hour trying to make their lack of progress sound like a pep squad rally. But she decided she was losing her touch; he hadn't bought it.

He hadn't even drunk the freshly brewed Mocha Java or eaten any of the cookies, which she had spread invitingly across the tray on the coffee table.

"Ah . . . yes, but this one lead, the one about the guy with the criminal record may pan out," she told him. "I wouldn't be at all surprised if he doesn't turn out to be our killer. And, of course, now that Detective Coulter has him in custody, we'll soon find out if . . . we'll find out where he's been keeping Christy all this time, and we'll be able to get her back."

"He has a record?"

Damn, she hadn't intended to let that slip, but, of course, he had latched onto it. "Mmmm, yeah, just one conviction, though. Not to worry."

"What was it for?"

"What?" She knew darned well "what" but asking was worth a few seconds of stall time.

"What was he convicted of?"

"It . . . ah . . . it might have been for writing bad checks, insufficient funds, something silly like that?"

O'Donnell's eyes searched hers, making her feel the need to squirm in her chair. She could practically feel her nose growing and her tongue turning black. As Granny had often warned her in childhood, it would probably fall out of her mouth at any moment.

Brian's eyes narrowed. "What do you mean, 'might have been'? Was that all? Just bad checks or something like that?"

Maybe it was Gran's presence upstairs in the guest bedroom, or maybe it was the fact that she had formally prayed last night for the first time in ages. Either way, Savannah decided she didn't really want to sully her freshly cleansed soul so quickly, so badly, with such a blatant lie.

"No, Brian. It wasn't bad checks. He was convicted of sexual misconduct with a minor."

"How minor?"

"A child."

He stared at her with stricken eyes. "Oh, God, *that* is what we're *hoping* for?" he said. "That's the best case scenario . . . that a convicted child molester murdered both of my niece's parents and took off with her?"

"Mr. O'Donnell, I'm so sorry, but I don't know what to say to you." Her head began to throb, until she could practically see double. "At this point, I don't know what the hell I'm hoping for."

As Savannah was walking Brian O'Donnell out to his car to say good-bye, Dirk drove up in the old Buick. The moment he climbed out of the car and slammed the door behind him, Savannah knew the tête-à-tête with Ian Warner hadn't gone to his satisfaction.

"Oh, great," Brian muttered. "I was hoping to avoid that jerk. He's really getting on my nerves."

"Dirk's a good guy; it's just that he possesses no social graces whatsoever and not a smidgen of couth. He rubs everybody the wrong way."

"How did it go?" Savannah asked as Dirk stomped up the sidewalk in their direction.

"It was a fuckin' waste of time. Nothing. Squat. That's how it went; thanks for asking."

"What do you mean 'nothing'?"

"He had an alibi. Several of his worthless friends will vouch for him. They say he was boozing it up with them."

"I didn't know that child molesters had friends."

"They do if their daddy owns a business the size of Warner Electric."

Savannah glanced at Brian and saw that he looked relieved. She supposed she should be, too. But she was wearing out her loafers, pacing around in square one.

"What are you grinnin' about?" Dirk asked Brian. "You think this is funny or something?"

"Dirk!" Savannah was surprised. Even though Dirk wasn't known for his diplomacy, he was one of the "good" cops. And, by Savannah's definition, that meant basically civil to anyone unless they gave him ample reason not to be. From where she stood, Savannah couldn't see any reason for him to be sarcastic with O'Donnell.

"Don't forget," Dirk continued, glaring at Brian. "So far,

you're the only one on my list who had motive and opportunity to kill both victims."

O'Donnell's face hardened, his jaws tightened. Savannah observed, with interest, that mild-mannered Brian O'Donnell had a temper, too.

"Okay, big shot," he told Dirk, "you've got opportunity and motive. How about some physical evidence? Last time I heard, you need a little of that, too, before you go around making accusations."

Not waiting for Dirk's reply, he turned and strode away toward his rental car.

"I'm working on it, buddy," Dirk shouted after him. "Be seein' you soon."

"Yeah, right." O'Donnell slammed his car door and peeled out.

With a mildly satisfied look on his face, Dirk turned to Savannah. "See what I mean. He ain't just a Mr. Hyde; if you get him mad, he can be a Dr. Jekyll, too."

Savannah sighed. "Dirk, you poor, illiterate dear. Dr. Jekyll was the good guy; Hyde was the nasty. You've got it backward."

"Who cares? You knew what I meant."

She took his arm and led him toward her front door. If ever anyone was in need of a ham and cheese on rye with dijon, it was Dirk. Now. From the way he was frothing at the mouth, it was apparent that his blood sugar level had hit bottom.

"You know," she said, "I don't appreciate you insulting my guests without my permission."

"O'Donnell was your *guest*? Since when?"

"He was on my property."

"He was standing on the sidewalk. That's public property,

which means he was fair game." Dirk shook his head. "Damn it, woman, don't give me a hard time. I'm having a really rotten day."

Savannah decided to add a Coke to the menu.

As Savannah walked into the examination room of the morgue, she was glad she had eaten a sandwich with Dirk. Because, upon seeing Earl Mallock lying on the table, his torso cut open and internal organs exposed, she figured it was a good day to diet.

The smell assaulted her nose and went straight to her gag reflex. Earl had been a bit ripe when they had found him in the shack. Time hadn't improved his condition.

"Savannah, good to see you. Want to watch?" Dr. Jennifer Liu stood over the corpse, scalpel in one hand, Earl's liver in the other. As always, she had a bright smile on her face, and her dark eyes glimmered with excitement. Dr. Liu simply *loved* doing autopsies.

"It's always fascinating," Jennifer had told Savannah once. "No matter how many you've done, each one is different. I love getting in there and seeing what I can find."

Savannah was infinitely glad there were people like Jennifer in the world. Medical examiners, morticians, and piano teachers—society needed them desperately. But Savannah had to admit that, whatever it took to do the job, she didn't have it.

Dr. Jennifer's young assistant, a fellow named Mark, was peeling Earl's face down from the top, revealing the bare skull with its perfectly round, black hole directly in the center of the forehead.

"Have you got a mask?" Savannah asked, trying not to inhale, only exhale . . . a tricky maneuver.

"Over there in the second drawer." Jennifer pointed with a bloody surgical glove. "Help yourself."

Savannah hurried to the cupboard and pulled out a small blue dust mask.

"Vicks?" she asked.

"Top drawer," Mark replied. He grinned and added, "Wimp."

"Up yours. Sideways." Savannah smeared a huge dollop inside the mask, then put it on, snapping the elastic around the back of her head. Instantly, her eyes began to water, but it was worth the sacrifice. Although no amount of Vicks could completely eliminate the stench, it cut it in half and kept her from gagging.

"What have you found?" Savannah asked, joining them beside the stainless steel table. She hung back a bit, telling herself it was because she didn't want to interfere with their work, but knowing it was because she—like all other healthy, living beings—had a natural and instinctive aversion to anything dead.

"Interesting stuff," Dr. Jennifer said, "huh, Mark?"

"Yeah, fascinating."

Mark didn't seem to relish his work. Savannah suspected the only reason he was an autopsy assistant was because it made him a popular guy at the local bars. He had an entire repertoire of morbid, corny jokes that resulted in him receiving more than his share of "stiff" drinks on the house.

"Like what?" Savannah asked.

"For one, I'd say that Mr. Mallock recently lost a lot of weight . . . and probably not the healthy way. His skin is a little saggy for a male his age. He also has stretch marks there on the underside of his belly and his upper thighs."

"That's what I understand, too," Savannah said. "I've been told he was quite heavy not that long ago."

"Another thing . . ." Dr. Liu looked pleased with herself. "He isn't a natural redhead."

"I knew that one, too."

"Oh." Jennifer hated to broadcast reruns. She much preferred to wow her audiences, rather than tell them something they already knew. "Okay, Miss Smartie Pants, I've got at least one thing that's going to surprise you."

"Really?"

"Yeah, let's go over here to the microscope while Mark opens up the skull for me."

"Yes . . . let's." Savannah hated standing too close when the saw was buzzing. Flying bone chips made her nervous.

As they walked away, Mark took a large, clear plastic bag and placed it over the head of the corpse. A few seconds later, the room reverberated with a noise that sounded like a chain saw cutting down an oak.

Savannah didn't look; the head was always the part that made her shoot stew if she wasn't careful.

"Over here," Jennifer shouted above the din as she pointed to the microscope. "Take a look."

Savannah leaned over the scope, squinted, and wondered as always, what she was looking at. Things certainly appeared different when magnified a zillion times. Once, Jennifer had shown her a common cat flea, and that night Diamante and Cleopatra had both been double-dipped, like a couple of chocolate-covered ice-cream cones.

"What is it?" she asked.

"Tissue from Mr. Mallock's wrists, near where the wire had

been twisted. Just like the sample I showed you that I cut from his ex-wife."

Savannah looked again, not understanding the connection. This material looked very different. "But Lisa's had those blue-black specks in it."

"That's right. Inflammation cells. Mr. Mallock's has none."

"What does that mean?"

"It means the wires weren't on him nearly as long. In fact, judging from the lack of swelling in the surrounding tissues, I'd say his wires were applied postmortem."

"*Postmortem?*"

Jennifer smirked, well satisfied with Savannah's degree of shock.

"You got it."

"But why would someone restrain a corpse?" she asked, thinking aloud. "Or maybe they just wanted it to look like the first murder. A copycat?"

Dr. Liu shrugged. "That's for *you* to decide. I just gather the facts, right? It's up to you and Dirk to catch the bad guy."

"We're trying, we're trying. What else do you have?"

"Two different kinds of wire."

"Seriously?"

Jennifer nodded her head. "The first one was common copper wire, like they sell in any run-of-the-mill electronic store. A thin variety."

"Electrical?" Savannah instantly thought of Ian Warner's shop.

"Yeah. But the second wire is even thinner. I'm not sure yet, but I'd say it's piano wire. And another thing. . . ." Jennifer reached for a nearby manila envelope and pulled out a coil of copper wire. "Look at this," she said, pointing to the end. "See how jagged and uneven the cut is?"

Savannah saw a number of gouges along the last four inches or so of the wire and the very end looked as though it had been sawn, rather than neatly cut.

"Yes, I see. What do you think it means?"

"I'd say the person who cut it used a knife. See the scrapes along the side? Those were probably made when he dragged the blade along the wire, before actually severing it. And see how it's sort of crimped?"

"Yes."

"Some people cut wire by looping it over the knife first, then sawing through."

"It must have been a pretty good knife," Savannah mused.

"One of those very effective survival knives, I'd say."

Mark's saw suddenly went quiet, and the women found themselves shouting in a silent room.

"Cap's off," he said, stepping back and giving a grandiose wave toward the body. "He's all yours."

"Ah, ha . . . now we can find the bullet," Dr. Liu said, all but rubbing her hands together with ghoulish delight.

Examining the front quarter of the scalp which Mark had sawn away, Jennifer carefully considered the small, round hole. "Yes, this is the entrance." She held it under Savannah's nose. "See, the bevel slants inward. The bullet always removes more material the farther in it goes. That's how you can tell if it's the entrance or exit."

Savannah marveled, not for the first time, at the wondrous design of the human body. Because of the dome shape, the skull was incredibly strong, yet surprisingly thin. She could see light through it as Jennifer held it up.

"And here . . . Mark, bring us a flashlight so that I can show Savannah exactly what I'm talking about. This always amazes me, the path that a bullet makes through a brain."

A flashlight. *Oh, great*, Savannah thought. If there was anything she didn't need right now, it was a better look.

But on closer inspection, she found that it was, indeed, amazing. The even, black tunnel of destruction had burned its way through Earl Mallock's consciousness, forever destroying a million complex biological processes, a million memories, and one life.

Dr. Liu lifted out the murdered brain and laid it carefully on the tiny dissecting table, beside the scale. When she returned to the cavity, she probed the empty bowl with her gloved fingertips. "And *here* . . ." She held up the tiny mushroom-shaped piece of metal that had done all the damage. ". . . is our bullet."

She squinted at it, turning it this way and that. "Mmmm. Not what I was expecting."

"Why? What is it?" Savannah found that her curiosity was contagious.

"I'd bet that it's a .45."

"What's unusual about that?"

"Normally, a .45 would have gone on through . . . created an exit wound. Maybe it was a low charge."

"Like target ammo?"

"Exactly. But there's another reason I wasn't expecting a .45."

"What's that?"

"I would have bet he was shot with the same weapon as Lisa Mallock. But she was killed with a nine millimeter."

Savannah held her breath for a long time, and it had nothing to do with the stench of death in the room. "No shit?" she said at last.

Dr. Liu quirked one eyebrow. "Are you sure they were killed by the same person?"

Savannah's head swam. "I don't know. I don't know anything anymore."

CHAPTER TWENTY

"I don't know what you're so excited about," Dirk told Savannah in his usual, pessimistic tone that irritated her to death. Leave it to him to pop her bubble at every possible opportunity.

"This is a *very* interesting development," she argued. "You just have to see the black side of every cloud." She poured herself another glass of Gran's homemade lemonade, leaned back in the chaise lounge, and took a long swig.

She needed it to cool off her temperament as well as her palate.

Ordinarily, this would have been a relaxing, pleasantly hedonistic experience, sitting in her backyard, beneath the grape arbor, sipping an icy beverage and listening to Gran hum through the kitchen window as she prepared her famous chicken and dumplings.

But Dirk's negativity could sour any occasion.

"I swear," she muttered, shaking her head, "if you won the lottery, you'd bitch."

"What's the point in winning?" He shrugged. "The whole thing's rigged, and besides, even if you won, the damned IRS would take most of it."

She studied him, continually amazed. "Point proved. But no matter what you say, I still think this helps to define our list of suspects. Before, we were only considering people who had motives to kill both Lisa and Earl. Now we know it may have been two different individuals."

"How does the list change?" He helped himself to a refill of lemonade. Savannah cringed when he set the cobalt blue antique pitcher down hard on the glass-topped table between their chaises. The man was hopeless.

"Well," she said, "we can rule out Vanessa. She may have hated Lisa, but she was in love with Earl."

"It wouldn't be the first time someone killed the one they love. Maybe she found out that Earl killed Lisa and figured it was because he was still hung up on her. Vanessa admitted she's the jealous type. Besides, she may have wanted to nab the kid . . . like it's the one she never had, or something like that."

"All right, I'll give you that one," Savannah admitted reluctantly. "But how about Alan Logan? He threatened to destroy Earl's family, just like he did his. Looks like someone did exactly that."

"He was a suspect before. He's one now. Nothing's changed there."

"And then there's the colonel. Gran says he was grief-stricken. He may have killed Earl because Earl murdered his daughter. I couldn't say that I'd blame him too much."

He sniffed. "Naw, the colonel's an old fart with arthritis. If you and me were huffin' and puffin' to hike back there to that shed, he never would've made it. He was barely able to get around his living room the other day."

Savannah heard a loud crash from the kitchen. A skillet or pan had hit the tiles. A moment later, Gran's head appeared at the window. "Dropped the diamond outta my ring," she said cheerfully. "Nothin' to worry about."

Yesterday, she had broken a glass, and a plate the day before. Savannah had decided not to concern herself. Dishes were replaceable. Gran was priceless.

"And then," Dirk continued, "there's that punk, Ian Warner. If he did it, then a whole houseful of people are lying for him. Which is possible, but not likely. Before, I figured he killed both Lisa and Earl to get to Christy. Now, I reckon Earl could have beat him to Lisa, but that don't change nothin'. It don't matter what Dr. Liu says about it bein' two different killers. Like I said, we're up Shit Creek without a paddle."

He settled back in his chair, drew a deep breath, and assumed that self-important, omniscient look that made Savannah want to slap him naked and hide his clothes.

"Yep . . ." he said, ". . . for my money, I'm still bettin' on the brother. He's the one with the most to gain with both Earl and Lisa dead and the kid missing. That way, he don't have to share with nobody."

"Three lives, for only fifty thousand dollars?" Savannah said, desperately refusing not to meander down that trail of thought.

"Get real, Van. People have been knocked off for a helluva lot less."

Savannah sighed, giving up the fight. Sometimes, it was futile to try to battle Dirk's cynicism. Like the mumps or German measles, it was contagious. If you were around it, eventually, you caught it.

"You're right," she admitted, chug-a-lugging the rest of the lemonade, wishing it were straight Scotch. "There's no point. The IRS probably would nab it all. Besides, quadzillions of people would write you tearjerker letters and beg for money, and . . . God, I hope I never win."

"Me, too."

Across the dark brown crockery bowl that contained the world's lightest dumplings, Gran studied Savannah with a curious look on her face.

"I heard what you and that Dirk character were talking about out there this afternoon," Granny told her as she ladled another helping onto Savannah's plate.

"Oh, you did, huh?" Savannah chuckled. "Is there anything you *don't* hear?"

"Not much."

"That's what I thought. And I suppose you have an opinion about what was said, or you wouldn't have brought it up, right?"

Gran smiled broadly. "Moss don't have a chance to grow on you, does it, sweetie-pie."

"Moss doesn't grow well in piss and vinegar . . . or so I've heard you say."

"That's true. And I *do* have an opinion about what was said in your backyard. I think your friend, Mr. Dirk Coulter, is a donkey's rump."

Savannah laughed. "Not many would argue with you about that."

"And I think he needs a bit of an attitude adjustment where old people are involved."

"And women . . . and kids . . . and cats . . . and . . ."

"But older folks, especially."

Taking a closer look, Savannah saw that her grandmother was genuinely offended, a rare occurrence. "What did he say that upset you, Gran?"

"Your rude friend called Colonel Neilson an old fart—which he ain't. He's a man who's managed to keep himself alive for seventy or so years, that's all. And fought three wars for his country and won himself a Congressional Medal of Honor in the process." Gran hesitated, toying with a bit of dumpling on her plate, her eyes full of hurt. "And what's worse, Savannah, is that you didn't even set Mr. Coulter straight for sayin' it. I'm surprised at you, honey."

Her grandmother's gentle rebuke went straight to Savannah's heart. She was right, of course.

How many times had she jumped on Dirk's case for uttering a racial slur, a sexist remark, an unkind observation about someone who was overweight, underweight, badly dressed, mentally or physically challenged, or just plain different in some way from himself.

But she had never thought to come to the defense of a person who was being denigrated because of his advanced years.

"Prejudice is prejudice, Savannah," Gran continued, "no

matter who it's against. It's just plain ol' ignorance: one person thinkin' he's better than any other one of God's creations. Ignorance and arrogance."

"I understand. I'm sorry, Gran. I should have said something."

"I've brought five children into this world, and they've blessed me with twenty-two grandkids besides. I'm here to tell you, they're every one different and I love 'em in different ways. But I love every single one completely, with all my heart and soul. It hurts me to hear one of 'em talkin' trash about the other one. And I'm not nearly as good a parent as the good Lord above. I can tell you, He feels the same."

"I'm sure He does, Gran. I'll talk to Dirk the very next time I see him. I promise."

"Well, you better. You inform Mr. Hot Shot Coulter, that he's gonna be old, too. It'll happen before he knows it, too, unless he kicks the bucket early, that is, and most people don't want to do that. You tell him that us old folks aren't any different than anybody else, except that we've been around longer. Just like younger people, we feel love and hate, sorrow and joy. Every day we decide whether to do good deeds or evil. And don't fool yourself, we're perfectly capable of both."

"Are you telling me that Dirk should reinstate the colonel on his list of suspects?"

"Hell, yes!" Gran's eyes blazed with a passion and conviction that, as always, made Savannah less afraid to grow old. "Don't you hear what I'm telling you, girl? To leave Colonel Neilson off that list is a downright insult! He belongs on there with the best and the worst of 'em!"

With the help of the Yellow Pages section of her phone book, Savannah located the bike rental agency that was nearest the abandoned Montoya Ranch where they had found Earl Mallock's body.

It was only a mile away from the cutoff that led to the old ranch house. She reminded herself to give Ryan a punch in the chops, at least verbally, for not mentioning this fact earlier. It irked her to think they could have ridden to the spread on the relative comfort of a dirt bike, rather than trudged over hills, through valley and dale.

"How long have you guys been in business?" she asked the swarthy, curly-haired fellow behind the counter. He was wearing a Grateful Dead tee shirt, but she decided he must be a second or third generation Deadhead. He didn't appear to be more than nineteen or twenty.

"Dad opened the place last fall," he replied as he scribbled down her driver's license number and expiration date on a rental form.

"So, you're new. That must be why my friend didn't know about you."

"Don't tell me you *hiked* the old trail all the way to the Montoya Ranch."

"I did. With these two feet and a twenty-gallon aquarium of water strapped to my waist."

"Really?"

He stared at her blankly; she determined he was a deadhead in more ways than one.

"No, not really. It just felt like it after the first hour or so."

"Well, you'll get there a lot faster on a bike. You do know how to ride, don't you?"

"Sure."

"Good. 'Cause Dad says we shouldn't rent to anybody who isn't experienced."

Five minutes later, Savannah sat on the bike in front of the shop, staring at the controls on the handles. "No problem," she mumbled once the kid was out of earshot. "Now, which one do you suppose is the brake?"

Two "hit-a-rock-or-some-damned-thing" spinouts, three "lose-your-balance" dump overs, and a first-class "bike goes east, rider goes west" dive, and Savannah was there.

Well, she was *almost* there.

The tin shed, trussed with yellow crime scene tape, was within sight, barely, across the open field. This time she was approaching from the rear, the opposite of when she, Dirk, and Ryan had come before.

And this was the end of the trail.

The young guy at the rental shop had described the beginning of the newly established dirt bike path. He had mentioned that hikers, tired of walking the long trail had begun to take bikes into the area. In an effort to stop the flow, forest rangers had erected the barricades across the old path, which the three of them had seen earlier.

Not to be undone, the bikers had forged another trail. And, although it wasn't as wide or well established, the path provided an only marginally treacherous route to the Montoya Ranch. This new path had only natural barricades: broken trees, unexpected rocks, the occasional bit of fauna.

Savannah concluded it was worth the bumps and bruises when she saw the tire marks, which she had been following, come to a halt, in the middle of nowhere, still a distance from the shed.

Other than that one structure, there was nothing for anyone to see in the area, no reason to come out here. So, why didn't they ride on up to the shed?

She had spotted the tire tracks as soon as she had started down the path. The marks had a unique distinction: an extra indentation, not caused by the tire itself, that was repeated regularly. It was a stone, wedged between the treads that created the demarcation.

Savannah was sure, because the imprint was exactly the same as the one left by the bike she was riding.

Someone else had recently rented this machine and driven it to this exact spot. And for some reason, they had elected to walk the rest of the way to the shed.

She got off the bike, released its kickstand, and followed the footprints in the loose soil. The prints were larger than hers, but that didn't surprise her. All of her suspects were male and had feet that were bigger . . . except for Vanessa, and Savannah had noticed that her shoes were in proportion to the remainder of the giantess.

As she neared the shed, the dirt became more compact and rocky, and the footprints faded. That explained why the police hadn't followed the trail from the shed out to the bike path, she surmised.

To her knowledge, until today, when she had found it, no one investigating the crime knew that there was another way into the location, other than on foot.

Savannah paused and listened to a couple of doves cooing

in an oak tree. The nearby stream burbled with a relaxing, peaceful sound that belied the violence done here.

But Savannah's thoughts couldn't be soothed by any of nature's gentle melodies. Because, until today, no one had considered that a seventy-year-old retired army colonel, an arthritis-plagued war hero, a grief-stricken father and worried-sick grandfather, could have made his way into this remote location.

Standing there, looking at the miserable little shed where the deed had been done, Savannah wondered if Colonel Neilson had killed Earl Mallock. She wondered if she would have done the same thing; she strongly suspected she might have.

Which left her with the most burning question of all: If she were able to prove that Colonel Neilson murdered his son-in-law, how could she bring herself to turn him in?

"Have a nice ride?" The young man's eyes flickered up and down Savannah's body as he spoke, taking in the dirt-streaked jeans, the mud-splattered blouse, her disheveled hair.

"Just friggin' ducky," she replied as she returned the bike and retrieved her generous deposit. Fortunately, the machine had fared better than its rider.

"Find the trail okay?"

"It was right where you said it was. Just behind the 'Absolutely No Trespassing' sign."

"You gotta be careful going up there," he told her, counting the bills onto her outstretched palm. "Some dude got himself murdered in a shack a few days ago."

"I know. That's why I was up there. I'm investigating the homicide."

"You're a cop?" he asked, his eyes wide with shock.

"Nope. A private investigator."

She could tell by the enthusiasm meter on his face that he was far more impressed by the title of P.I. than law enforcement officer.

"Wow, cool." He leaned across the counter toward her, his smile eager. "Can I help you with anything? I keep a close eye out all the time. I notice all kinds of stuff."

"Can you tell me who else has rented this bike lately," she asked, hopeful. "The one I was riding today."

"Sure. Some crazy chick with purple hair. She loaded it down with groceries and camping stuff from her car, then took off. I figured she'd be up there for weeks, considering all the provisions she took. But she came right back that afternoon."

"Which afternoon was that?"

Savannah couldn't help being hopeful. Maybe it was Vanessa, after all. She had to admit she would be relieved. She liked the colonel, Brian O'Donnell, and even Alan Logan. If it had to be someone . . . and it did . . . she hoped it was Vanessa, her least favorite.

"A gal with purple hair?" Savannah tried to sound surprised. "I guess you *would* notice something like that."

"It looked like she was trying to hide it under a baseball cap. But it was sticking out on the sides."

"What day, exactly, did she rent the bike?" Savannah was so excited, she could hardly feel the pain in her butt or the bruise on her thigh.

The kid hauled a stack of receipts in a binder out from under the counter. "Let's see now. It was about the fifth or the sixth. Yeah, here it is. It was the morning of the sixth."

"Oh." Her hopes fell. Suddenly, her injuries began to throb. "That was a week or so before the murder."

"I guess it doesn't have anything to do with it, then, huh?" he said, looking equally disappointed to have let her down.

"Is that the last time you rented it out?"

"I'm not sure. Let me take a look at these and . . ."

He thumbed through the pink sheets, then stopped, excited. "Wait a minute. Here's another one for that bike. It was rented on Thursday."

"This last Thursday?"

"Yeah. Hey! Wasn't that the day that guy got blown away?"

"Yes, it was. Can you tell me the name of the party you rented it to?"

"Sure." He consulted the ticket. "It was a guy named Charlie Delta."

"Charlie Delta?" Bells went off in Savannah's head. "Do you recall what this 'Mr. Delta' looked like?"

"Yeah, now that I think about it, I do. He was an older guy with gray hair. It was chopped off flat on top, one of those dumb-lookin' crew cuts, like the Beach Boys used to wear, you know, way back in . . ."

CHAPTER TWENTY-ONE

Savannah stood at Colonel Forrest Neilson's back door, her heart in her throat, and a slice of Gran's famous beef liver in her hand.

The colonel wasn't at home. Of that she was sure, because she had just seen him drive away in his Lincoln. But, unfortunately, he hadn't taken Beowulf along.

"It'll work, I tell you," her grandmother had said as Savannah had left home fifteen minutes ago with two pieces of dinner leftovers zipped into a plastic bag. "Dogs love it. Just stick it under his nose and he'll be yours forever . . . or at least until he finishes gobbling it down."

"That's a good Beowulf," Savannah told the dog as she presented her offering to him. "Come on, you handsome devil. Bite the liver, and not the leg."

With incisors bared and eyes gleaming, the dog took one step closer to her. The growl that issued from him sounded as though it were rumbling out of a deep cavern. With a nerve-jangling revelation, Savannah realized this was probably the most dangerous animal she had ever encountered . . . including that copperhead that she had nearly stepped on barefoot as a kid while picnicking beside the Mississippi River.

But just when she was sure the dog was going to chomp a plug out of her, his nostrils flared and began to twitch.

"Yeah . . . that's it. Smells great, doesn't it?"

Beowulf seemed to agree. Gingerly, he put out his tongue and licked the edge of the meat.

The long, fringed black tail began to wave from side to side. A good sign, Savannah thought with a modicum of relief. Maybe she would have the opportunity, like every other "normal" person, to die of a terminal illness, in an automobile crash, or of old age.

That was comforting. She wasn't sure they let you into heaven if you expired from being eaten by an Akita who seemed to think he was a mountain grizzly.

Once she was sure she had the dog's full attention, she dropped the meat onto the porch and took a tentative step closer to the door. As Gran had predicted, the liver ploy had worked, and Beowulf paid her no mind as she proceeded to try to pick the colonel's lock.

"Dang it," she muttered after the third attempt failed. Back in the olden days, when she had held a search warrant in one hand and her badge in the other, this sort of nonsense hadn't been necessary. It wasn't easy, being Jane Q. Citizen.

Click. She heard the tumbler move. "Bingo," she said, twisting the knob. The door slid open.

She ventured another quick glance at Beowulf, but he was in doggy-ecstasy, licking every molecule of liver from the cement with his long, red tongue.

Quickly, she slipped inside the house, making sure the door was securely closed behind her. She couldn't afford to have the dog follow her, because she only had one more piece of liver left, and that was to help her make her escape.

First, she tiptoed through the house, checking to be certain that no one else was about. In every room, she felt watched by the dozens of clock faces and wondered what the lord of the manor would say if he could see her now.

Best not to think of that at the moment, she told herself. She had always hated this part of the job. Even with a badge and a judge's authorization, she felt uncomfortable invading a person's home . . . if that person was someone she liked.

And, whether she wanted to admit it or not, whether he had murdered his former son-in-law or not, she did like the colonel. She couldn't help it. The man radiated a quiet grace, strength and confidence of a bygone era. He was a hero, straight out of central casting, and she was in awe of him, no matter what he had done.

Besides the fact that she was violating Neilson's privacy, she didn't relish going on a search when she wasn't sure what she was looking for.

A cursory glance into each room told her nothing, except that the colonel was obsessively neat in his housekeeping habits.

In the guest room closet, Savannah found a collection of

Barbie dolls and girls' clothing. But that was to be expected of a man who doted on his granddaughter.

"Christy, where are you, sweetie?" Savannah murmured as she touched one of the dolls, which had long red hair like its mistress. "Please be safe until we can find you."

With a heightened sense of urgency, Savannah hurried into the living room, where the colonel had served them refreshments before. She didn't have time to dawdle. For all she knew, he had just slipped out to the local market for a quart of milk and was already on his way back.

The last thing she needed right now was to spend time in the county jail for breaking and entering. No . . . that would make Captain Knothead Bloss far too happy.

Again, she was drawn to the medal, proudly displayed in its case. In all the years of dealing with the public, Savannah had never gotten over the dichotomy of the human spirit. It seemed even the best among us could commit the worst of sins.

Working her way around the room, she pulled out drawers, opened the closet, checked beneath furniture. But nothing seemed out of order.

As she approached the piano, she flashed back on her conversation with Dr. Liu over the body of Earl Mallock.

"Piano wire," Jennifer had said. "His wrists and ankles were bound with piano wire."

A buzz against her ribs made her jump. It was the cell phone in her jacket pocket . . . as though her nerves weren't tight enough as it was. If she'd been smart, she would have left the damned thing in the car or fed it to Beowulf along with the liver.

She pulled out the phone and flipped it open. "Yeah?" she said irritably.

"Oops, I'm sorry, Savannah. Are you busy?" Tammy said, her Long Island twang more pronounced than usual. She always reverted when under stress.

"A little."

"Where are you?"

"The colonel's. And let's just say . . . I didn't receive an engraved invitation to be here . . . if you know what I mean."

"You broke in?"

Savannah sighed. "Tammy, this is a cell phone, remember?"

"Oh, yeah. Sorry again."

Tucking the phone beneath her chin, Savannah began to set some of the pictures on top of the piano aside.

"Did you . . . ah . . . find anything yet?" Tammy asked.

"Nothing yet." Carefully, Savannah lifted the shining ebony lid of the baby grand. "Is there something I can do for you?"

"Not really. Why?"

"You called me. Remember?"

"Oh, right. Sorry. I just wanted you to know that Dirk is on his way over here. I told him I thought you'd be back by now. I guess I blew that, too."

Savannah scanned the row of glistening wires, precision spaced, stretched taut and, no doubt, perfectly tuned. "It's okay, Tammy. I should be there soon. Just tell him to hang on. Wait a minute. . . ."

One wire was missing.

High up in the treble range, a gap, like that of an absent

tooth, grinning at her. Savannah shivered with an awareness she didn't welcome.

"Shit," she whispered. "Not exactly what I was hoping for, Colonel."

"What?" Tammy sounded completely confused.

"Let's just say I may have found something. I've gotta go, and Tammy . . ."

"Yes?"

"You say you're sorry all the time. It's driving me around the bend."

"It is? Oh, I'm sor—"

"Stop it, or, every time you say it, I'm going to deduct a quarter from the generous salary that I'm not paying you. Understand?"

"Um . . . I think so."

"Good. See you soon."

Savannah shoved the phone back into her pocket and carefully replaced the photographs atop the piano, knowing that a neatnik like Neilson would notice if anything were out of place. She didn't want anyone, except Tammy and Dirk, to know she had ever been here. Unless she had found something, she hadn't intended to tell anyone.

Was this something? She wondered. It certainly wasn't incriminating evidence. There had to be plenty of pianos in the town of San Carmelita with missing wires. But it was definitely something.

At the front window, she glanced outside and saw that the street was still empty. But the creepy feeling was even stronger than before. Like a disease-carrying insect, it crawled up her back and around her neck, making her feel the need to go home and take a long, hot shower with lots of soap.

Murder always made her feel that way.

It wasn't natural. No matter who committed it or why, it violated the laws of God and man. And her basic instinct was to stay as far away from it as possible.

Not feasible, considering her chosen line of work.

Just as the eerie feeling began to crescendo, the house exploded in a cacophony of bells, chimes, buzzes, and cuckoos. It was 6:00 P.M. on the Pacific coast and in Colonel Forrest Neilson's house, there was no way to miss the event.

Savannah's pulse rate tripled and her knees felt like warm gelatin as she sagged against the windowsill and waited for the din to cease.

How could he stand living with this? she wondered, as the sounds went on and on. She and her two companions must have stayed less than fifteen minutes the other day, she decided. They must have just missed witnessing the phenomenon.

The ornately carved grandfather clock to her right was the loudest of all, tolling out the Westminster Chimes with bass notes that reverberated through her body.

She found herself humming the familiar tune, until it stopped, abruptly, in mid-chime.

Strange, she thought. In a house where everything appeared to work perfectly, this was an anomaly.

The clock had an open well, with no glass to shield the chains and etched brass weights. Two of the shining weights were barely visible, hanging in the space above the lower body of the clock. But the third one on the far right had dropped out of sight. The other chains were hanging straight, but the one to the third weight was loose, as though something were lifting it, rather than pulling it down.

More than any of the others in the house, this clock had to be the colonel's pride and joy. It was obviously older and more valuable than the rest. Savannah couldn't imagine him neglecting its service or allowing it to be in disrepair.

Kneeling in front of the clock, she lifted the shining brass latch and opened the lower casing.

Once she could see inside, she knew what had halted the downward progression of the weight. It was resting on a small, wooden case.

Instantly, she recognized the type of box, and her hopes for a happy solution to this puzzle fell, even as her investigator's excitement rose.

It was a gun case.

Carefully setting the box on the carpet, she opened the lid and looked inside.

Nestled in a sculpted bed of aged red velvet, was one of the most beautiful pistols she had ever seen. It was a chrome-plated, .45 caliber, four-inch-long reduced barrel, Colt Commander. A trophy gun, given to an officer by his men.

The engraving on the side confirmed her theory.

"TO CAPT. F.L. NEILSON WITH GRATITUDE AND DEVOTION,
FROM THE MEN OF FOXFIRE COMPANY."

"I knew I should throw it off the end of the pier," said a deep male voice behind her. Savannah jumped to her feet and whirled around to see the colonel standing in the kitchen door, watching her with a sad, sick look on his face. "I even drove down there at midnight to toss it in . . . but when it came right down to it, I just couldn't."

"I understand," Savannah said. "I don't think I could have either. It's a beautiful piece."

"It means more to me than that medal over there." He nodded toward the glass-topped wooden case. "The president who pinned that on me didn't even know who I was . . . what I was all about. But the soldiers who gave me that pistol, they knew me better than any human being ever has, including my own wife. They fought with me, side by side. You can't get closer than that."

For the first time since Savannah had met him, she thought he looked even older than his seventy years as he walked over to his easy chair and collapsed onto it.

"You might as well have a seat, Miss Reid," he said, waving a hand toward the sofa. "It appears you and I have a lot to talk about."

Savannah glanced down at the pistol. She hadn't taken it out of its box, and she had no idea if it was loaded or not.

But, loaded or empty she decided that, if she was going to sit on the sofa and have a chat with Colonel Forrest Neilson, it was a good idea to take his gun with her.

"Oh, Dirk. Come on in. I'm glad you're finally here," Tammy said as she ushered Dirk across the bougainvillea-covered porch and into the house.

Dirk was surprised, almost shocked. Since when was Tammy Hart happy to see *him*?

Her face was a bit red; maybe she had gotten too much sun.

"I'm really starting to worry about Savannah," she said, gripping his arm.

"I'll tell you right now, that's a full-time job with no benefits. Believe me, I've done it for years. Don't even get started."

"I talked to her about forty-five minutes ago on the phone, and she was at Colonel Neilson's home."

"What's she doing there?"

"Snooping, I think. She said she didn't have an invitation."

"Yeap, that's what she calls it, all right. She broke into a colonel's house . . . a friend of the chief of police. I swear, I—"

"Dirk, she told me she had found something, but she didn't say what. And she said she was coming home soon. Where is she?"

"Knowing Savannah, there's no way to tell. But she's the only woman I've ever known who can wind up in hot water and deep shit at the same time."

Tammy wrinkled her pert nose and pursed her lips as though she had just sucked on a sour lemon. "Oooo, that's gross. Must you be so crude, Detective Coulter?"

Dirk chuckled. Other than the fact that they had no idea what sort of trouble Savannah had gotten herself into, or what he would have to do to get her out, things were back to normal.

"Where is your granddaughter, Colonel?" Savannah asked.

"Safe. That's all I'm going to tell you right now," he replied.

"Did she see you kill her father?"

"No, of course not. What kind of a man do you take me for? I waited outside until she had left the shack to relieve herself in the woods. That's when I did it. She never even saw the body."

The two sat in relative silence for a while, listening to the ticking of the clocks. Savannah watched while he stroked Beowulf's ear and scratched the animal's neck as it leaned against his leg. The dog didn't seem at all aware of the turmoil his master was feeling.

"When I decided to kill Earl," Neilson continued, "I told myself that I wouldn't care if I got caught. It was something I had to do, no matter what the cost.

"But now," he continued, "now that I've been exposed, so to speak, I find that it matters very much. Miss Reid, I'm an old man. I don't want to spend my few remaining years in prison."

"Perhaps you should have thought of that before . . ." Savannah didn't like the self-righteous tone of her own voice. While she might be morally right, who was she to judge this man?

"Do you think I didn't? I thought about it long and hard. But like I said, it didn't seem to matter at the time. He killed my little girl, Miss Reid. She may have been a woman, a stranger to you. But she was my Lisa. That bastard tortured her. Before he died he told me that he was trying to get her to admit that she had committed adultery. But Lisa was a good woman, a decent person. She never . . . but he . . ."

His voice broke and tears flooded his eyes. Savannah had the decency to look away.

"I know what he did," she said. "And I believe I know—at least in part—why you did what you did, too."

"You can't know it all . . . the guilt, the self-condemnation, the regrets. When they wanted to prosecute him, years ago, during the war, it was because they knew what kind of an animal he was. He mistreated his prisoners, just like he did Lisa. But I helped to get him off. I had to, he was my soldier. That's why I had to be the one to execute him. I had to be the tribunal and the firing squad. He was my responsibility. I had to take care of it the only way I could."

Savannah had to ask to satisfy her curiosity. "I was wondering, sir, about the piano wire bindings."

"I wanted to mislead you and the police into thinking it was the same killer. I couldn't find out what kind of wire he had used on Lisa, but in Vietnam he had used piano on the prisoners. So, I thought it was a good bet. Besides, I thought it was ironic justice somehow for him to be discovered in such a demeaning position, the same as he had inflicted on Lisa and those POWs."

"But you bound him *after* he was dead?"

"Of course I did. I'm not a cruel person, Miss Reid. I'm not a monster, like he was."

Savannah quietly digested that information for a moment, deciding that it had the ring of truth. Then she drew a deep breath and continued. "Colonel, I can't even imagine the pain you've been through, losing your daughter in such a terrible way. And I won't presume to understand all of your motives and actions. But Earl Mallock wasn't your soldier anymore. We have laws, and we have peace officers to enforce them. Whatever your reasons, what you did was premeditated murder."

"You call it what you want. I call it justice."

"It doesn't matter what you or I call it. It's up to the courts now."

"So, you're going to arrest me?"

For once, Savannah was almost relieved not to have that

badge hanging on its chain around her neck. "I'm not a cop any-more, Colonel," she replied. "Thankfully, it isn't my duty to ar-rest you."

"But you're a conscientious, law-abiding citizen, Miss Reid. Just as I was until a few days ago. Do you feel it's your duty to turn me in?"

She sat, quietly studying him, searching her own heart. The colonel didn't look like a war hero. He looked like a tired old man with an ashen face and beads of sweat shining on his wrin-kled forehead.

But then, one never knew for sure what was going on in-side another human being, Savannah reminded herself.

"Are you going to try to stop me?" she asked him. If they were laying their cards on the table, they might as well see the entire deck.

"Do you mean, would I try to kill you, too, rather than let you turn me over to the authorities?" He shook his head. "No, Miss Reid. I've killed for my country. I killed for my daughter. But I won't commit murder or any other crime to keep from suf-fering the consequences of my own actions. If that's what you feel you have to do, I won't try to stop you."

Savannah looked into those ice blue eyes, and realized they weren't as cold as she had once thought . . . as she wished they were.

Under the circumstances, she didn't want to like, admire, or respect this man. It clouded her judgment, made it difficult to be objective.

Was it her duty to turn him in? Of course it was. He was a killer, plain and simple.

But it wasn't so plain. And it certainly wasn't simple.

Either way, Savannah had to make up her mind. Because, from where she sat, she could see out the front window, and a very determined-looking Dirk was coming up the walk.

CHAPTER TWENTY-TWO

Dirk wasn't overly concerned as he strolled up the sidewalk toward the colonel's front door. So what if Savannah was a little overdue? What else was new?

It wasn't until he heard her yelling that he kicked into high gear.

"Dirk! Dirk, Dir-r-r-rk!" She sounded serious. Very serious.

He bolted to the door and tried the knob. Of course, it was locked. Dirk always expected the worst, because that's what he usually got.

"Dirk!"

She had gone from serious to desperate.

A hundred images flashed across his mind. Most of them having to do with her struggling with a seventy-year-old man.

And, judging from the sound of her voice . . . losing. With her black belt in karate, it didn't seem likely, but . . .

He mentally cringed, waiting for the sound of a gunshot.

"Savannah! Savannah! What the hell's goin' on in there?" He tried to force the door, but it was one of those big, solid, reinforced types. And his lineman's shoulder had seen better days, better years.

"Get in here!" she yelled, sounding breathless. "Back door!"

He sprinted around the side of the house, slipping on some freshly dug dirt in a flower bed. His knee wrenched. Pain shot up to his hip, but he only barely noticed.

He grabbed the back doorknob, twisted and threw it open with so much force that it bounced off the wall and hit him squarely on the forehead.

Even through his own groans of pain, he could hear the dog barking and Savannah panting as she struggled.

"In here!" she cried between strangled gasps.

He ran into the living room, then nearly skidded to a stop, trying to figure out what his eyes were seeing.

The colonel lay sprawled in the middle of the floor on his back. Savannah was kneeling beside him. It looked like she was beating the living crap out of him. There were no weapons in sight, except for a pistol in a fancy box, lying several feet away beside the sofa.

"Don't just stand there!" she shouted. "Help me!"

"Looks to me like you've got everything under control," he said dryly. "You're the one on top."

Now that he could see she was all right, he was relieved and a little pissed for all the effort he had gone through. Besides, his knee was starting to throb.

"Damn it, Dirk. He had a heart attack. Make yourself useful and call an ambulance. Then help me with the CPR, before I have one myself."

Suddenly, everything made sense, and Dirk felt like a fool.

Oh, well, it wasn't the first time, he thought as he yanked his cell phone out of his pocket and punched out 911. And knowing him, it certainly wouldn't be the last.

"Is he going to make it?" Savannah asked the army hospital doctor who looked too young to be anyone's physician.

Funny, the older she got, the younger they seemed to be making doctors, lawyers, and politicians. The kids were running the world these days.

"Are you friends or family?" he asked, holding his clipboard tightly to his chest beneath crossed arms.

Savannah looked at Dirk, who was standing next to her in the hall outside of the Intensive Care Unit, looking as impatient as she felt. She saw him start to reach for his badge, and she grabbed his hand.

"Friends. *Close* friends . . ." she said, ". . . of the family."

Dr. Kid didn't appear to completely believe her, but he looked bored and eager to be finished with this interview. "Your friend is stable," he said. "That's about all I can tell you right now until we get the results of some tests. From my preliminary examination, I'd say it was a fairly serious heart attack. While we don't know what damage was done, I would caution you to prepare yourself."

She gulped. "For what?"

"Is he gonna croak or not?" Dirk wasn't one to mince words.

And he had never minded alienating people. In fact, he seemed to take a morbid pride in his talent to do so.

Dr. Kid lifted his chin until he was staring down his nose at Dirk—not an easy feat, as Dirk was at least four inches taller. "Yes, he's going to 'croak'," the doctor replied without the candy coating or further explanation.

"*Sooner* or *later?*" Savannah asked, trying to sound sweet, but it came out saccharine.

"Yes," was the reply.

"Thank you so much, Doctor." She reached for his hand and gave it her firmest shake . . . the one that was guaranteed to make the recipient wince. He did. "I just can't tell you how helpful you've been."

Dropping his hand as though it had something distasteful smeared on it, she turned and strode down the hall. Dirk quickly caught up.

"Yeah, he's helpful, all right," she muttered. "About as helpful as a pissant in an outhouse."

As they left the building and headed across the parking lot to the Buick, Dirk stopped and grabbed Savannah by the elbow.

"Hold on, Van," he said. "Now that the dust has settled, I gotta ask you. What happened there at the colonel's house today?"

"What happened?"

"That's what I said. And don't stall by repeating my own question back to me. That's *my* trick."

"It's every man's trick . . . and you didn't invent it. Men always act like they're the first to come up with something."

"Oh, yeah? Well . . . women always change the subject."

"We do not."

"So, what happened at the colonel's?"

To his surprise, her blue eyes filled with tears and her lower lip began to tremble.

She was going to cry. *Savannah* was going to cry right there in front of him. She had done it before, but it was a rare occurrence . . . and it made him feel completely miserable, helpless, and inept.

"Can I . . . ?" She choked, then tried again. "Dirk, can I please get back to you on that? I've got some thinking to do."

Right there, right in the middle of the hospital parking lot, in front of God and anybody else who wanted to watch if they were nosy . . . Dirk put his arms around his former partner and pulled her to his chest. Gratefully, she snuggled in and buried her face against the front of his shirt.

"Sure, kiddo, take all the time you need." He pressed a quick kiss to the top of her dark, glossy hair and thought for a moment how nice it smelled. "Just as long as you spill your guts to me by . . . oh, say . . . tomorrow morning."

Savannah sat in her floral chintz easy chair, Diamante on her lap, Cleo curled around her feet, a piece of half-eaten chocolate cheesecake on the table beside her. Raspberry liqueur sauce dripped tantalizingly down the sides, and onto the cut crystal plate, but—for the first time in the history of the world, or at least as long as Savannah could remember—she wasn't interested in food.

She gave the dessert another sideways glance. Nope, not even a niggle of appetite.

Not a good sign, she thought. Any situation that couldn't

be vastly improved by a piece of cheesecake had to be a tough one, indeed. She must be more worried and upset than she had thought.

Across the dimly lit living room, the time glowed in green numbers on the VCR. It was ten past four in the morning and she hadn't slept all night.

You're gonna feel like shit tomorrow, she told herself.

It's already tomorrow, came the sarcastic reply.

See, I told you so. She had to have the last word in an argument, even if it was with herself.

The slow creak of an upstairs door and the soft steps on the staircase told her that Gran was sleeping about as soundly as she was. Or *wasn't* . . . as the case might be.

A moment later, she saw her grandmother's feet, the hem of her robe, and then the lady herself as she descended the stairs.

For half a second Savannah felt guilty, afraid she had awakened the older woman, who probably needed her sleep. But the guilt quickly faded to relief at not being alone with her problem.

"What's the matter, Chicken Little?" Gran asked as she sat on the end of the sofa nearest Savannah and pulled her feet up, tucking them beneath her. "Is the sky falling?"

"Not yet. I'm deciding whether to pull it down or leave it there."

"Pull it down onto your own head?"

"On someone else's."

Gran nodded sagely. "Mmmm . . . making a decision that's going to affect another person . . . that's always a hard one."

"Especially if you happen to like that person, and if your decision is going to have a major impact on his life."

Reaching for the uneaten cheesecake, Gran said, "You were a police officer for years, Savannah. I would have thought you'd made hundreds of decisions like that."

"I suppose I did. But usually, the choice had to be made in a matter of minutes, sometimes only seconds. I didn't have time to think it through. I just acted on instinct."

"Maybe that's what you should do now. Listen to your heart, Savannah."

"It isn't talking."

"It's always talking. If you can't hear it, it's because you aren't listening."

Savannah sighed, leaned her head back on the chair, and closed her eyes. "I'm just so afraid that I'll make the wrong decision and it'll turn out badly."

"From where you stand now, you can't foresee the future. You can't possibly know if it will turn out well or not. But even if it all goes to hell in a handbasket, that doesn't mean you made the wrong decision."

Savannah opened her eyes and studied the dear old face, loving every line. "What do you mean?"

"People are always judging their decisions by the outcome, and that's just plain foolish. There have been lots of decisions made in this world that have caused a heap of human suffering and misery. But that doesn't mean they weren't the right choice to make at the time."

Savannah thought that one over, while stroking Diamante's satiny head. "So, if you don't base your decision on what you believe the outcome will be . . . what's the deciding factor."

"You go with what you feel is the morally right thing to do."

"What if you're a bit fuzzy about that?"

"You do the best you can and, as long as your heart is being as honest as it can, you trust that the Almighty will take up the slack. It's all any of us can do."

Savannah thought of Earl Mallock, lying on the floor of that tin shed, a bullet through his brain. "But Gran," she said, "I know someone who did exactly what you're saying. He made a decision which he thought was morally upright, but he was wrong. It can't be a moral act to take another human being's life . . . except as an act of self-defense or in defense of society."

"I agree with you. But the person you're speaking of . . . whoever this individual might be," she added with a sly smile, ". . . didn't agree. If he's a man of honor, he did what he felt he had to do, and he'll understand that you've gotta do the same."

Savannah felt a sinking sensation in her stomach, as though her half a piece of cheesecake had been made of rocks instead of chocolate.

"I don't like it, Gran," she said. "Not at all."

Granny Reid buried the fork in the decadent confection and scooped up a generous bite of cake and raspberry sauce. "Yeah . . . well . . . what's 'liking' got to do with the price of tea in China?"

It wasn't even six o'clock in the morning when Savannah knocked on Dirk's trailer door. He took a long time to answer, as she had expected he would. Along with a love of food and nabbing criminals, she and Dirk shared another common bond: Neither one was a morning person.

"What the hell?" he asked as he cracked the door and stuck his head out. "Oh, it's you."

"Lovely to see you, too," she replied.

"What time is it?"

She looked up at the sky which was only just beginning to streak with the first rays of sunlight. "Dawn-thirty. Rise and shine, big boy."

"I'm risen, but there's no way I'm gonna shine, for you or anybody, this early."

He stepped back and threw the door open, waving her inside.

She wasn't surprised to see he was wearing only his boxers and an undershirt. Modesty wasn't high on Dirk's list of virtues, and he had told her once that he considered robes an extravagance and pajamas sissy.

"I need coffee," she said, plopping down on his sofa.

"And I need three more hours of sleep. Looks like we're both outta luck."

He sat down beside her, ran his fingers through his hair, and rubbed his eyes. "Sorry, I haven't had a chance to get to a market. Want some water?"

"Bottled?"

"Tap."

"No, thanks. I don't have any of Ryan's iodine tablets on me."

He leaned back and draped his arm casually across the top of the sofa. His expression wasn't casual. "Okay, spit it out. You didn't come over here at this hour for coffee. You've got a cupboard full of that gourmet shit in your own kitchen."

She took a big breath. "It's about the colonel."

He nodded. "I thought it might be."

CHAPTER TWENTY-THREE

"Earl Mallock murdered Lisa, just like we thought," Savannah told Dirk, who had pulled on a pair of jeans in honor of the occasion. "And Colonel Neilson killed him . . . 'executed' him, is the way he put it."

Dirk leaned forward on the sofa, acutely interested. "He actually confessed to you?"

"Yes, there in his house, just before he had the heart attack."

He nodded thoughtfully. "A confession. Now *that's* something I didn't have."

"What do you mean? You didn't know it was the colonel!"

"I did after I had the lab run an overnight ballistics check on that Colt .45 of his. It matches the bullet that killed Mallock. I wonder why he didn't get rid of it?"

"He said he took it out to the end of the pier and was going to toss it. But he couldn't."

"Understandable."

They sat quietly for a moment, and Savannah's ire began to rise. "Okay . . . so you've got the gun, but you don't know about the piano wire, smart aleck."

"The one missing from Neilson's baby grand? Oh, yeah. Been there, done that. You aren't the only decent detective around here, you know."

"Well! Well . . . I . . ." she sputtered. "I was there first! I was the one who found the damned gun for you. And it wasn't easy, either; he had hidden it in the big grandfather clock."

"Would've been the first place I'd have looked."

"Bullshit!"

"Bull, true."

She sat, glaring at him, breathing hard, nostrils flared. "You know, Coulter," she said in a deadly quiet tone, "I've never really liked you. Not even a little bit. I want you to know that."

He smirked. "Can't say as I'm all that crazy about you, either. Though you are kinda cute when you're pissed."

"I am not!"

"Cute?"

"Pissed. I don't have anything to be pissed about, except you trying to take credit for my work. I broke this case and you know it. If it hadn't been for me, you'd still be harassing poor Brian O'Donnell."

Dirk sobered. "Oh, yeah . . . I've gotta apologize to that guy. I was pretty hard on him."

Savannah reached for a ratty blanket that had been tossed on the end of the sofa and draped it around her shoulders. Suddenly, she felt chilled.

"What are we going to do about Colonel Neilson?" she asked.

"He committed a murder."

"I know. But that doesn't answer my question."

"Doesn't it?"

"You're going to arrest him." It was more of a statement than a question. She knew Dirk all too well. Why had she even asked?

Dirk sighed. "The hospital called about two hours ago. He'd just had another heart attack. He slipped into a coma. They don't think he's going to come out of it."

Savannah imagined the colonel, lying helpless on his white hospital bed, and she thought of how unfair it was that people were housed in such vulnerable machinery as the human body.

"If he does come out of it?" she asked.

Dirk stared at his thumbnail. "I'll arrest him. I'll have to, Van."

"And if he doesn't? Dirk, his reputation, his grand-daughter . . ."

Dirk rose and walked over to his kitchen sink. Opening the cupboard below, he squatted and pulled out the colonel's small gun case. "If he doesn't, I guess you and I will take a romantic moonlight stroll on the pier, kiddo."

She smiled at him. Loved him. For the compassion and the goodness he tried so hard to hide. "It's a date."

As Savannah drove down her street toward home, Dirk sitting next to her, she said, "I wonder what our surprise is. Tammy sounded excited."

"I don't think my system can take many more surprises this week," Dirk growled.

"She sounded happy."

"She sounded ditsy. With her, it's hard to tell the difference."

Approaching her house, she saw a classic, silver-gray Bentley parked in her driveway. "Hey! Ryan's here, and maybe Gibson. They must be part of the surprise."

"Oh, thrill," he drawled. "I'm getting terribly excited. I think I'm having a hot flash," he added with an obnoxious lisp.

"You know, Coulter, I really wish you would try to be a little more tolerant," she said. "And a whole lot kinder."

"Yeah, yeah. I'm working on it."

"Work harder."

They parked, got out of the car, and by the time they were halfway up the walk, Tammy had thrown the front door open and was dancing a little jig on the porch.

"You're here, you're here," she said with giggles interspersed.

"You're a ditz, you're a ditz," Dirk muttered under his breath. But Savannah heard and gave him the usual jab in the ribs with her elbow. "If you don't stop doing that, I'm going to start wearing a gougeproof vest."

"What's up, sugar?" Savannah asked as she bounded up onto the steps.

"Just come inside."

When Savannah entered the living room, she found Ryan

and John sitting on the sofa, wearing smiles as broad as Tammy's.

"Good morning, Savannah," John Gibson said as he rose to kiss her hand. "Detective Coulter." He gave a curt nod in Dirk's direction. Dirk responded with a grunt.

"Apparently it is a good morning," Savannah replied. "Does someone want to tell us why?"

"Ryan and John just got here about half an hour ago, and I called you right away," Tammy said breathlessly. "You see, I had a feeling the colonel might have been the one who murdered Earl. And after I talked to your grandmother early this morning—I called to talk to you, but she said you were already up and out—she and I were both sure it was the colonel and—"

"Tell-a-Gran," Savannah muttered. Gran was sweet, she thought, but discretion was not her most prominent virtue.

"I beg your pardon?"

"Never mind. Go on."

"So," Tammy continued, "I kicked into high gear and did some serious research there at home with my computer and modem. When I found what I was looking for, I called Ryan and John and they took it from there."

She grabbed Savannah's hand and led her through the living room, into the kitchen, and over to the back door. Dirk followed as quickly as he could without appearing to be overtly interested.

"Look at what they brought for us." Tammy pointed through the window in the back door.

Savannah stared through the glass, blinked, and looked again. But it wasn't easy to see, because the tears were already beginning to well.

There, sitting at her small picnic table beneath the grape arbor was Granny Reid. Dressed in a caftan that was sprinkled with tiny daisies, a handmade wreath of daisies from Savannah's country garden in her hair, she wore a happy, contented smile that made her look at least a generation younger.

She was sharing a pitcher of lemonade with Christy Mallock, who wore a similar daisy ring around her red curls. One of Savannah's J.C. Penney catalogs was open on the table before them, and each held a pair of scissors. They were "cutting out paper dolls," an activity that brought back a flood of fond memories for Savannah.

For a moment, Savannah couldn't move, couldn't speak, couldn't even breathe. Then she whirled around and grabbed Tammy about the waist, lifting her off the ground.

"Thank you, thank you," she said between sobs.

Then she turned to Dirk and did the same thing . . . except for the lifting part. She tried, but he was much larger and made of denser stuff than Tammy.

Ryan and John had followed them into the kitchen. They were hugged and profusely thanked next.

Even Dirk had moist eyes as he grabbed Ryan's hand, then John's and gave them hearty shakes.

"Where the heck did you find her?" he asked, too relieved to care that he had been beaten to the punch.

"An old army buddy of the colonel's. A lieutenant colonel who feels he owes Neilson his life."

"How did you talk him into giving her to you?" Savannah asked.

Ryan winked at her. "We quietly suggested that if he did, he might not get into trouble for hiding her all this time. With the colonel in the hospital, he felt it was the best thing to do."

"Another thing," John added, "we promised we would deliver her safely into the arms of her Uncle Brian."

"Brian, oh, yes," Savannah brightened at the thought. Good news to tell him, at last! "Someone needs to let him know what's happened."

"He's on his way over," Tammy said proudly. "But we thought you should be the one to tell him."

Less than twenty minutes later, Savannah had the deeply satisfying pleasure of introducing Christy "The Snow Fairy Queen" Mallock to her Uncle Brian.

If Brian O'Donnell had seemed the least bit remote or unemotional before, Savannah decided that it had all been an exercise in self-control as he folded his niece into his arms and kissed her cheek.

For a child who had been through such a horrible ordeal, Christy seemed remarkably open to him.

"Are you really my mommy's big brother?" she asked as they sat down next to each other on the picnic bench.

The adults gathered around, feeling like intruders on this tender occasion, but unable to pull themselves away.

"I sure am," he said. "That's why we all have red hair and brown eyes . . . and lots of freckles."

"Mommy says they're angel kisses."

Brian cast a quick look at Savannah, who felt her heart catch.

"Then that's what they are," he replied, his own voice husky.

"My mommy's dead," Christy said with childlike candor. "Daddy killed her, just like he said he would."

"Did you see that happen, sweetheart?" Brian was sliding easily into the role of father; Savannah could tell by the way he held his niece and the gentleness of his caress as he smoothed her hair back from her face.

They all waited tensely for the girl's reply.

"No, he did it in the other room. But I heard the gun go off. It was really loud. And I knew what he did."

"I'm so sorry you had to go through that, honey." Brian kissed her forehead.

"Then my daddy took me into the woods to this little bitty house. And I thought he was going to hurt me, too, because he got mad and said I looked just like my mommy."

Savannah had a quick, terrifying vision of what might have happened if Colonel Neilson *hadn't* decided to take care of "his soldier" on his own. It didn't bear speculation.

"But my grandpa saved me. He hurt my dad before he could hurt me. I think my daddy's dead, too, but I'm not sure."

She waited, obviously expecting an answer.

"That's true, Christy," Uncle Brian said. "I won't ever lie to you. He's dead."

She nodded matter-of-factly. "That's probably good. But my grandpa's in the hospital."

"I know. We're all praying he gets well."

"Me, too. But that lady said I can't live with him all the time, cause he has to take care of himself and Beowulf." She nodded to Gran. "She said I might get to live close to Disney World."

Brian laughed and reached into his hip pocket, pulling out

his wallet. "You sure are. Only a few miles from Disney World. And you're going to live with her . . ." He opened the wallet and showed the girl a picture. "She's my wife, your aunt. And these are my three sons."

"*Three* boys!" Her mouth fell open and her amber eyes widened. "I always wanted a brother or a sister, but *three* of them? And they're all boys!"

"They all have red hair. Just like you."

"And freckles?"

"Between us all, we probably have a million, billion freckles."

Christy laughed. "Our family will look like *One Hundred and One Dalmations!*"

"Our family."

Savannah played the term over and over in her mind for the rest of the day and night, even after she had gone to bed. Having heard those words come from Christy's lips, she knew she could sleep, trusting that the child would be okay in the end.

Later that night, about ten o'clock, Brian's wife had flown in from Orlando to accompany Christy and Brian on their trip to Florida.

Having met her, Savannah knew that—although she would never take Lisa's place in Christy's heart—Mrs. O'Donnell would be a loving and devoted mother to the child.

"Are you still awake?" Gran asked, sticking her head into Savannah's bedroom. She was wearing a purple satin robe with a lace shawl collar. A daisy was still stuck behind her ear. She had never looked more beautiful to Savannah.

"Yep, still awake," Savannah replied.

"I just wanted to pop in and remind you . . . in case you'd forgotten."

Savannah grinned. "I hadn't forgotten, Gran. Really. I'm looking forward to it as much as you are."

"Bright and early?"

Savannah looked doubtful. "How bright? How early?"

"Dawn-thirty."

"Al-l-l-l right. Dawn-thirty."

Gran literally shivered with excitement and danced a little jig. "Good night," she said. "Sleep tight."

"And don't let the bed bugs bite," Savannah added, finishing off the litany.

As she cuddled into her pillows, she heard her grandmother strolling back to the guest room, singing, clear and strong:

"M—I—C. . . . See you real soon.

"K—E—Y. . . . Why? Because we *like* you!

"M—O—U—S—E   E   E   E   E!"

Please turn the page for
an exciting sneak peek of
G. A. McKevett's
newest Savannah Reid mystery
SUGAR AND SPITE
on sale now
wherever hardcover mysteries are sold!

CHAPTER ONE

"I don't quite understand this," Tammy Hart said as she watched Savannah add three eggs to the skillet and several slices of bread to the toaster. "*You* help *him* nab the bad guy and *he* rewards *you* by letting you fix him breakfast?"

The "him" she was referring to was sitting at Savannah's kitchen table, a satisfied smile under his nose. Dirk was always happy when food was imminent. Especially if that food was free. And in keeping with her Southern heritage of hospitality, Savannah made sure that everyone in her presence was stuffed like her Granny Reid's Christmas turkey. Heaven forbid anyone should feel a pang of hunger. It wasn't to be tolerated.

"So I'm a sap for a pretty face," Savannah said.

"And what does that have to do with Dirk?" Tammy shot a contemptuous look toward the table and its occupant, who was still dressed like a street bum.

Savannah chuckled and took a sip of the hot chocolate she had poured for herself . . . laced with Baileys . . . topped with whipped cream and chocolate shavings. Savannah suffered few hunger pangs herself, as was evidenced by her ample figure.

Tammy, on the other hand, was svelte, golden tanned, golden blond, the quintessential California surfer beach beauty.

Savannah loved her. Anyway.

So the kid was scrawny and ate mostly mineral water, rice cakes, and celery sticks; everyone had their faults.

Savannah retrieved several jars of homemade jams and preserves from the refrigerator and shoved them into Tammy's hands. "Put these on the table," she told her.

The younger woman took the jars and looked at the labels disapprovingly. "Gran's blackberry jam . . . probably full of sugar."

"I'm fresh out of sea-kelp spread," Savannah muttered under her breath, and swigged the hot chocolate.

Tammy sashayed over to the table and plunked the jars in front of Dirk, who gave her a cocky smirk. "Now I have to cook for him, too?" she complained. "It's bad enough that you're his slave, but now I have to—"

"Oh, stop . . . enough already." Savannah snapped her on her teeny-weeny; blue jean-covered rear with a dishtowel. "I'm not Dirk's slave, but you *are* my assistant, so assist. Butter that toast."

"With real butter?"

Savannah sighed. "Yes. Cholesterol-ridden, fat-riddled butter. I'm fresh out of tofu."

"I'll go shopping for you."

"No, thanks."

"Why are you having breakfast at four o'clock in the afternoon, anyway?" Tammy dipped only the tip of the knife into the butter and made a production of spreading the one-eighth of a teaspoon over the slice of bread.

"Because we didn't eat this morning," Dirk replied, watching the meal's progression with the acute attention of a practiced glutton. "We were working, remember?"

"Spraying the genitalia of youthful offenders," Tammy said with a giggle. "That's work?"

"Savannah did that all by herself. Thank God, or I'd be up on charges. You shoulda heard that guy screeching when they were scrubbing him down in the emergency room."

He and Savannah snickered. Tammy shook her head, pretending to be appalled.

"There are advantages to going freelance," Savannah said as she dished the eggs, some link sausages, and thick-sliced bacon onto the plate, then ladled a generous portion of cream gravy beside a scoop of grits. Where she came from, grits might be optional but gravy was considered a beverage.

Dirk's eyes glistened with the light of hedonism as he picked up his fork. "Van, you've outdone yourself. This looks great."

"Yeah," Tammy said as she sat down to a bowl of long-grain rice across the table from him. "She's good at CPR, too. And if that doesn't work, I'm pretty good at angioplasty." She hefted her knife and punctuated her statement with a skewering motion.

Savannah was reaching into the cupboard for a box of marzipan Danish rolls for herself, when she heard a buzzing coming from Dirk's leather coat, which was draped across one of her dining chairs.

"I see you've got it set on VIBRATE again," she said, digging through his pockets and handing him the phone. "Your love life in a slump?"

"Eh . . . bite me." He flipped it open and punched a button. "Coulter here."

"He's sure grumpy when somebody gets between him and his dog dish," Tammy whispered to Savannah. "Reminds me of a pit bull I knew."

Savannah didn't reply. She was watching the play of emotions over Dirk's craggy face: irritation, fading to surprise, softening to . . . she wasn't sure what, but she was fairly certain the party on the other end was female.

"Ah, yeah . . . hi," he was saying. He turned in his chair, his side to her and Tammy. His voice volume dropped a couple of notches. "I'm . . . ah . . . here at Savannah's. No, not like that. We were working together this morning. No, really."

Savannah didn't like the sound of that. Why, she wasn't sure. She and Dirk weren't anything "like that," but she didn't like to hear him saying so . . . so clearly . . . to another woman.

Another woman? *Where did that thought come from?* she wondered. *To hell with that,* she quickly added to her mental argument. *Who is he talking to?*

"Yeah, I was going back home right after . . ." He looked wistfully down at the plate of goodies on the table in front of him. "Actually, I was leaving right now if you want to. . . . Yeah, that's good. Sure. See ya."

He flipped the phone closed and rose from his chair. The look on his face reminded Savannah of a sheep after an embarrassingly bad shearing. "I . . . ah . . . gotta go," he said. "Sorry about the"—he pointed to the food—"ah, breakfast. But I really should—"

"No problem," Savannah said as she snatched the plate out from under him and carried it over to the cabinet. "If you gotta go, you gotta go. Obviously it's an important meeting."

"Ah, yeah, it is . . . kinda." He slipped on his jacket and fished for his keys. "I'll see ya later, okay?"

Savannah nodded curtly.

He grunted a good-bye in Tammy's direction, then headed toward the front of the house.

"Don't let the door slap your backside on your way out," Savannah called after him.

Another grunt. The sound of the door slamming.

"Well," Tammy said, recovering from her shock. "I never thought I'd see the day that Dirk Coulter would walk away from a free meal . . . especially one *you* cooked," she told Savannah.

From the kitchen window, Savannah watched his battered old Buick Skylark as it pulled out of her driveway. He was practically spinning gravel.

"Hmm," she said thoughtfully as she took his heavily laden plate from the cabinet and carried it back to the table. She sat down, picked up his fork, and dug in.

"That's all you've got to say?" Tammy asked her. "Hmmm. That's it?"

"I'm thinking."

"And eating." Tammy watched disapprovingly as Savannah shoveled in a mouthful of grits, dripping with butter.

"I think best when I eat."

"That explains your mental prowess," Tammy mumbled.

"Shut up. I've almost got it."

"Got what?"

"The plan of action."

"You've gotta know, huh?"

Savannah snorted. "Only if I intend to sleep tonight." She downed a few more bites, then jumped up from her chair. "Be back later," she said as she snatched her cell phone off its charger base.

"What's the story?"

"He forgot his phone."

"That's *your* phone."

She shrugged. "We bought them at the same time. They look so much alike. It's an honest mistake."

"Going out there is a mistake," Tammy grumbled as she followed her to the front door. "There's nothing honest about it."

"I don't recall asking for your editorial comments. Go on the Internet while I'm gone. See if you can drum up some business for me so that I can continue to pay you that high, minimum-wage salary you've grown accustomed to."

Tammy sputtered, stood between her and the door, then moved aside with a sigh of resignation. "That's it? The phone story? It's a bit thin."

Savannah grinned and tossed her purse strap over her shoulder. "Yeah, well . . . Dirk's a bit thick. It'll work."

CHAPTER TWO

As Savannah pulled her 1965 Camaro into Dirk's trailer park, she grimaced at the cloud of dust that was settling on her new red paint. There was a nice mobile-home park down by the beach, but Dirk was far too tight to spring for that. He had parked his ten-foot-wide in the Shady Vale Trailer Park fifteen years ago, and once Dirk was parked anywhere, he tended to stay until he rusted.

Shady Vale was inappropriately named. Flat as a flitter, without a tree in sight, the property's picturesque description must have been a figment of some developer's imagination.

Dirk's neighbors were mostly transient, and more than once he had been forced to arrest one of his Shady Vale-ites for everything from armed bank robbery to blowing up half the park while cooking up a nice batch of methamphetamines in one of the trailer's kitchens.

The only residents who had been at Shady Vale longer than Dirk were the Biddles. They were a cantankerous, nosy old couple who watched the comings and goings of everyone in the park, as though they owned the dusty gravel road themselves. From their #1 spot at the entrance, they saw every arrival and had an opinion as to whether that person had legitimate business in Shady Vale.

Their trailer was right next to Dirk's, which was parked in spot #2, and Savannah was hoping she could avoid her usual argument with Mr. Biddle or an interrogation from Mrs. Biddle. If luck were on her side, she might be able to recognize Dirk's mystery visitor's vehicle and find out who his guest was without having to use that ridiculous cell-phone ruse.

But the new silver Lexus parked beside his Buick didn't ring any bells. Since when did Dirk have a girlfriend . . . let alone one that could afford to drive a new Lexus?

Looks plumb out of place in this neck of the woods, Savannah thought as she slowed down to see if the car had vanity plates. But the series of random letters and numbers told her nothing.

She saw Harry Biddle sitting in his broken-down lawn chair, swigging a beer, scratching the roll of hairy belly that was protruding from beneath his gray undershirt. As she drove by he watched her with a lascivious gleam in his eye that made her want to crawl out of the car and slap him goofy. Half a slap would probably do the job.

Feeling like an adolescent whose curiosity was about to

land her in trouble, Savannah parked her Camaro behind the Lexus and got out. Harry perked up when he saw her walking in his direction, until she turned toward Dirk's trailer.

"Wouldn't go in there right now," he said, his ugly, snaggled grin widening.

"Yeah, why not?" she asked, knowing she wasn't going to like the answer.

"Let's just say, he's already got hisself some company." He waggled one bushy gray eyebrow suggestively. "I think three'd make a crowd, if you catch my drift."

"Well, catch mine, you old coot. Mind your own business."

"Or then . . . maybe you three are into that kinky stuff. . . ."

"And maybe you're a dork with a dirty mind and a grubby undershirt."

Leaving Mr. Biddle behind to mutter obscenities into his beer can, Savannah strode to the door of Dirk's trailer and rapped a shave-and-a-haircut greeting. Might as well be friendly. Might as well be casual. Might as well pretend she wasn't there to snoop.

Dirk might even believe it.

He didn't. She could tell right away by the irritated look on his face when he opened the door. Considering his less than cordial mood, she pushed past him before he could ask her to enter . . . or to leave, which was far more likely.

"Gee, I hate to drop in on you unannounced like this but . . ."

Savannah's voice trailed away when she saw who was

sitting on Dirk's 1973 vintage, beige-and-gold-plaid sofa. It was the last person she expected to see.

The former Mrs. Dirk.

The hated and often maligned—though not often enough in Savannah's book—ex-wife who had run away with a shaggy-haired, twentysomething rock-and-roll drummer several years ago.

"Polly!" Savannah replaced her look of shock with a carefully constructed facade of nonchalance. The act probably would have been more convincing if she hadn't been choking on her own spit. "What are you doing . . . I mean . . . what a surprise. I didn't expect to ever see you again."

"You mean, you *hoped* you'd never see me again."

"Yeah, that too."

Polly leaned back and propped her arm along the top of the sofa. She looked as casual as Savannah was pretending to be. Her long legs were stretched out before her, every inch of them bared by her short-short shorts. Savannah noted with just a bit of catty satisfaction that her knees were starting to sag a little.

So was her heavily made-up face. Foundation applied with a trowel, spider eyelashes, red lips that had been painted too far outside the natural lipline to fool anyone . . . except some fool like Dirk. He had admitted to Savannah that he had actually thought Polly was a real blonde for the first year of their relationship. Savannah could spot Golden Sun Frost a mile away . . . especially when it was on a swarthy-skinned woman who, undoubtedly, had been born with dark brown hair.

Like most of the men who had crossed Polly's path, Dirk had been taken in . . . in more ways than one . . . by a used-to-be-pretty face and a not-too-bad body, and lots of skillfully worded female flattery. Those had always been Polly's greatest weapons when hunting.

"Hope I'm not interrupting anything," Savannah said smoothly. She was pretty sure by the frustration on Dirk's face and the way he was pacing the ten foot span of trailer floor that she had. If she hung around long enough, she might just put a stop to this nonsense all together.

Some might call it interference; she called it charity. The guy needed to be saved from himself. On a nearby TV tray lay a single red rose. Probably a pre-Valentine gift from her to him or from him to her. The thought completely irked Savannah . . . either way.

"No problem," Polly said smoothly. "I'm sure you'll be leaving soon. Right? I mean, now that you see Dirk has company . . ."

"And now that you've seen who that company is," Dirk growled as he nodded, not so subtly toward the door.

In her peripheral vision, Savannah could see Dirk's cell phone sitting on top of the television set in the corner. She sauntered across the room in that direction.

"Actually, I had a good reason for dropping by, old pal," she told Dirk. "I brought you something. It's in my car."

She craned her neck to look out the window at her Camaro. As she had hoped, they did the same and she took the opportunity to sweep the cell phone into her jacket pocket.

"What is it?" Dirk said. She could hear the suspicion in his voice. She didn't really expect him to buy this pitch. The best she could hope for was that he would be a gentleman and not call her "liar, liar, pants on fire" to her face.

"Your cell phone," she replied. "You left it at my house. I figured you'd need it."

Dirk shot her a "yeah, right" look and glanced around the room. He didn't see his phone. But that wasn't unusual for Dirk. The guy would lose his rear end if it weren't stapled to his tailbone.

"So where is it?"

"In my car."

"Why didn't you bring it in with you, Savannah?" Polly asked, flipping her lush, golden mane of split ends back behind one shoulder.

"Forgot." Savannah held out her car keys to Dirk. "Why don't you go get it? I think I left it on the passenger's seat."

He grumbled under his breath and headed for the door. "Aren't you coming with me?" he said, not bothering to hide his anger.

"In a minute, darlin'," she said, much too sweetly. "You go ahead. I'll be along shortly."

He looked from her to Polly and back, then shook his head. "I don't think it's a good idea to leave you two broads alone."

"Go on, Dirk," Polly said, stroking one of her legs as though checking for razor stubble. "I'm not afraid of Savannah. We're old friends, right?"

"You may be old," Savannah replied. "I'm barely middle-aged. And just for the record, you and I have never been friends." She tossed the keys to Dirk. "Go get your phone. I'll be right out."

Reluctantly, he exited the trailer, leaving the door ajar. Savannah waited until he was out of earshot. Then she took a few steps closer to Polly.

In spite of what Polly had said, she did look a bit worried, just enough to satisfy Savannah's perverse streak.

"I don't know what you're doing here," Savannah said. "After the number you did on Dirk, I can't imagine why you would come back into his life, or why he would allow you to. But if you use him and hurt him again, like you did before, I swear, I'll beat the tar outta you. And if you think I mean that figuratively, you're wrong."

A flicker of fear crossed Polly's eyes; then she reached for the pack of cigarettes on a nearby TV tray and lit up. She blew a long puff of smoke in Savannah's direction before answering. "Now what is this I hear? Do I detect a note of jealousy? Was I right all those years ago . . . you really do have a thing for Dirk?"

"Yeah, I have a thing for Dirk. It's called friendship. Loyalty. Concern for his well-being . . . all things you wouldn't know about."

"I think you want him all to yourself." Polly released more smoke through her nose.

How perfectly lovely, Savannah thought. *Quintessential femininity. I'd like to snatch her bald.*

Savannah reached over and, before Polly knew what was

happening, grabbed the cigarette out of her hand. She crumbled it between her fingers and dropped the remains into a glass of white wine that was sitting next to the ashtray and a bottle of half-drunk beer on the TV tray. Dirk's beer, no doubt. Polly's wine.

"If you hurt Dirk again," Savannah said, using a voice she usually reserved for suspected murderers and child molesters, "I'll hurt you. My interest is not romantic; it's self-preservation. I'm not going to listen to him bellyache for two long, miserable years like he did when you left him before. If I have to pick up the pieces of Dirk, Miss Priss Pot, somebody's going to have to pick up pieces of you. You got that?"

Polly didn't answer. But Savannah could tell by the wideness of her spider eyes and the way her too-lipsticked mouth was hanging open that she had heard and believed . . . at least a little.

Savannah left the trailer, slamming the door behind her, and nearly ran, chest first, into Dirk.

"My cell phone isn't in your car," he said, his nose inches from hers, his voice as low and ominous as hers had been a moment before. "But then, neither one of us really expected it to be, right, Van?"

Savannah reached into her left jacket pocket and took out his phone; hers was still in her right. "Oh, silly me," she said. "Here it is. I guess I remembered to bring it in with me after all."

When she handed it to him, he looked puzzled and apologetic enough to make her feel a little guilty. "Oh, you really . . . oh, thanks, Van."

"No problem. Watch yourself, buddy, with that gal." She nodded toward the trailer. "Remember last time?"

"Yeah, I remember. But it ain't like that this time. She just wants me to help her, to take care of somethin' for her."

"That's all she's ever wanted, Dirk, from anyone. She's a leech. That's the problem."

"Naw. I can take care of it. Don't worry."

Don't worry, yeah sure, she thought as she left him, got in her Camaro, and drove away. Dirk wasn't stupid—not by a long shot. But he had a blind spot where women were concerned . . . especially women he loved.

Why else would he buy a stupid story about a cell phone?

Savannah had no idea what line of bull Polly was going to try to sell him, but she was pretty sure he'd buy it, too.

Savannah had just dropped off to sleep when the telephone rang, exploding in her right ear and sending her pulse racing like a scared rabbit's. She grabbed the receiver, dropped it on the floor, picked it up, and smacked herself on the teeth with the mouthpiece. She could swear she tasted blood.

"What?" she shouted, ready to kill whoever was calling her at—she squinted at the red, glowing numbers on the bedside clock—1:22 a.m.

"Van . . ."

Savannah didn't need Gran's extrasensitive radar to detect the distress in that one word. She sat straight up and flipped on the bedside lamp. "Yeah, Dirk, what's going on?"

"It's Polly."

Savannah had a half a second to utter a quick, silent prayer, one that she instinctively knew was pointless. *God, let*

*her be okay. They just had a fight, right? She's alive, but they just
argued and—*

"She's dead."

Let it be natural causes, or . . . "A car accident?"

"Murdered."

ABOUT THE AUTHOR

G. A. McKevett is the author of five Savannah Reid mysteries: *Just Desserts*, *Bitter Sweets*, *Killer Calories*, *Cooked Goose* and *Sugar and Spite*. She loves to hear from readers and you may write to her c/o Zebra Books. Please include a self-addressed stamped envelope if you wish a response.